I0680633

The Potter's Daughter

Daniel Arthur Smith

The Potter's Daughter

ISBN: 0988649314
ISBN-13: 978-0-9886493-1-6

Also Written by Daniel Arthur Smith

The Literary Short Story
Opening Day

The International Best Selling Men's Adventure Novel
The Cathari Treasure: A Cameron Kincaid Adventure

* * * * *

For Susan, Tristan, & Oliver, as all things are.

* * * * *

.

CHAPTER 1

Abby sat on the split log bench sliding her skates back and forth into the grooves of the snow beneath her. She pressed her palms upon her thighs and extended each leg, one at a time, in a slow rhythm. Her knees rose and fell in time with deep soft breaths. Though her legs were tight, the skates felt good. Tense since arriving in Willow Lake, she thought a long skate would give her an opportunity for a much needed work out. Abby took in a deeper breath and rolled her head from one side to the other then stretched back, exposing her thin neck above her scarf. She peered through the branches of the willow above and slowly exhaled. The willow had noticeably grown since the last time she looked up from this bench. Her eyes ran up the trunk through naked branches to the top of the tree some fifty feet above where she sat.

Fixed high in the willow tree were two thick steel cables. Abby traced one back to the house and the other to the studio. Abby's father feared that one day the willow would slip down the embankment into the lake. He had assured Abby that the equal tension on the cables would maintain the willow's upright position. Though Abby doubted her father's laymen engineering she never outright disputed him.

Adding one more contention would not benefit either of them and to her the cables fastening the tree were trivial.

Abby gave her legs a final stretch. She adjusted her pink knit cap firmly and pulled her chestnut ponytail out of her scarf. Leaning cautiously against the weeping willow Abby raised herself off the bench then with small crunching steps moved down the embankment onto the ice directly below.

The lake had little snow cover and would be easily traversed yet the only skating Abby had done in years was around the small city rink at the park. A rink that would fit thrice into Bellen Bay and Caroline's house was far around the point and half way across the long Willow Lake. Already so late in the day Abby pondered if she had underestimated the effort involved in skating as far as her cousin's after so many years off the lake. She set out into the bay to counter any mounting hesitation. To skate across the lake may be more of an undertaking than she had imagined yet standing on the shore would not get her there any faster.

Abby balanced on one blade then effortlessly switched to the other gliding over the frozen lake. When she rounded the point to turn toward her cousin's she could see that the eastern sky across the lake was already a dark hue of blue and the details of the trees along that shore were becoming indefinable. Above the sky was grey while to the left in the western horizon remnants of soft sunlight were disappearing fast.

Rather than hugging the shoreline, Abby headed out toward the center of the lake.

The openness of the frozen lake and the brisk air was a welcomed change from her father's mess back at the house on shore. For Abby's father bachelorhood had become a liberty from household responsibility. When she had arrived at her father's house on the lake, most every inch was covered with newspaper or clothing. Before the house could be cleaned, Abby spent a day simply organizing the mess. All of the laundry needed to be done and there was not a clean dish in the kitchen. What little was in the refrigerator had to be thrown out. Her father had never been stellar at keeping house yet his skills had deteriorated to almost nonexistent in the twenty years since her mother had passed.

Abby's father did not bide well with her ordering him around. Often she had to seek him out in the studio when he was supposed to be helping her in the house, and though he would perform the tasks she asked of him, she could hear him grumbling under his breath.

Out on the ice there was no mess, no father to chase down, and Abby did not dwell on why she was in Willow Lake instead of the city.

In the catharsis of the skate, Abby felt she could go the entire length of the lake.

When Abby reached Caroline's, yellow lights twinkled within the eastern tree line, headlights and shops animated the village at the northern tip of the lake, and the last remnant of day silhouetted the western tree line with a strip of tangerine sky.

* * * * *

CHAPTER 2

Caroline's husband Brian greeted Abby as she skated up to the lakeside.

"Took you long enough," said Brian. He offered his arm out for Abby. With his help, she pulled herself up from the ice onto the terrace to remove her skates.

"I'm sorry. I had a late start. I hope Caroline's ok."

"Quite alright. Caroline has almost everything wrapped up and she is excited to see you. We both are," said Brian.

"You are so sweet. That must be what Caroline sees in you."

Abby sat on a stone bench then unlaced her skates. The house stood on a hill above her overlooking Willow Lake. During the day, the house was hardly visible from the lake below. She looked up at the lights of the kitchen and could see Caroline and the five-year old twins trying to see out the large glass doors. Abby waved as she crossed the weathered boardwalk between the terrace and the steps of the house. Through the surface of the snow bordering the walk pruned shrubs shivered in their burlap wraps among the parched straw colored ornamental foliage.

As Abby and Brian topped the steps Lily and Andrew ran out of the kitchen door bundled in heavy winter attire.

They scuttled toward Abby then squeezed her legs tightly when they reached her.

"Hey! Let's get inside before we freeze to death," said Abby.

Abby led the group stumbling into the kitchen where Caroline was preparing for the party. Food in different stages of preparation covered every counter. The aroma of cooked meats and spices filled the room and the sweet smell of a baking cake lingered above the oven.

Caroline's blonde hair was held back with a headband and the oversized collar shirt she wore had flour on the tails and cuffs.

Caroline embraced her cousin. "Hey sweetheart," said Caroline. They kissed the others cheeks three times, like they had learned years ago on their summer abroad in Holland. "Back on the skates, huh? How is it out there? The edges were a bit creaky last weekend."

"Seems ok now, I'm sure this last cold snap took care of that," said Abby. She removed her cap, scarf, and down vest and took the hot mug of coffee Brian offered her, "Thank you, nice and hot."

Lily ran toward the den, kicking a few strewn wooden blocks in her wake, "Abby come with me!"

"No! Come look at my room. I got new bunks. We can play sleepover," said Andrew as he cast off his wool hat and mittens and tossed them onto the floor.

Brian grabbed the mittens off the floor, "Forget it, we've got to go. You can see Abby later today." Brian turned an eye to Abby, "Sorry hon, we were just on the way out the door, trying to give my darling wife a little uninterrupted time to prepare for tonight's festivities."

"Oh God, I'm so sorry. Happy Birthday Brian," said Abby, "I nearly forgot."

"Don't sweat it. I know you've got a lot on your plate right now." Brian leaned over and kissed her on the cheek. He assumed things were tense at home with her father.

"Come on kids. Let's get to the pool before it gets too

late," said Brian.

"It's started snowing. Look Mom, it's snowing," said Lily as Brian shuffled the kids back out the kitchen door where large flakes were beginning to fall.

"Indoor pool?" asked Abby.

"Indoor pool at the community center, at the fairgrounds behind the Stone Tavern," said Caroline.

"Willow Lake is booming, first fine dining at the reopened South Point Inn, now a community pool."

"All the amenities of the city."

"And the kids are getting so big. I can't believe it. It seems like it was just yesterday you were out to here," Abby made a circle with her arms far away from her belly.

"I guess I was, and it feels like yesterday," said Caroline pouring herself a cup of coffee.

"So how are you and Will fairing over at the studio?"

"Well, you know Dad. He has a charming way of stressing me out."

"I'm really sorry about that hysterical call before you left the city, I guess I kind of lost it huh?"

"No, I think I needed it. It snapped me out of the state of denial I was in. I think I thought if I ignored it, it would go away, but you were right. He's getting noticeably worse. I called Dr. Roberts last week. He said Dad's tremors are happening more often than he's letting on, of course. He suggested I start looking for someone to help him around the house."

"Hmm. What do you think about that? I can imagine what Uncle Will will think."

"Yea, he'll hate it. But I'm sure not going to hang around to take care of him, and I can't have him burdening you guys."

"Oh, he's not a burden. It's just been a little tough lately, that's all. Hey, did you ever take that Asian cooking class you were talking about? I have all the makings for these fantastic spring rolls. Do you mind? I'm a bit behind schedule?" Caroline pulled a plate of shredded vegetables and a stack of wonton wrappers from the refrigerator and set them in from of her cousin.

"Sure. I'll give it a try. I never told you what happened in that class. I went to a few, but the whole group, except the teacher, were married couples and I felt out of place."

"Was the teacher cute?"

"He kept hitting on me."

"Well?"

"Well nothing! He was older," Abby paused, "and I'm not looking."

"What do you mean you're not looking?"

"Just that, is that so bad? Oh yum, give me a lick." Abby reached over Caroline's shoulder and dug her finger into the bowl of chocolate frosting her cousin had taken from the refrigerator.

"No, of course not. But you can't stay single forever, that small apartment of yours has to get lonely."

"Yea," said Abby in a singing pitch, "but dating is really not going anywhere."

Abby meant what she said about dating. Though the city was chock full of interesting people and she had tons of great friends, all of the men she dated turned out to be flawed. These flaws usually became apparent when she thought everything in the relationship was going well.

There was the graphic artist with the chiseled chin and the hazel eyes that could talk about color and design for hours and could have been a catch had he not had such a profane mouth. The musician with the dark curly hair and the thin frame that declared women were not capable of the passions necessary to create true art, meaning that he thought women were inferior altogether. Then there was the media exec a friend had set her up with, a philanderer that could not keep his eyes, much less himself from wandering.

"All of the men I am meeting are coming up losers," said Abby.

"Hmm. Well that's lousy. How are things at the

Museum?" asked Caroline.

"Well, actually pretty good," said Abby.

Abby was glad that Caroline had changed the subject from dating to the museum.

Last Friday had been the most incredible day at work. Abby was assigned the Renoir exhibit and her boss Olivia hinted that she would be up for promotion when Olivia left for maternity leave. Abby imagined herself a managing curator. She would wear her hair up and abandon her plain ponytail. She could buy real cosmetics, discard her jumble of drug store brands, and carry a proper handbag instead of her battered leather backpack. She saw the promotion as an excuse for her to get serious.

The new exhibit Abby had been chosen to work on fascinated Caroline.

The Renoir exhibit would be a premier show at the museum. This would be the third exhibit project for Abby and the largest. The exhibit would feature over 100 paintings and drawings from Renoir and other artists representing the development of impressionism. The project management for this exhibit would take months of planning, collecting, and marketing. To Abby, this was a sign her career was definitely on track.

The girls chatted for some time. Caroline asked questions and listened for details that she would never hear in discussions on the lake. Coffee turned to chilled white wine as they went on to talk about other artists they loved. They talked until Brian and the twins returned to dress for the party, and then they talked some more until they themselves went upstairs to dress.

* * * * *

CHAPTER 3

On the western shore of Willow Lake, three structures huddled amid the evergreens. The shoreline studio dwarfed the tool shed nestled in the trees opposite the lakeside yard and the main house stood recessed between the two. From the house and the studio large bay windows peered out across the lake to the eastern shore. At the lakeside, a weeping willow towered over the compound.

Kiln rooms added to the side of the studio housed industrial electric kilns and gas-burning giants. The old wood-burning kiln which Will preferred stood half dug into the ground by the tool shed. Despite the old kiln being Will's preference the oven did not get much use anymore.

Inside the studio were two large tables with urns ranging in size at different stages of completion. On the far wall were stacks of clay sacks and the smaller tool and paint storage rooms. The bathroom was in the corner. Everything was coated in a fine layer of clay dust giving the room a distinct grey accent. Lined up and evenly spaced under the large window stood five pottery wheels. Sitting at one was Will.

Will had spent most of his sixty-seven years in this greyed studio and was as much a part of the workshop as the clay and urns themselves. All of his memories came from this place. Bellen hands had built the Bellen studio. Will had grown up in the studio and there he had raised his children.

The potter's wheel is where Will felt most comfortable. The wet clay felt moist against Will's hands lightly running between his fingers. Delicately the clay was brought to life by his seasoned touch. Will had learned how to be a potter from his father and in turn had taught his son.

For generations the Bellen name was synonymous with hand crafted ornamental urns. Since Will's grandfather had built the studio, trucks had come to Willow Lake four times a year to pickup urns ready for consignment. Will was proud that Bellen urns had been taken as far away as China and India.

The urns were all of sizes and degrees of ornamentation. The cremation urns were always in demand and there were standing orders with the best interior design firms for several of the tall highly decorated urns to be displayed in the lobbies of hotels, custom homes, or large city apartments. Some urns were special order. Will's father used to boast that President Roosevelt had two tall urns put in the White House that were made with his own hands, the hands of a Bellen.

Over the years the highly detailed urns tended to be more popular and brought in the most money. Urns Will did not like that much because he thought they appeared contrived. Each grape vine, humming bird, and floral decoration was created with such skill and artifice that they ironically lacked naturalness and spontaneity. Will's favorite urns were tall and plain. That is what he was about to create.

Though the shop had electric wheels, for the tall urns Will always used the manual kick wheel with the pedal on the floor just as his father did. When Will's son Michael was alive, the two would have competitions. Will on the manual wheel and Michael on the electric. The contest was to see which of the two could raise the clay to the tallest urn. Will had played the same game with his own father.

The clay Will was working with started as a blob and was that no longer. Will reached over to get the wet sponge while holding his other hand effortlessly still on the side of the clay. The wheel hummed. The pedal pumped up and down. Will's upper body was postured statuesque, the clay waiting to dance before him. Will squeezed the sponge above the clay as the water uniformly engulfed the form. The time was right. Leaning into the wheel, Will put his other hand lightly to the side, beckoning his partner. The clay responded and began to lift from the wheel, agreeing to join him. Will led, the clay followed. His right hand caressed below the rising nape of the rim. His left hand stroked the side at the waist.

The clay began to dance.

If Will respected the clay, if his hands were steady, the clay would become a tall plain urn.

* * * * *

CHAPTER 4

After Will finished the urn he stood up from the kick wheel, turned toward the lake, and reached inside of the pocket of his flannel shirt for a Camel cigarette. Camel shorts without the filters had been his cigarettes of choice for many years, yet after Emily died twenty years ago, he switched to the light filters and then only smoked those sparsely in the studio or at the Stone Tavern. Will put the cigarette in his mouth then reached into his pants pocket for his Zippo without removing his gaze from the frozen lake.

There were three snowmobiles crossing the lake from Peters Beach, Will was not focusing on them.

Will's mind was drifting from the completion of the urn to the inevitable thought that he was capable of completing a piece at all. How effortless the wheel had been for him, as throwing the clay had been countless times before. Surely the tremors were no reason for everyone to be so concerned, he was after all as able bodied as ever.

Just under six feet tall, Will was as solid at sixty-seven as he had been at forty or twenty. He was moderately stocky and shared the crystal blue eyes and the sandy brown hair of every Bellen man before him. Grey was the color of his hair now, yet all there, and a color that blended well with his studio. Will was quite proud of that. A little grey did not debilitate him.

Will thought Abby was audacious. His daughter was always welcome to her childhood home. Taking time away from her job was a bit much though. If Abby had her own issues to work out, he would support her just as long as she did not project them on him. Abby having an early mid-life crisis was not his fault. Abby did not have to meddle in his life for distraction from her own. Meddlesome is what they all were. Little Caroline calling Abby in the city burned him a bit too. Abby should be taking care of her life and he should be taking care of his.

Will threw down his half smoked camel and crushed the tobacco on the dusty cement floor, his eyes still fixed across the lake. Shrugging off thoughts of Abby and Caroline, he turned to one of the worktables in the center of the room. Under the worktable were a set of cabinets that held dyes, sponges, and water bottles. Along side of the supplies were two bottles of red wine and some paper cups. Will pulled a half bottle of wine out of the cabinet along with a paper cup. He opened the wine and filled the cup.

Alone in his studio Will began to sip from the paper cup.

* * * * *

CHAPTER 5

The party was a celebration for Brian's fortieth birthday. Brian's favorite jazz music permeated every corner from the surround sound system. Paper lanterns donned the stairwell and were hung in strategic points of the house so that the fireplace and a few scattered candles appeared as the primary light. The twins had helped make decorations and a banner that read 'Happy 40th Brian'. Balloons were scattered across the ceiling.

Caroline had borrowed a young bartender from the Stone Tavern to pour drinks and a neighboring high school girl to take coats. Champagne flutes were filled with peach or mango belinis and given to guests as they arrived. Proseco filled other flutes for continual toasts to the man of the hour. Bob Jensen, owner of the Stone Tavern and close friend of Brian's, walked among the guests with a bottle in hand ensuring everyone was well provided for.

Brian looked ahead to each year as something new and was pleased at forty as he was at thirty and would be at fifty.

Abby was not sure she would feel the same as Brian when she turned forty and thought that when her time came the celebration would be a wake for her youth and vitality. This party contrarily celebrated Brian's ongoing adventure and the conversations he was having with his guests reflected as much. Brian spoke of plans for his home, his family's cross-country vacation, and most of all planning for his guests. Some of the guests at the party had Brian and Caroline design or renovate their homes and many more would have liked them to.

If Abby was afraid that forty was a tiresome ending point then Brian was there to assure her that he was still peaking. Listening to Brian discuss architectural designs with the guests was exhausting to her. So much so that she mentioned to Caroline, " How can you actually pull off all of those amazing things Brian is talking about? How can you do all of that?"

"Ah," said Caroline. "There is someone I would like you to meet."

Caroline lightly pulled Abby's arm and led her across the room.

"You discovered our secret. Well not so secret. When Brian and I do a design, we actually don't do the magic by ourselves. We call on a third," said Caroline. "Abby, I would like you to meet Mitch Carlson, the magician."

Abby let her eyes synch with Mitch's dark brown eyes and was charmed by the quick to react curve of his lips. His brownish black brushed back hair, a bit shaggy, went well with his white-collar shirt that hung loosely outside of his blue jeans. Abby guessed that Mitch was some type of artist or craftsman by his dress and the relaxed air of confidence that shadowed him. She had grown up with two such men.

When Mitch took Abby's hand to greet her, she noticed that his skin was tough like coarse leather yet his muscular touch though firm was gentle.

"So you make it all happen?" asked Abby.

"Well the building part, Caroline and Brian handle the design," said Mitch.

"You sell yourself short," said Caroline. "If it weren't for Mitch we would be doing theory of design rather than implementing it. Mitch has been working with us since we got out here, every design has his mark on it."

"I love you too hon," said Mitch, "You make me all gushy inside."

"Seriously," said Abby, "All of these projects sound exhausting."

"Excuse me, the Franks are just getting here," said Caroline as she stepped away leaving the two to talk.

"It's not exhausting at all, really," said Mitch. "Abby, you're the cousin from the city?"

"That's me."

"Your famous around here. Working at the art museum, I love that place!"

"Really?"

"It's one of the only places I care to see when I'm in the city. There and O'Malley's," said Mitch.

"Well of course O'Malley's, there's days I'd rather be there than the museum."

Both laughed and clinked their glasses together in an ad hoc toast.

"El Greco," said Mitch, Abby interrupted, "—El Greco, yes!"

"El Greco," said Mitch, "one of my favorite exhibits a few years back."

"That was a good exhibit, I was an assistant curator on that one."

"Well, I must say you did a good job."

"Thanks for the compliment," Abby paused, "You don't know what I do there, do you?"

"Not at all," said Mitch. They both laughed again. "Could you tell me what exactly a curator does because I did sincerely find the exhibit both enjoyable and memorable? "

"Well in a nutshell a curator manages or executes all of the effort to put on an exhibit. There is a lot of research, planning, gathering media and of course what needs to be exhibited, then there is marketing, most people do not associate curating with marketing, let me tell you, " Abby nodded her head.

"So you organize the entire exhibit."

"The entire exhibit."

"Where does the research come from if you are already the biggest museum in the city?"

"We do have amazing archives. We have to go through all of that stuff. Oh, we teach too sometimes. I taught a class last year," said Abby. She took another drink.

"How do you go about gathering artwork from around the world?"

"That is a bit tricky. You see most stuff comes from private collections and --," Abby stopped.

The sound of a revving engine and breaking glass came from the driveway. Some of the guests moved toward the atrium to look out the glass plate wall to see what was going on outside. Abby scanned the room for Caroline then saw her already walking toward the window see what the disturbance was. Caroline glanced back at Abby for a second, and then out the glass plate wall of the atrium. Then without turning her head away from the ongoing action outside Caroline stretched her arm toward Abby then wiggled her fingers.

"Excuse me," Abby said to Mitch and then walked to where Caroline was standing.

The loud revving truck engine could be heard shifting gears and there was a clinking of glass bottles falling on top of each other. Abby looked out the window and her teeth slowly started to grind. She saw a 1961 blue Chevy pickup that, because so many guests had already parked, had tried to park on the snow covered edge of the driveway and had ended up on top of the recycling bins, already half full of containers from the party. The driver was making a loud awkward unsuccessful attempt to correct his mistake.

Abby knew the pickup was a 1961 Chevy not because she was any type of auto aficionado. Abby knew the owner of the truck and what condition he was in behind the wheel.

"I'll go get him," said Abby.

Caroline was by Abby's side as Abby stepped out the

door of the atrium. The two women looked down the driveway from the elevated porch to the truck. The truck did not appear to be stuck in the deep snow. The driver was relentlessly trying to find a parking space to his satisfaction and was revving the engine to power through the snow. The pickup was going two feet back and then two feet forward and then two feet back again. The recycling bins and landscaping beneath the snow had fallen prey to the parking maneuvers.

"Will Bellen!" yelled Abby.

The truck was revving loudly.

"Will Bellen, get out of that truck!"

The revving stopped.

"Will! Turn off the key!"

The truck was now in a position where the driver's door was blocked by the pine trees that skirted the yard.

There was a pause and then the engine of the truck stopped running. The silence was peaceful. Abby and Caroline gazed at the sleeping blue pickup sitting in the snow and waited. Against the snow in the shadow of the pines, the truck took on a cerulean hue. With a heavy creak the passenger door opened. Out into the snow climbed Will Bellen. He thrust himself forward to make a couple of spry steps then teetered. Will put one leg forward, unsatisfied he thrust the same leg a little farther out into the snow then fell back on the other leg finally coming to rest with a gentle sway. Having achieved the great feat of standing up Will flashed his crystal blue eyes at the girls and showed all of his teeth in a grin.

* * * * *

CHAPTER 6

"Sorry I'm late," said Will.

"You're drunk!" said Abby.

Will's eyebrows raised and his jaw dropped open. Abby's jaw clenched tighter.

"Are you Ok Uncle Will?" asked Caroline.

"Couldn't be finer."

Will reached into the truck, pulled out a bottle of wine, and then held the bottle into the air.

"I had two of these," said Will, "one seemed to dry up."

"Your intolerable Will Bellen!" snapped Abby.

Will was unfettered by Abby's reaction to his entrance.

"Well if you are not going to invite me in, I'm coming in from the cold," said Will and proceeded to the atrium choosing to tromp directly through the deep snow covered yard rather than by way of the driveway where the snow was clear.

Abby wanted to go back into the party and let Caroline deal with her father. There would be no speaking to Will rationally. Abby's clenched jaw, ironically a trait from her father, made speaking tough.

When Will got to the steps of the porch he took them two at a time, though Caroline and Abby were not sure that

19

was his plan. He stumbled, almost dropping the wine, before setting the bottle on the top of the porch in front of him.

"Whoa," said Will.

The women reached out their hands for Will then each grabbed an arm. They pulled him to the top of the porch where he stood on his own balance. The odor of smoked camels filled the porch and the women could see the purplish hue of Shiraz on Will's lips.

Will bent over, picked up and then presented the bottle of wine to Caroline. "So how are you this evening my dear Caroline?"

"Fine uncle Will. Are you sure your ok?"

"Dandy. What's the weather like sunshine?"

"Partly cloudy, storm's a comin'," said Caroline.

Will winked at Caroline, "So where's the Birthday boy?"

"You have some explaining to do," said Abby.

"He's inside. C'mon in, I'll get him," said Caroline.

Caroline opened the door and walked through. Will moved to follow her and was stopped by Abby.

"Let me brush that snow off your legs," said Abby.

"Ok, ok."

Will had caked snow around the calves of his blue jeans tromping across the yard. From the inside of the door, Abby grabbed a small broom that was kept for that purpose and brushed the snow off for him. When she finished Will lifted his cool crystal blue eyes to her and asked, "Are we ready now?"

"Yes, old man," said Abby. Her brows furrowed.

Will stepped into the atrium followed by Abby. In a low voice to the back of Will's ear Abby said, "I can't believe you were driving drunk on Willow Lake Road. You're crazy."

"It was fine," said Will, "no unsafe conditions."

Abby did not like him using that term.

Winding twenty-one miles around Willow Lake was Willow Lake Road. Willow Lake Road many years ago had been a two-track road that after the war became a two-lane dirt road and on the map became County Road Twenty-Three. Summer people did not like stones chipping away at their foreign cars so a few years later County Road Twenty-Three was coated with asphalt and on the map became Willow Lake Road.

Each summer Willow Lake road had at least one fatal accident, a motorcycle collision, or someone just driving too fast around one of the many curves, usually not a local, and each winter there were far more fatalities because of 'unsafe conditions'.

Asphalt gathers precipitation, moisture from the air, that when cold creates a layer of ice. County trucks then put salt on the asphalt melting the ice, ice that turns to water, water that is absorbed into the minute cracks and crevices only to resurface when the effects of the salt wear off forming yet a new layer of ice. The new ice brings to the surface all of the oil and sediment that was in the road creating black ice. Black ice is slicker than normal ice, virtually invisible, and in a word, deadly. Since the asphalt had been put down, the death toll rose and the blame is the layer of black ice. The police accident reports give a simple explanation when the black ice is blamed not requiring too much paperwork, 'unsafe conditions'.

When Abby's brother died, his jeep flew off the road, hit a tree, and then smashed into the rocks at South Point. The accident report read 'unsafe conditions'.

Will had used that term to shut Abby down successfully. She would not be getting in the way of his good time. He removed his coat and scarf then handed them to Jenny, the neighbor girl Caroline had hired to help at the party. Then he entered the large main room, peeked around, made smiles to familiar neighbors, and made comments under his breath to Abby as to which smiling face was an idiot and which owed him twenty dollars. Will's beige wool sweater complimented his silver hair and contrasted his blue eyes in a way that made them look brilliant. Will spotted the bar and walked there directly. Abby did not follow him.

Abby picked up the white wine that she had set on the maple side table then headed toward the kitchen at the other end of the house.

Set out on the kitchen island was a buffet. There was a bright orange ceramic plate with small chicken and egg meatballs covered in a ginger teriyaki sauce. A baby blue square ceramic plate held enoki mushrooms wrapped in bacon. There were many swiss, cheddar, and havarti cheeses with thin herb flavored crackers next to sopressata sausages, salami, tuna salad, potato salad, and a local favorite, cream cheese and green onion wrapped in sliced ham. Abby picked up a small plate and fork and allowed herself to become distracted.

Especially enjoyable were the meatballs, they were downright addictive. Lightly grilled in the ginger teriyaki sauce they tasted like candy.

"They're delicious right?" said Mitch. He had walked up to Abby from the side and she had not seen him. Abby cleared her throat with a drink of wine.

"They are. I'm drowning my sorrows in them," said Abby.

"Everything all right outside?" asked Mitch.

"It's all trouble you don't want any part of," said Abby.

Mitch raised his beer up to his chest, cocked his eyebrow, and with a comical Bogart impression said, "I don't mind a reasonable amount of trouble."

"Sam Spade, nice," said Abby.

"When I was a boy I wanted to be Sam Spade," said Mitch. "As far as I was concerned being a private detective was top of the heap. Do you like Sam Spade?"

"What curator wouldn't be intrigued by a golden falcon encrusted from beak to claw with rare jewels created by the Knight Templar of Malta in 1539?"

"Touché," said Mitch.

"Plus there's Sam Spade, that's one of my favorite movies of all time."

"Cheers," said Mitch. "Cheers," said Abby.

"Is the real Maltese Falcon in a museum somewhere?" asked Mitch.

"Not at all," said Abby, "but it was based on a real sculpture called the Kniphausen Hawk made in 1697. No romantic story like the Maltese Falcon, but it was still covered in jewels."

"I'd rather have a good story over the jewels," said Mitch.

"Agreed," said Abby.

Mitch finished his beer. "Can I get you another glass of wine?"

"I would love one. However, after seeing that parking fiasco I'm pretty sure I'm on driving duty," said Abby.

Across the room, Mitch and Abby could see Will's face glowing as he was describing something to the Lumsdens'. In an exaggerated gesture Will was making a large circle with his hands from above his head to his waist and then from his chest to the extent of his arms, all the time holding a three quarter full wine glass. His eyes were fixing to and from Hank and Mary Lumsden's faces to judge their reaction. Either they were totally enthralled by the story or waiting for the red wine to come jetting out of the glass straight into there faces.

"So you're driving him home?" asked Mitch.

"I think it's best," said Abby.

Trying yet again to use the voice of Bogart, Mitch said, "You're a good man, sister." Abby answered with her own Bogart impression, "Don't be too sure, I'm as crooked as I'm supposed to be."

* * * * *

CHAPTER 7

The buckwheat batter sizzled into perfect round circles upon the hot skillet. Caroline always made perfectly round pancakes. As a child, her parents took the family to the Lakeside Diner every Sunday after church. The cook used the skillet to flip the cakes way up in the air astonishing all of the wide-eyed children in for Sunday breakfast. She had to use a spatula to flip them, which frustrated her just a little. Every time Caroline had tried to flip pancakes with the skillet, they ended up hanging off the edge of the pan or landed on the stove.

The twins were singing along with a man in an animal suit on the television when Caroline called to them to get ready for breakfast. Their song switched from the sing along to an assailing yell as they ran toward the kitchen to reap the strawberry jam and maple syrup that would be covering the silver dollar pancakes their mother had made for them.

Andrew and Lily climbed onto the stools at the island counter and, paying no attention to their small forks, began eating the little stacks on their plates.

"Pancakes, how yummy!" said Mitch as he walked into the kitchen with Brian.

"Have some. There's plenty," said Caroline. She handed Mitch a small plate and gestured toward the platter stacked with the silver dollars.

"Thanks Mom. Don't mind if I do," Mitch took the plate and sat down on the end stool next to the twins.

"You threw a great party last night," said Mitch to Caroline as she handed Brian a plate.

"We were so glad you came," said Caroline. She put the mixing bowl into the dishwasher. "What did you think?"

"About the plans for the Walker house? Well Brian just showed them to me and I think they are amazing as always, but the material costs are going to go way up."

Caroline cut him off, "—No, not about that."

"What do I think about what?"

"Oh never mind." Caroline frowned. "Hey are you going up to the Johansson house this morning?"

"Sure am, why?"

"Would you mind dropping something off for me?" asked Caroline.

"No not at all."

Brian's eyes met with Caroline as she walked into the other room. She scrunched her nose at him and grinned.

A moment later Caroline came back holding a paper bag, "Could you please drop these at the Bellen house? It would be a big favor. Abby forgot these and I want to get them to her along with some food for her and her Dad."

"For Abby eh? Well I guess."

"Thanks Mitch, I would really appreciate it. I have to get the twins ready for school and need to express mail those papers to the Walkers and--,"

"—Ok, ok no worries. I have to run to the garage first but I can drop the bag off after that."

* * * * *

Abby heard the whistle of the teakettle. She pulled her sweater over her head and walked into the kitchen. She was startled to see someone standing on the porch. The shadow could not be Will because she had just seen him out by the lake. A soft knock came on the door and Abby peered through the light lace curtain. Mitch was standing on the porch in a dark brown Carhart jacket and bibs. He held a ruffled brown paper bag under his arm and was gently knocking with two coffees stacked in his hand. Abby opened the door with her usual 'always happy to see you' smile.

"Hi there," said Abby. She sincerely was happy to see him.

"Hey there," said Mitch. "I'm sorry to bother you." He offered her the paper bag adding, "Caroline asked to me drop this off."

"Thanks."

"No bother at all."

Mitch peered past her to the whistling kitchen.

"Oh," Abby glanced over her shoulder, "I was just about to have a cup of tea. Would you like one?"

Mitch smiled and gestured toward the two coffees that he held in his hand. "Right," said Abby. "Well come on in then."

"It's no problem?" asked Mitch.

"Don't be silly."

Abby opened the door farther and waved her arm back into the kitchen.

"Well here is the kitchen. Let me take your jacket and have seat at the table," said Abby. She hung Mitch's jacket on one of the hooks by the door then took the kettle from the stove.

Mitch raised a coffee cup toward the painting above the table, "That painting really captures the morning view of the lake."

Abby paused and gazed at the painting, "The lake is lovely with the sun shining down on the surface." She then returned to the counter to prepare the tea.

"That's pretty much the way the lake is right now. It's a

beautiful day out there," said Mitch.

"That is something I do miss about being out here."

Abby stood at the counter for a moment then removed the steeped bags. She brought two cups of Earl Grey tea to the table and set one in front of Mitch.

"You have to try this. I am sure the coffee is getting cold by now."

"It is," said Mitch. He actually had just bought the coffee at Lakeside Diner before coming over.

Mitch tasted the tea, "Its delicious."

"It's because of the honey. I mixed it in with the milk."

"Is this honey from Mr. Wilkin's hives?"

Abby nodded, "A local treasure."

"It is indeed local treasure," said Mitch. He pushed the bag forward, "So Caroline sent these."

"Alas, the package. What's in there?"

"Your skates, some food from the party. Caroline said to drop it by, so…"

"Mission accomplished. My skates. Nice. Thank you so much."

Abby took the bag from Mitch. She put the food containers on the table and placed the skates on the floor. Abby had not needed the skates at all still she truly appreciated Mitch dropping them off and was truly enjoying his company.

Mitch asked Abby about working at the museum. She told him about her job and the chance of the promotion. Mitch in turn told her about working with Caroline and Brian. Like old friends, their conversation flowed easy and time flew quickly. The teacups emptied and neither minded.

* * * * *

CHAPTER 8

The Bellen studio had developed some refined systems over the many years in operation. The pottery moved through a make shift assembly line. From the wheels, the pottery was placed on one of the tables near the entrance of the studio. All of the detail work such as the grapevines and ivy were adhered to the urns and then after drying all were loaded into one of the kilns. After firing, the kilns were unloaded to the tables on the far side of the room to be painted and if needed glazed before being fired again. Will had started the new order this morning with this first urn, so he had to make room on the tables by filling the kiln.

Five four-foot high urns were detailed, dried, and ready for firing. Will prepared the kiln and then went to the table to begin loading the urns. The urns were ornamented with flora and fauna and these particular urns composed a set, each one with different flowers and birds. The first urn Will picked up had long stems of honeysuckle and hummingbirds. Will was able to create the clay hummingbirds in minutes. The detail of the honeysuckle still took a good part of an afternoon. Each petal was made separately and then added to the flower on the stem. Will wrapped his arms around the urn and effortlessly lifted, the entire weight bearing on his strong legs. He carried the piece into the kiln and then returned to the table to get the second urn. This urn had beautiful sparrows and cherry blossoms.

Will put all of the weight on his legs again and lifted the second urn carefully then turned toward the kiln. A tremor began in his forearm. Will squeezed the urn hard and tried to hurry his legs, to no good. His forearm then his hand went weak. The urn began to slip. Will was powerless to do anything. Quickly he tried to kneel to bring the urn closer to the ground to avoid a crash. Will's arm gave out first. The urn fell from his grasp onto the cement floor with a loud thwacking sound.

Down on one knee Will stared at the at the large triangle shard of grey clay with the cherry blossoms still intact and closely bound to their branches. Across the floor were spread pieces of sparrow and blossom. Will inspected the pieces where they fell while he massaged his weak arm. The hand that had failed him was shaking slightly. He squeezed his palm tightly to steady the shaking. Then in a quick motion, without getting up from the floor, he grabbed the large shard with both hands and threw the clay at the wall letting out a loud wail as he did so. The shard fragmented into small pieces upon hitting the wall. Will's face was red. Needled pains shot through his weak arm. He picked up another large piece next to him and threw this shard less forcefully than the first. The shard landed short of the wall and broke apart on the floor.

The studio door swung open and in came Abby and Mitch. Will was still kneeling over the broken urn. Abby could see there was broken urn all over the floor at the end of the studio. She knew exactly what had happened. If the urn had just broken her father would have simply mended the clay before firing. The debris was a tell tale sign that urn broke because of an episode.

"Are you alright Dad?"

Abby knew the answer before he spoke.

"Yea," said Will, "I tripped."

"Are you sure that is what happened?"

Will raised his voice, "I said I damn tripped. Isn't that enough for you people? It's this damn floor."

"Yea, alright Dad. We heard a loud noise and just came to see what the hell happened."

Will was still rubbing his arm, his head bent toward the floor, "I guess I better get the broom and clean this up."

"You remember Mitch?"

"Of course. I'm old, not senile. Hey there Mitch."

"Hey there, Will," Mitch replied. "You need help cleaning up?"

"No," said Will, his voice calm and softer. "No, you kids go ahead."

Mitch turned to Abby.

"I should probably get going anyway," said Mitch.

"Thank you for bringing the skates by," said Abby then quickly added, "And thank you for the conversation. It was nice."

"Me too, I mean thank you for the tea, and the conversation," said Mitch.

Mitch turned and walked out the doorway. "What a girl," he thought as he made his way to his yellow pickup. The conversation really had been refreshing and Mitch felt that he had connected with someone in a way he had not in a long time. As Mitch got into the truck, a smile crept across his face. Abby was waving good-bye from the door of the studio. Mitch waved to Abby, backed his truck out of the driveway, and kept smiling.

Abby walked back into the studio and discovered her father still on the floor. Will had not moved from his kneeling position. Walking over to the side room to grab a broom she said, "I don't remember the last time I saw you smash an urn. I've seen you repair worse."

"Well I dropped it. Is that what you want to hear? Damn, it's not the first time I dropped a piece of damn clay."

"Colorful language," said Abby as she started to sweep up the remnants of the urn strewn across the room. "I bet you can't even get up."

"I can get up."

Will lifted himself from the floor hobbling a little on his right leg as he did.

Abby walked toward him, "Let me help you."

"I don't need help!"

"I think that is exactly what you need."

Will raised his voice again, "I think you need not worry about it."

"Well how long do you think it will be 'til I have to? Give me a heads up so that I can know 'now it's the time to worry!'" Abby threw down the broom and stormed out of the studio.

Will had never been one to yell yet lately his voice was rising quite a bit. Yelling was something Abby was not accustomed to and certainly not going to stand for.

Will slowly walked over to where Abby had thrown the broom. He bent forward and picked the broom up with his good hand. His other arm was not shooting pain anymore. Will opened his hand stretching his fingers wide and then pensively he closed them together into a tightened fist. A fist that still felt weak.

* * * * *

CHAPTER 9

Walking into the Stone Tavern Abby was washed with a wave of warmth. The whole place had the smell of burning wood and stale beer. The room was full of people shooting pool, leaning at the bar, and sitting at the yellow lacquered pine tables. A group of men and women standing at the bar wore full body snow suits, some blue and others black, all undone to the waist with the sleeves hanging behind them like tails. They were the owners of the small fleet of snowmobiles parked in a line outside of the tavern.

In the corner of the room was a small stage that held the house band's equipment and a space cleared for dancing. The equipment consisted of microphones, monitors, and a single bass drum kit. Tonight the two men on stage in blue jeans and t-shirts were not using any of the equipment. They sat on stools with acoustic guitars and were playing a mix of originals and alternative rock covers. They switched off on vocals, sometimes harmonized, and chose their material well. The music was not the kind to dance to, though the melody did tempt one to sing along if caught off guard.

Sitting in the center of the room between the pool table and the hearth were Caroline and Mitch. Mitch was pouring the last of the beer into Caroline's glass mug. Brian was behind them carrying a fresh pitcher from the bar over to the table. Abby removed her vest as they exchanged hellos - kisses three times for Caroline - and then hung the vest on one of the pegs that jutted out from the large wooden pillar next to the table.

Caroline touched Abby's arm, "Glad you could make it."

"Wednesday at the Stone Bar," said Abby as she sat in the empty chair at the table. "How could I miss it?"

"Well it could be karaoke night," added Brian and they all laughed.

Wednesday night at the Stone Tavern was a regular occurrence for Caroline and Abby when they were young. In the winters of their youth the tavern was the only place to unwind during the week. In the summers, the tavern was a great kickoff to the local cottage and beach parties. For Caroline and Brian the tavern was a regular occurrence since they had moved to the lake. A time to swing back a couple of mugs and commune with the other locals as they discussed hunting and fishing, building and tearing down, and how the bad winter of fifteen years ago compared to the winter of thirty years ago. The Stone Tavern's smell, the warmth, the conversations, and the faces of the old timers holding up the end of the bar were very much a part of home as the lake.

Brian poured Abby a mug of beer then refreshed his own. Abby needed to slip a second hand under the heavy glass mug when she took the handle so she could have a steady sip. Abby took a drink and let the foam momentarily sit in her mouth before swallowing. She truly enjoyed beer on the rare occasion. She preferred wine yet pitcher beer from the tap was an old indulgence from her childhood. The beer tasted delicious in the warm room.

"You came just in time," said Caroline. "These fellas have been talking about the new snowmobiles outside since we got here."

"Well a man has to have an appreciation of machinery,"

Brian retorted.

"There was a new one?" asked Abby, her eyebrow lifted.

"Exactly," said Caroline lifting her mug to toast her friend.

The discussion at the table stayed light as they drank their beer and joked with each other. There was a new project coming up that was still in the architectural stages. Abby enjoyed hearing Brian passionately explain archways and stairwells though most of the conversation was Greek to her. As she listened to the architect and the carpenter's vision of the project to come, she noticed that both were wearing wool sweaters. She caught herself thinking how handsome Mitch looked in his. The sweater added to his musculature giving Mitch a statuesque quality that she had not seen in him before. Caroline touched her hand then winked when Abby glanced at her.

After another pitcher of beer, Brian and Mitch went to the pool table leaving Caroline and Abby alone.

"So what do you think?" asked Caroline.

"About what?"

"About Mitch, I know he likes you."

"Maybe so," Abby did not want to give in to Caroline's line of questioning.

"I am sure of it," Caroline stated in an exaggerated voice.

"He is a nice guy and all but --,"

Caroline cut her off "—But what?"

'But what,' what indeed, the sentiment echoed in Abby's head. That was a question Abby had not asked herself and maybe because she had enjoyed the beer or maybe the warmth in the room or maybe she had just been in denial because right now she realized that she did in fact like Mitch. Not just like, she was also attracted to him. Up until now there had been no question as to 'but what', the question had been moot.

"Caroline," a non-answer suggesting that Caroline was joking. Caroline's face went falsely serious. Abby added, "He lives here and I live in the city."

They shared a giggle, which made light of the conversation and took a bit of the tension away that was building up in Abby's mind. Caroline was obvious in her intentions to set Abby and Mitch up and that did not bother Abby that much. Caroline thought well of Mitch and Abby both and that Caroline proposed a match was a compliment to either of them. What did bother Abby was that she herself was considering Mitch at all. The last thing she needed would be to get involved with someone. Abby was beginning to feel elated and overwhelmed. She gazed over to the pool table where Mitch was leaning over to shoot. The light above the table shown amber on Mitch, shadowing his contours, he was a handsome man.

Abby winked at Caroline, "He is kinda cute." They both smiled.

After the pool game Brian returned to the table, "Well I'm out. Who's next?"

Caroline spoke first, "Abby wants to play."

Abby matched eyes with Mitch, already racking the balls for the next contender, smiled and stood from her chair taking the cue stick from Brian in the same motion then walked directly to the pool table, grabbed the chalk from the edge, and chalked her cue.

"You've done this before," said Mitch.

"Once or twice," replied Abby coyly.

Mitch finished racking the balls and slid the rack into the slot at the end of the table.

"Lady breaks," said Mitch.

Abby leaned toward the table, moved the cue ball to the right of center, and then aligned herself for the shot. She pulled her arm back and then in a single motion thrust forward. A white streak struck the balls at the other end of the table. The pool balls initially made a loud crackling sound as they clacked together and then spread across the table dropping three balls into three pockets.

"Let's see," said Mitch, "A three, five, and an eleven, two solids and a stripe, ladies choice. You have done this before."

The four was lined up with the pocket and Abby bent to take a sure shot. Shooting too quickly at the ball, Abby failed to hit the ball square and rolled the four across the table away from the pocket.

"There goes beginners luck," said Abby.

"It's alright. I thought they sent over a ringer."

"Far from it, I haven't played in forever."

Taking his turn, Mitch shot at the fifteen and put the ball in the corner pocket. He then lined up for the twelve.

"Sounds like your project up at the Johansson house is really coming along," said Abby.

"You should stop by and see it tomorrow, if it's on your way."

Before making his shot, Mitch raised his head and their eyes met, only for a second. The acoustic duo was singing an old folk harmony. Abby was sure she felt a spark and so did Mitch. Mitch's eyes returned to the green field of the table and fixed upon the twelve. He pocketed the ball with a quick blow from the cue. Abby complimented the obligatory, "Nice shot." This sounded flirtatious to Mitch, and though not necessarily intentional, encouraging. He then shot the cue ball down the length of the table toward the thirteen sinking the thirteen and the fourteen.

Abby decided a little banter might be necessary and was coming up short. "Tomorrow? I suppose I could swing by. Maybe around lunch?"

Mitch lifted his eyes from the table, "Yea, lunch would be great. You know how to get there right?"

"I know," said Abby.

Mitch missed his next shot giving Abby a chance to redeem her game.

The next shot was easy as the two-ball was on the edge of the corner. The second shot that Abby needed to make was a bit more of a challenge. The four was still sitting next to the pocket and was easily her best bet since she had no obvious other shots and there was no direct way to hit the four without banking the shot. She stood at the corner of the table getting her bearing on an angle and then shifted to the other corner doing the same thing. Abby then kneeled down to see the cue balls perspective, furrowed her brow for a moment, and nodded her head.

"Not a clue, do you?" said Mitch.

"Nope," answered Abby.

"I'll tell you what," said Mitch, "I will walk to the end of the table and place my finger on the edge of the table. All you have to do is aim at my finger."

"You'll do that?"

"Yes, I will," said Mitch.

"Well ok then."

Mitch walked to the end of the table. He held his arm up and pointed at the four-ball, then pointed at the side pocket, and then he hovered his finger for a moment while he gauged the cue ball before placing his finger on the edge of the bumper.

"Gently," said Mitch.

Abby leaned across the table and pushed her cue stick toward his finger gently as he had said. The ivory ball went to the bumper and to the aubergine ball. Upon being struck the ball slowly spun around into the side pocket.

"Well how do you like them apples?" Abby asked.

"There you go," said Mitch.

Abby saw a shot she thought would be easy. The seven-ball was at the corner of the table and a straight shot from the cue. Abby walked around the table circling Mitch at the end where he stood. "Easy shot," said Abby as she passed him. Abby took the shot. The cue ball bounced off the bumper next to the seven, missing the ball, and raced down the other side of the table right into the eight ball. The eight ball and the cue ball went into the opposite corner pocket.

"Ouch," said Mitch. "A little too much spin I guess."

Abby wrinkled her nose at Mitch, "I guess."

* * * * *

CHAPTER 10

Mitch and Abby went back to the table to join Caroline and Brian. Bob Jensen, owner of the Stone Tavern, was at the table. Bob was complimenting the couple on the party and goading Brian as to whether he felt any 'worse for the wear' at forty. After Bob stepped away, the pitchers began to pour.

The acoustic duo finished another harmonic number then announced they were taking a long break then began talking amongst themselves. Mitch excused himself and walked over to the stage. Abby could see that Mitch and the duo were friends by the 'bro-hug handshakes' they exchanged. She saw them scan the table then focus back on her and suspected that Mitch was requesting some sort of song.

One of the musicians walked the three steps to the back of the stage with his guitar in hand and took a violin out of a case. Caroline tapped Abby on the arm when, instead of putting the guitar down, the musician handed the instrument to Mitch.

"You're going to love this," said Caroline.

Mitch sat on the musician's stool and the violinist stood to Mitch's left while the other musician picked up his guitar and took a seat back on his respective stool.

Mitch spoke into the microphone, "I got the boys to do one more quick song."

Mitch looped the thick black leather guitar strap over his neck. "This is to make up for winning a pool game," said Mitch fixing his gaze at Abby.

Mitch began to strum the guitar slowly. Abby felt the warmth of her cheeks flushing and was giddy in her stomach.

"We don't have a drummer so we'll need everyone's help when the time comes. You'll know when."

The violinist serenely followed in behind Mitch. Mitch began to sing a slow, sappy, sweet verse. Abby had a sudden urge to head for the door. The verse was a simple rhyme scheme and a few lines that switched from serious to comedic.

'If you had a chance
  to meet this girl
You would know
why I feel this way.
Mary Love is the loveliest
girl in the world
now she is gone away.
But she left with Mark,
John, Paul, and Rob
so with them I wish she'd stay'

The bar filled with laughter and the violinist changed to a quicker rhythm that, with the accompaniment of the guitar, created an upbeat jig. Two couples near the dance floor got up and began to dance and Mitch repeated the verse in time with the music and went into new facetious verses. Abby had thought Mitch's demeanor calm and cool. Contrarily his exuberance had the whole room clapping in time. The bow of the violin melodically sped across the strings with a melancholy cry that fit the song well. The song was a comedic dreadful story of a man abused by a lover, named Mary Love, which he could not escape. No matter how many times she would cheat and leave, she would always come back. The man attempted to hide everywhere, yet to no avail, which came out in the chorus:

'You can try to hide in the valley below,
You can try in the mountain above, but,
You cannot hide,
You cannot hide,
You cannot hide from Love.'

Mitch and the guitarist had both stood up by this point and were tapping to the rhythm. Another couple was dancing and the air had turned electric. The music of the last verse slowed then rose to a crescendo for the last chorus then stopped abruptly to everyone's applause.

"Thank you everybody," said Mitch. He winked at Abby and then shook the duos hands before returning to the table.

"Told you you'd love that," said Caroline.

"Who wouldn't," said Abby.

The three at the table clapped again as Mitch approached to sit down and Brian picked up the pitcher and topped off Mitch's beer.

"Aren't you talented," said Abby.

"That's the only song I know," said Mitch.

"I doubt that."

"Well maybe a couple more," said Mitch.

"I bet you do," said Abby.

"He does, don't buy the modesty act," said Caroline. "Let's see if he's talented enough to read a menu. I'm famished."

"Ha, ha, ha," said Mitch in a mock laugh as he took the menu Caroline offered him.

Instead of reading at what was on the menu, Mitch was peering over the top at Abby. Her cheeks were full and she was glowing after all of the laughter. Mitch realized he had stared too long into the light and had to avert his eyes when Abby began to lift her head from the menu. Abby had not noticed. When Abby lifted her head, she saw Mitch intently studying his menu.

"Do you know what you're having?" asked Abby.

"So many choices I'm not sure. It all looks good," said Mitch.

"You should try the child's menu," said Caroline.

Mitch mockingly laughed again, "Ha, Ha. You are full of them tonight."

"Maybe if you looked at the menu a bit more instead of Abby you would find something," said Caroline. She had noticed Mitch's prolonged gaze in Abby's direction.

"Probably a burger," said Mitch. "Yes, a burger and sweet potato fries."

* * * * *

CHAPTER 11

Will pulled his truck up to the Stone Tavern and parked in the space at the end of the snowmobile pack. He stepped out and looked across the road to see if the liquor store was still open. The fluorescent light that hung low in the store was on however that did not necessarily mean anything since they left the lights on all night over there. The watch Will kept on the dashboard of his truck had not worked in five years or been worn in fifteen, even then only on occasion. Walking across the road, he leaned his neck forward to see any signs of movement a bit sooner. The face of the wall clock read ten minutes to the hour. Will took this as a good sign. When Will opened the door a little bell signaled the counter that someone had just arrived in case they were stocking shelves, in the back, or with a customer.

The Willow Lake liquor store was just that and nothing else. This was the only place to buy liquor for twenty miles. The store interior did not need to be upscale or wood trimmed. The wine section did not need the ends of giant casks on the wall. The advertisements were even at a minimum because they were not really needed. The liquor store had been set up by the liquor control commission and was as basic as a store could get.

Inside of the liquor store aisle after aisle of alcohol, the vodka, the whiskey, the brandy, and gin were lined up on the shelves with full cases behind them, in more of a storage facility fashion than a display. Along the side and back walls, from floor to ceiling, were all of the varietals of wines, the Cabernets, the Chardonnays, the Pinots, and the Chablis from wineries from around the world. The variety of wine labels to choose from represented a vast collection of wineries, corporate and boutique, with catchy names like 'Red Juice', 'Farmers Dream', and 'Devil Dog'.

Will chose his wines for taste and price. The Argentinian Malbec had a faux French label to appear authentic and the Shiraz had a large black turtle on the label. Both were under ten dollars and did not taste like varnish. That pretty much made them his wines. In what now had become a ritual he swiped one of each off the shelves and went up to the counter. After setting the bottles down next to the register Will stepped back three steps and picked up a half pint of ginger brandy, elixir as he called the drink, and tossed the bottle hand to hand as he stepped back to the counter. Will knew what the total would be before Dennis, the cashier, rang the bill up. Will reached into his pocket and pulled out two twenties and placed them and the ginger brandy next to the wine. Dennis bagged the bottles and slid them across the counter. Will did not wait for Dennis to ring in the twenties. Will scooped up the bag and muttered goodnight as he turned to the door.

Will's walk back across the street was direct. His thumb punched the button to the handle of the passenger door and as the door swung open, he pulled himself inside. Will dropped the bag on the passenger side floor of the truck. Immediately he reached for the ginger brandy. He cracked the top and poured some down his throat. A jolt shot through him. He cringed. His body tightened up and then went loose as he shook off the initial bite. A numbing quiver crept up his spine. Will put the bottle to his lips and took another drink. This one went down smooth and brought him momentary euphoria.

Will slipped the brandy into his inside coat pocket, shut the door to the pickup, and then headed to the Tavern door. Stepping inside Will went right to the end of bar, waved over Jodi the bartender, and ordered a beer and a sidecar of whiskey. While waiting for his drinks Will said hello to some fellow locals at the bar, undid his coat, and proceeded in small talk with Terry Enders. The talk was automated though because all Will could really think about was getting the beer and whiskey. A beer and a shot were part of the formula that would calm his nerves and steady his hands so he could get back to work on the urns. Urns that were Bellen urns only if they were made by Bellen hands. This was all part of a ritual.

"What's taking Jodi so long to pour a damn beer and a shot," Will thought to himself as he continued the small talk then half-heartedly laughed at a comment he really did not hear. The world around Will was secondary and out of focus. To watch Jodi talking to someone else at the end of the bar was frustrating for him when he had not even been served yet. Will clenched his jaw. Jodi had just taken some money from another customer and was about to ring them up.

Terry was still going on about some hockey game and how he thought some coach had made an unfair call. Will was not paying much attention to Terry anymore. Terry realized this and tried to get Will's attention.

"Will, what do you think?"

A pause.

Terry asked a second time, "What do you think Will?"

Terry began to ask a third time and Will snapped at him in a raised voice, "I don't really care what call he makes Terry. I just want Jodi to get me a beer!"

"I hear ya," said Jodi across the bar. "I'm comin' right over."

"That's fine," said Terry. "No point getting uppity."

Everybody else on that side of the bar heard Will as well, including Abby.

Abby and Caroline looked at each other and then up at Will fidgeting at the end of the bar—tap, tap, tap with the hands. Jodi was holding a pint glass with one hand and the beer tap down with the other, as if that would make the beer pour any faster. As soon as the beer neared the top of the glass Jodi eased up the tap at a pace just slow enough to put a head on the beer yet fast enough to let Will know that he was working with a sense of urgency.

"Why thank you Jodi," said Will when the beer was placed in front of him.

"No problem Will," said Jodi, holding the rocks glass in one hand and pouring whiskey with the other.

Jodi set the rocks glass next to the pint.

Will raised his brow and said to Terry, "Now that wasn't so hard was it."

"Lay off him and go home," said Abby. She was now standing just behind Will. "You need a drink so bad you need to be a bully?" she asked.

"Whoa, now hold on there," said Will.

Terry turned toward the television at the other end of the bar and everyone sitting at the bar in earshot pretended not to hear. Mitch, Brian, and Caroline were a few feet away and were coming closer until Abby held out her hand for them to halt where they were.

"Whoa nothing," Abby's voice was quiet, "you might think you can get away with being nasty in your studio but this is the real world. How dare you bully these nice people?"

Will was caught off guard and did not quite know what to say. Will started to stutter a sentence, "Well just a minute Abby, I was just --." Abby cut him off, "—Just a minute nothing. Go home Will. Go home. This has to stop. You don't understand what you're doing to yourself." Abby turned and walked to the door. Mitch and Brian followed.

Caroline sidled over to her uncle, "Listen to her uncle

Will."

"Storm's a comin'," said Will with a wink. Caroline raised her eyebrows, looked to the door, back to her uncle, smiled, and then she too walked out the door.

When Caroline joined the three outside Abby was moving both of her arms up and down to shake out whatever negative energy she felt could be expelled through her fingertips.

"Are you ok?" asked Caroline.

"It's not me," said Abby. "It's him, and he doesn't see it."

"I know," said Caroline, "That's why I called you to begin with."

"You were so right. He's like this every day?"

The door to the bar opened and out walked Terry Enders. Terry could not avoid Abby because she was right in front of the door.

"Hey there, you okay?" asked Terry.

"I'm fine Mr. Enders," said Abby. Long since retired, Terry had been one of Abby and Caroline's schoolteachers.

"I'm sorry my father was so rude to you."

"Abby dear," said Terry, " Your father has been there for me when I've needed him many times over. We all need to blow off a little steam sometimes."

"He upset every one in the bar," said Abby.

"The only person he upset in the bar, just walked out and is talking to me right here," said Terry. "Your father is a good man. Good night."

"Good night," said Abby.

* * * * *

CHAPTER 12

Will gazed up from the split log bench through the leafless willow branches. He marveled at how large the willow had become since Emily had planted the tree twenty long years ago. Though chemotherapy had made Emily feel ill, she had found the strength to go out to the bench in the early mornings to watch the sunrise. Often Will would wrap a blanket around her cold shoulders and hold her frail body to keep her warm. Emily found comfort next to him.

Emily knew Will had concerns about the progress of the treatment so she told him that she had decided to plant and watch a tree grow tall. Watch as the tree aged with them. Will had suggested the now fifty-foot tall weeping willow and told Emily the seedling would thrive next to the lake. Will did not tell Emily why the fast growing willow tree had been his choice, yet she knew. Will's hope that Emily could see the seedling grow to a tree kept her going. Shivering and weak Emily had put the roots deep into the ground.

Sitting on the bench, gazing through the branches of the tree that had thrived next to the lake for those almost twenty years Will lost himself in thoughts of Emily. Thoughts where Emily was still alive, always exuberant, never weak, never dying. He felt her presence there. He felt their youth. He was not alone.

* * * * *

William Bellen and Emily Allen met during her college break when Emily took a summer job, detail painting for Will's father. Will barely said a word to Emily the first weeks she worked at the studio. The studio was electric when Emily was there. Her detailing on the urns was as dazzling as Emily herself. Emily wore her chestnut hair to her shoulders making her hazel eyes all the more friendly and inviting, like her laughter, and she always wore a sleeveless blouse and Capri pants that came half way down her calves. Will did not say much to her. He could not think about anything else.

Will tended the big wood-burning kiln, the only kiln at that time, and fed the oven's voracious appetite for small logs. The temperatures in June and July that year had already been high and were twenty degrees higher working next to the kiln. Often Will did not wear a shirt when he chopped the logs by axe and then fed them into the kiln. Emily had secretly been sketching him from the window of the studio. She had taken notice of Will's young frame, oily and covered with a fine mist of soot that made the tone of his body glisten.

Will's fascination with Emily had distracted him to near stupor. Will's father was getting frustrated with all of the clay that Will was breaking, not much pottery was getting into the kiln or getting too far away. Will's father finally resolved to coax Will into asking Emily to have lunch.

When Will approached Emily with the sodas and sandwiches he had made himself and asked her to have lunch on the dock, she did not hesitate to say yes in fear he would change his mind.

"Perfect timing," said Emily. Emily grabbed Will's hand and practically dragged him out to the lakeshore.

Capitalizing on the opportunity to make an impression,

Will began rattling out all of the conversation he had held back for the last two months. There was no pause for Emily to say anything. She thought the sweet boy's behavior incredibly cute. Still Emily feared that Will was going to give himself the hiccups.

Emily decided she needed to calm him down. Though what she did next would not exactly slow his heart. Will's speech did slow, first to a crawl then a stop.

As Will professed how modern kilns could change the family business, Emily stood up on the dock, pulled off her white blouse, tossed the shirt down, then undid her Capri pants and shimmied them to her feet. Emily stepped out of the crumpled pants one foot at a time. Standing in her bra and panties, Emily fixed her eyes on Will. Now silent, Will sat on the dock with his legs crossed, a sandwich in one hand and a soda in the other, his mouth open.

"It is so hot today Will, let's go swimming," said Emily. She ran to the end of the dock and dove into the clear water of the lake. Emily surfaced fifteen feet away, her head bobbing above the water.

Will was still sitting on the dock with his mouth open.

"Well," said Emily.

"I'm coming."

Will tried to stand so quickly that he forgot his legs were crossed. He tumbled over the side of the dock, blue jeans, t-shirt, soda, and sandwich in hand.

Will stood up next to the dock, the water at his waist and t-shirt soaked, still holding his soda. Emily, concerned for Will's safety, wanted to call out to him to ask if he was ok. Instead, she could not help herself from laughing uncontrollably.

"What's so funny?" asked Will, the corners of his mouth pushing his cheeks up to his dripping ears.

Will placed his soda on the dock. He waded a few feet out into the lake and then, still wearing his clothes, dove toward Emily. Will surfaced when he got to Emily. She immediately started splashing water in his face to which he splashed back. They played in the water and then went up to the soft green grass by the shoreline where they dried themselves in the warm air of the hot July day.

Through the rest of July and all of August, a day did not go by that Emily and Will did not have lunch together.

Emily had come to Willow Lake with her twin sister Mary and the two shared a cabin on their parent's property that was the size of a small house. To make spending time together easier Will and Emily set Mary up with Will's friend Tom. Tom's parents owned the IGA grocery store kitty corner from the Stone Tavern. The four of them went boating, swimming, and had late night bonfires with six-packs of beer and steaks from the IGA.

When not with Mary and Tom, Emily and Will would explore the many trails in the wooded hills surrounding Willow Lake sometimes disappearing for the whole afternoon. This prompted Will's Father to go on about both of them slacking on the work that needed to be done around the studio. He really could not be happier for both of them.

On rainy days Will and Emily stayed in the studio and marveled at each other's artistic skills. Will had been raised a potter and, a master of the kick wheel, could bring up tall pots, squat pots, vases, and cups. While at the wheel Will explained to Emily what he was doing. Emily took her turn at the wheel next to Will and made mess after mess. Will came over to Emily, put his arms around her, placed his hands gently below hers, and guided her. With Will's guidance, Emily was able to even out the ball of clay to the center of her wheel and then indent the center in the right way so that the sides began to rise. Will explained to her that this was the dance of the clay. As he spoke, her neck quivered. When the spinning wheel stopped, Emily held a small pot and Will held Emily. Their eyes were closed, frozen in the moment.

Emily in turn helped Will with his sketching.

Will always carried a notepad and a pencil in his back

pocket. He was ready for a fiddlehead fern at the edge of a trail or a cardinal perched in an almost hidden tree. Every small bird, leaf, and flower was captured in his sketchpad as an ornate possibility for his pieces. Will's sketches matured to full designs and lines of pottery and he would explain to Emily how important he thought the ornamentation could be if done the right way.

Will was not only sketching butterflies and trees. At times Emily would look up from her sketchbook to find that she had become the object of his study. Her body would go warm under Will's blue gaze. On Will's square jaw, a constant sultry smile that Emily could not resist to mirror.

Emily sketched everything. For Emily each page in her sketchpad was a prototype for a painting. Emily sketched with pastels when she could because the true subjects for Emily's paintings were not the objects themselves rather the colors in the light within and around them. She lived in a universe of varying shades of illumination and her passion was to capture them.

Will's father commented that he did not ever remember seeing Will sit still for so long as when Will posed for Emily by the lake. When Emily gave Will the watercolor portrait he told her that the radiating color made him look some how courageous and that the wondrous waterscape could have been some far off sea and not Willow Lake at all.

Emily stayed up late with Will as he tended the kiln. She told him of her plans to collect sunrises from different places around the world. They spoke of Notre Dame and the Seine, the Pyramids and Sphinx, Crete and Knossos, and The Great Wall and The Forbidden City. Will wanted to go to all of the places where Bellen pottery had gone before them to gather sunrises as well. Will and Emily together listed all of those places they would pass along the way so as not to miss the sunrises of the Mediterranean or Caribbean while their ships sailed in the early hours.

William Bellen was a sweet, kind, generous boy and

Emily Allen was falling in love. William had no need for a fall. Will's heart belonged to Emily Allen the first time she stepped into the studio.

Will and Emily never talked about September. When time came for Emily and Mary to go back to school, Will and Tom stayed up with them all night and then saw them off. There were no tears or long faces. The boys saw the girls off with the same upbeat energy and humor that had been with them all summer. The girl's car was not even out of site when the boys put their hands on their hips and looked at each other. Will scratched his head. Emily and Mary were both feeling the same way. All four of them already feared the absence of each other's company.

Emily and Mary wrote the boys often telling them about the classes they were taking, the activities they were involved in, and campus gossip that really meant nothing to anyone in Willow Lake. Occasionally Emily sent Will sketches of the world around her and he would pin the puppies, hippies, and university buildings on the wall. Emily even sent a sketch of Mary once. Will gave the portrait to Tom. Tom bought the beer that night.

Will and Tom were not big on writing so they decided to climb into Tom's car to go see the girls. The girl's parents allowed them to live in a small off campus bungalow their senior year. Emily made buttered noodles and bread - the bread burnt - and Mary made chicken. Will and Tom bought the biggest bottle of cheap red wine they could get. Friday night was a feast and Saturday was a headache. Will and Tom had never been to the university before so the girls said they would give them a tour of the campus, which never happened. None of them left the bungalow until Sunday when the time came to drive back to the lake.

Tom's car turned out to be not very dependable. Returning back home to Willow Lake the car broke down and would not run again. This did not deter Will and Tom. They made their next few visits to see the girls by hitching to the university until Tom's father took pity on them.

Tom's father had said that he appreciated the boy's determination yet there would be no benefit to anyone if they were found frozen at the side of the road. The boys themselves had thought that would happen on more than one occasion. Tom's father lent them his car every other weekend to get them through the coldest months.

The year could not go by fast enough for Will. When the weather got warmer, Will started hitching again so that he could see Emily as often as he could. Emily missed a few classes yet still graduated in May without her parents being the wiser. Then Emily and Mary went back to the lake for another amazing summer.

The four easily fell back into the routine of boating, swimming, late night bonfires, shared six packs of beer and steaks from the IGA. Will and Emily worked side by side each day and Tom and Mary spent their time together at Mary's cabin.

In the fall, Will took on some shifts at the IGA and Tom added some shifts to his normal schedule. The girls wondered why the boys were spending so much time working rather than spending the precious little summer that was left with them. The boys told them that they were trying to scrape together the money for a car so that they would not have to hitch the extra distance this winter to see girls in the city. The city was much farther than the university.

What Will and Tom did not know is that the girls were going to surprise them by staying at the cabin through the winter. They had fulfilled their obligation of finishing school and had bargained with their parents for a year off before starting their next endeavors.

The boys had a surprise for Emily and Mary all of there own, they were not saving up for a car. At a late night bonfire at the end of August, under a full moon, the boys executed their plan. They had borrowed two canoes for a morning fishing trip. After a full fireside meal, they asked the girls if they wanted to go canoeing. Each took a girl in their canoe and they paddled out together onto the lake. The lake was bright as daylight. The girls suspected nothing when the boys made an excuse for each canoe to go a separate way. The boys had done well to hold their ardor and let the evening do their talking. In the middle of Willow Lake with blankets wrapped around them and moonlight shining down, Will proposed to Emily and Tom proposed to Mary. To the relief of the young men, both of the girls said yes.

Tom Anderson and Mary Allen were married and moved into the cabin until a house could be built some years later. William Bellen and Emily Allen were married and moved into his father's family home.

Will and Emily loved the western shore and every morning the couple would have their morning coffee in front of the big bay window overlooking the lake, warmed by the fuchsia, tangerine, and lilac hues that escorted the rays of the sun.

The next few years the two were happy alone with each other, and with Will's father. The children were neither planned nor unplanned. They had wanted children and let fate happen. Michael, Will's protégé to carry on the Bellen craft, came first followed a bit later by his sister Abby, every way was the shadow of her mother. Where Michael shared his father's cool demeanor, Abby's electricity filled the room like her mother.

As a girl Abby would wake each morning and patter out of her room to find her father in his chair reading the daily paper and her mother at the table with her watercolors and brushes, often trying to capture the hues of the morning sky. The sunrise was to Emily what Mont Sainte-Victoire was to Cezanne. Abby's mother would set everything aside to greet her daughter and pour her juice. Emily and Abby would then discuss their day's agendas, decipher a dream Abby had the night before, or go over homework to be turned in that day. At some point Michael would roll out of bed and sleepily join the group. Will intermittently chimed in to report a news story he found interesting or outrageous, usually having to do with the local community or politicians. Will considered both 'backwards'. Then he would go to the stove and start to prepare the morning feast of eggs, potatoes, bacon, and on weekend's stacks of pancakes.

Breakfast was the Bellen family's time together. Young families lead busy lives and the Bellen family was no different, rising early because they would rarely convene again as a family until the following morning.

* * * * *

CHAPTER 13

The lakeside trees diminished as the rocky shoreline crept up to the road around the last bend to South Point. There were three spots on the lake where Willow Lake road ran next to the shore, in the village, Peters beach, and at the rocks at South Point. Now out of the shade of the trees the winter sunlight shown on Abby as she drove her father's truck. To her left nestled in the trees across the rocky shore lined cove Abby could see the deck of the South Point Inn. Perched on the hill above her, ever watching the lake as in her childhood, Abby could see the Johansson house. At the end of the bend, the blue pickup turned right onto Johansson drive and then ventured away from the lake up and around the hill.

From the lake the house appeared brilliant white against the snow, up close the paint was chipped and faded in many spots, revealing stripped patches of black and grey wood siding beneath. Having been untended for years, unremembered stalks of tall grasses and clovers, brown and withered, poked out through the snow around the base of the house and the yard. By the side of the house, the doors of the three-bay garage were open. Two bays were filled with lumber, large sheets of compressed wood, and stacked in the back with what Abby thought might be drywall and hardwood flooring. A large table saw stood in the third bay surrounded by sawdust and wood chips. When Abby stepped down from the pickup truck she could smell the fresh cut of the sawdust mixed with the oil of the saw and leading from the bay into the side door of the three-story house she could see the trail of wooden dust. Coming from somewhere inside the large house Abby could hear saws and the rhythmic stomp of a hammer so she headed toward the side door.

Yesterday Mitch excited Abby. How could she not be attracted to someone that spontaneously performed a song in her honor? She certainly felt physically attracted to him at the bar although that might have been the beer. Abby feared today may be different.

When Abby stepped through the door Mitch greeted her by yelling across the house.

"Hey there Abby!"

"Hey Mitch!"

"We're up front. Watch your step coming out of the mudroom and across the kitchen, and head into the sitting room!"

Bright lights bounced off fresh white paint in every room Abby walked through. The sitting room was a large room facing the lake with a large angled fireplace on the corner of the outer wall. A chandelier cast out yellow light onto the walnut floor and left a dim shadow in the fireplace. Abby decided that the chandelier was faux crystal because there was far too much to be real. From the sitting room, Abby could see Mitch's reflection in the next room from a dimly mirrored set of shelves behind a bar. Mitch was standing in front of the bar talking to one of the carpenters. He looked stunning to her. Abby's heart beat noticeably faster. She felt a definite attraction today.

From where Abby stood, she could see the lake vista.

Newly seated bay windows faced north and east. Through the north window Abby could see the cerulean midday sky blanketing the horizon. The eastern window overlooked the terrace and the glassed-in porch.

Abby gestured toward the outside terrace, "Can I go out there?"

"Sure. Just a second though, it might be better if I come out with you. It's a bit rickety in spots."

Mitch finished his conversation with the carpenter then joined Abby.

The two went out on the porch and then out the door to the wooden deck terrace.

"It seems solid enough," said Abby.

"For the most part. I wouldn't trust these old wooden steps though. Most of them are rotten. They'll be replaced this summer after the new gas lines are run for the pool."

"Pool?"

"An infinity pool. Right here under the terrace," said Mitch.

"And overlooking all of that," said Abby. Abby rested her eyes closed then inhaled deeply taking in the brisk air and the whole of the lake and countryside. She opened her eyes and relaxed her shoulders, "Not a bad day at the office."

"Except for the ice road across the lake," said Mitch, "It looks pretty much the same as it did a hundred years ago."

The ice road ran from the IGA in the village to the South Point Inn on the other side of Willow Lake cutting the distance and time off the trip from one side of the lake to the other December through March. The ice road was the road that fisherman used to get to their ice shanties in the center of the lake and snowmobile enthusiasts made part of their route when riding the trails. The ice road also created a direct route of travel to the ski lodge on Mount Frisia. Abby did not like the ice road much and could not wait to get from one end to the other when she needed to travel across the lake because the thought of driving over the ice in something as heavy as a vehicle always churned her stomach.

A slight wind chilled the terrace. "That's from the lake," said Mitch. "Let's go back inside. I'll give you the grand tour."

The two went back into the house that now seemed far warmer than when the two had stepped outside.

"So who is paying for all of this?" asked Abby.

"An investment group from the city hopes that the place will become a premier spa, bed and breakfast sort of thing."

"Ah, how nice."

Mitch showed Abby the rooms on the main floor she had missed coming in. Then he took her upstairs and showed her the bedrooms to be decorated in contemporary style, each of course with a separate bath. Three tradesmen were at different phases of construction as Abby walked through the upstairs rooms. A lot of the interior was complete still Abby could see there was trim work, painting, and stucco yet to be done.

The third floor consisted of luxury spa suites overlooking the lake. These two and three bedroom suites were larger than Abby's fourth floor city apartment and loaded with amenities. In the middle of the grey marble bathrooms were stone hot tubs and glassed-in showers that had water jets floor to ceiling in every corner. The views were better in the luxury suites then two floors below. On the horizon to the north, Abby could see Fremont and to the east, she could see skiers on lift to the top of Mount Frisia, the large hill at the lakes southeast corner.

"You know these will fill up," said Abby.

"You still haven't seen my pet project," said Mitch.

* * * * *

CHAPTER 14

Mitch led Abby back to the main floor library then through a sheet-curtained door that led into a large room built on to the side of the house. If Abby had closed her eyes, she would have thought she walked into the center of a pine grove. The large room was entirely pine paneled except for one wall that had a very large velvet curtain. Three rows of large cushion armchairs filled the room. The trim across the top, bottom, and sides of the wood panels was embedded with the details of routed design work, and seated within the center of the wall panels were custom sound cushions.

"This theater has been my pet project," said Mitch.

"It's amazing," said Abby. "How much of it did you do?"

"Practically all of it, except of course the curtains, chairs and movie equipment."

"Did you design this?"

"Not exactly," said Mitch, " I kinda played it by ear – like jazz, ya know?"

"Whadda ya mean jazz?"

"You know," said Mitch, " I had to build this theater so I picked a place outside the library in the fall when I could still get a good foundation down. Once I had the foundation I had the bass line." He slowly drew a horizontal line through the air to illustrate his point. "I already knew the melody in as much as a theme. I mean the room was to be a theater. The movie equipment had a set of requirements. The rest I just made up as I went a long – like making up notes." Mitch made a rapid conducting motion, "Like jazz, I filled in the spaces in between the bars."

"Heavy," said Abby.

Mitch took Abby's hand, eased her down into a cushion chair next to him, and in his Bogart voice said, "The stuff dreams are made of."

Abby and Mitch took in the room.

"That's a great perspective," said Abby. "I've never seen a theater like this before. Pine paneled."

"I like tackling work like this, creativity in limits, your cousins make good partners."

"I can see why they like working with you," said Abby. She inspected the pine details. "How did you get the detailing so ornate?"

"Having Brian show me Roman and Greek reliefs until my eyes popped out and then a lot of hours practicing with the router. I enjoy the way the wood smells when you work with it, how the process relaxes the mind. It's Zen like I think."

"I can appreciate that," said Abby, " sometimes I get so caught up in my work it gets to the point where it takes over everything else."

"That's not exactly what I mean," said Mitch. " I don't think about it that way. Getting caught up in something that takes over."

"Well," said Abby, "my work can be an escape from the world around me. The city isn't like out here, you have to find a place to hide from it sometimes. It can suck you in and thrash you. You have to work to keep yourself sane. Isn't that what you mean?"

"I don't know if I am trying to hide from the world. I want to be part of my work, what I'm doing, not a slave to it," said Mitch.

"What's the difference if you enjoy what you're doing?" asked Abby.

"I dunno, but I think you got something there," said Mitch. "I don't suppose you want any tea."

Abby did want a cup of tea and was pleased that Mitch remembered.

When they exited the theater to the library Mitch gestured for Abby to step to the left.

"I forgot to show you the guest entrance," said Mitch.

They went through the foyer to the porch and looked out the window to the circular end of the drive.

"Step out the door and look to the side," said Mitch.

Abby did and saw on either side of the double oak doors two four-foot high, three-foot circular urns with embossed ivy decoration.

"I think they're Bellen's," said Mitch.

"They seem to be close, but I have never seen this design before. I wish we could see the mark on the bottom."

"Unfortunately they weigh half a ton. We're going to move them inside later, we'll take a look then."

"I can't wait to see," said Abby. Mitch and Abby went back inside.

They went to the kitchen where Mitch filled an electric kettle with water and then put the plug into a wall socket next to the stainless steel stove. From his lunch pail, Mitch produced milk from a short blue thermos and even some honey.

"You were pretty sure I was going to stop by," said Abby.

"Not in the least."

"I hope you aren't trying to impress me."

"Well, yea."

"Good job then."

Mitch put out two ceramic mugs and a box of Earl Grey.

"So you must think of Willow Lake pretty nostalgically. I mean you grew up here and everything but it has to be pretty far removed from where you are."

"It's removed alright."

"How are things in the city?"

"Things are fine, the job is good," said Abby. "It's not here."

Mitch raised his brow. "This back-water you mean?"

"Yea, that's what I mean," said Abby. "No of course that's not what I mean. I mean it isn't here. Simply that. Here everybody knows you. You're not from here, I am. Everybody knows my business, my past. There, I blend. I get to choose who I want to be, how I want to be. I don't get that here."

"So you don't like the 'every body knows your name' thing, eh?" asked Mitch.

"It's not that in so many words."

"What do you mean? I kinda like it." Mitch leaned his back against the counter picked up a spoon and began to stroke the end.

"It's just that here I am 'Will Bellen's' little girl, and there, I'm 'Abby Bellen woman-of-the-world'."

"I thought Caroline said that you girls had a great time growing up."

"We did, it was great, and I wouldn't trade it. But I had to get out of here. I mean after," Abby hesitated, "after my mom died, and then after high school. I had to get out of here."

"Your Mom, right, sorry. Caroline told me about her, said she was some kind of firecracker artist. Caroline said she was an inspiration."

"Yea she was all of that all right."

"That had to be rough dealing with the cancer, being a teenager, losing your mom. Good thing you had this whole community to support you."

"To support me, to remind me everyday, to treat me like I was broken. That's exactly why I had to get out of here."

"You still won't catch me in the city, but I think I get it."

"What do you get?"

"I get the 'where nobody knows your name' syndrome, I guess it works for everybody that moves around. Nobody knows you so you can invent yourself." Mitch turned and placed the spoon he had been fiddling with into a mug and unplugged the electric pitcher that had already heated the water to a boil. "Here you felt you were 'Will Bellen's daughter'," said Mitch, " there you invented Abby Bellen, the great curator."

"And you Mitch Carlson, you're not from here, who were you before you reinvented yourself?"

Abby opened the Earl Grey.

"No great mystery Abby," said Mitch taking a tea bag from Abby. "I was a coffee drinker."

* * * * *

CHAPTER 15

Will went into the house to get more coffee. The coffee can Will kept by the automatic drip in the studio was empty. He opened the yellow cupboard above the counter and pulled down the can kept there only to find few grounds inside. "How long since we had coffee in the house?" he thought. Shuffling further behind the sugar packets and cubes, the pink and yellow sweeteners, and the honey, produced no coffee. Will pulled out three boxes of tea instead. Holding two boxes in one hand and the other at arms length he tilted his head back to read the label. This did not satisfy Will so he reached into his pocket and put on his wire frame glasses for another look.

"Ok then," mumbled Will, "herbal assorted mint, raspberry... no." Will set the box on the counter and inspected the next. "Bergamot. Ughh." Will set down the Earl Grey and turned to the last box that read 'Black Breakfast Tea'. Will smirked and nodded his head. He tapped the box on his palm and scanned the kitchen.

The kettle was on the back of the counter. Will grinned, set the box of black tea down by the stove, and then filled the kettle with water from the tap. He put the kettle on the stove and then sat down at the table to wait. From the driveway came the sound of the pickup. Abby walked into the kitchen to see her father sitting peacefully watching the stove in anticipation. Abby stood for a moment contemplating whether to leave him for a while or to get the conversation over with that she had been dreading.

"Hey there, what are you doing?" asked Abby.

" I, am having, a cup of tea," said Will, as if he had been planning a cup of tea all morning.

"Mind if I join you?" asked Abby. She removed her coat.

"Please do, please do," said Will graciously. "I heard the old truck pull in. I hope it ran all right for you."

Abby hung her coat on a hook next to the door, "Yea it was fine, thanks."

Will brought his elbows to the table, clasped his hands, and then began tapping the ends of his fingers together. "Hey, Abby, about the Stone Bar --."

Abby interrupted, "That…"

Will now regretted mentioning the bar. He had not even had a cup of tea yet.

"I'm sorry," said Abby.

Will did not miss this window. "You're sorry," he opened his hands to her, "no I'm sorry honey. I forget myself sometimes."

"It's ok," Abby turned away from Will and walked over to the open tea cupboard.

"I forget myself too," said Abby.

Abby saw the empty can of coffee and understood Will's sudden inclination for tea.

"You wanted a black tea?" asked Abby.

"Yea, the 'Black Breakfast Tea', that's the one I like," said Will.

Abby took out the honey and two tea bags, one Earl Grey and one black tea, and placed them into two cups. She then put the rest of the tea back into the cupboard and closed the door.

Abby realized that Will had not had an afternoon

caffeine fix and decided she should ease off, or at least be subtle. She was right to think both were relieved to put yesterday's incident behind them. Still Abby's back was to Will as she straightened the counter and sorted his dishes from lunch.

Will dropped one hand onto his knee, put his back to the wall, and began tapping the table with the other as he watched Abby straighten the counter.

"So what did you think of that big old monstrosity up the hill?" asked Will.

"You should see the place. Brian and Caroline really know a thing or two and Mitch is doing a great job. I think it's going to be a real nice resort. It'll stir up a lot of business for the village and lodge."

"Can't say we don't need it, lodge almost went under again last year, new owners bailed, sold quick. That house is still going to be an eye sore though. I grew up with that thing looming over the lake, been empty most of my life, half my fathers too. Gives me the creeps," said Will, he shook his jowls, "Ahuhuhuh."

"Well, it's not going to be empty any more," said Abby.

"Still gives me the creeps."

"There were some old urns up there," said Abby, "a lot like ours but different somehow, nothing I've ever seen you make or in the scrapbooks."

"They're ours all right. Your great grandfather made them custom. Thick as hell so he could carve down the ivy."

"I'll have to tell Mitch he was right."

"That's how we ended up out here you know."

"I thought we were on the lake further back than that."

"The property was in the family further back but we didn't start hauling urns out of here until your great-grandfather built the studio and wood kiln to make those urns in particular. His pottery studio had been in Fremont. This isn't the Bellen's first," said Will. "Built the business selling to all the rich people on the hill here, and in the city, then other cities, and so on, and so on."

The flames licked the bottom of the kettle which started whistling at first a low pitch and then higher. Abby pulled the kettle off the burner and poured hot water into the two waiting cups to steep the tea.

"So those were the first urns?" asked Abby.

"Oh no. He made urns back in Fremont, that's how he got the commission," said Will, "but it was a small part of his business. He made a lot of salad bowls and cups, practical things people could use. My Dad said he had a good contract making clay insulators when they ran the first electric from the dam through Fremont, less then a penny a piece, but a fair amount of money at that time. But the lake business changed everything."

Abby faced Will, "I never knew."

"Yea, well, I guess I told your brother."

Abby turned her back to Will again and prodded the tea bags. Michael had been the protégé, the obligatory male apprentice in the Bellen line of clay artisans that went back farther than Will's grandfather, all the way back to northern Italy as far as she knew, and Will would be the last in the tradition. That was made clear to Abby when Will stood above Michaels casket.

Not because Abby did not know her way around the Bellen studio. That is where Abby and her brother spent their childhood. Her earliest memories were playing with clay while her father worked. Her father had made a child-size kick wheel Abby was able to spin with skill and ease before she could read or write. Michael, however, had the benefit of Will's mentorship. Will would take Michael with him around the studio and teach him about the craft. Abby would eventually always learn from Michael what their father had taught him. Michael loved to show off any bit of knowledge or new technique to his sister. Michael would spend as much time as he could to be sure Abby learned the new skill and in trade, Abby would teach him the skills she learned from her apprenticeship with their Mother.

"Yea, I suppose you told Michael," said Abby.

Will tapped his fingers a little faster as the tea was taking too long. "Well, they've ordered some new urns," said Will, "you're cousin and Brian. Urns and pots, some discs. Good amount of work."

"That's great," said Abby. "What would you like in your tea?"

"Oh, uh. Like yours, I like it like the way you make yours."

Abby added milk and honey to the tea, took the cup to the table, and sat across from Will. He was quick to have a sip despite the steam. Will curled his lip, "This is great, good tea."

"It's tea," said Abby. Abby decided this was as good a time as any to have the conversation she wanted to have with Will so she started, "so I need to get back to the city in a week."

"So soon," said Will, his blue eyes formerly somber now lighting up as he took another sip of tea, "that's a shame. You just got here."

"Well, I'll clean this place up before I go."

"You don't have to do that."

"And then, I'm bringing someone in to look after you and to help keep the place up," Abby had taken her shot and was poised for Will's reaction.

There was a pause, Abby expected that, and then Will took another sip of tea. "You know," said Will, "I should drink more tea. Yes, I think I will. It tastes so much better than coffee." Will examined the sides of the cup as if there were some label of confirmation, "feels good too."

"You heard what I said. I'm bringing somebody in to help you out."

"Black Breakfast Tea, that's the stuff," said Will.

Abby's jaw clenched, "I am going back to the city and you can't be trusted to take care of yourself. Don't pretend you don't hear me."

Another pause.

Will set down his cup of tea onto a saucer and put his hands flat on the table on either side. His blue eyes went foggy as his brow furrowed over them. Abby watched Will's lower jaw recede, making his lip pout.

In a low voice Will said, "Go back to the city." Then in almost a whisper, "No ones coming around here. I can damn well take care of myself."

"Is that what you call this, no food, your clothes, the dishes, this house."

"I get along just fine," said Will. He stood up and put his hand behind his head, fingers scratching a neck that did not itch.

"Just fine, is that what you call it?"

"Yea, just fine."

"Well I'm just getting started. You don't eat, I don't know how much you're drinking, and from what the doctors tell me --."

Will cut off Abby mid-sentence, "—That will be just about enough, we don't need to talk about doctors."

"When are we going to talk about it, Will?"

"We're not, doctors don't have a lick of sense. Any idiot can tell ya I'm just getting old." Will held up both hands, "And I don't want anyone poking around here. That's the end of it."

"That's not the end of it. I'm not going to let you destroy yourself," said Abby. "Regardless of what you want."

"Regardless, of what I want? Fine way to talk to your Father. Your Mother would never stand for this, I tell you that."

"What would she say about you self-destructing?"

Will was cornered, "So what of it!"

Abby had never heard her father raise his voice out of anger. It was time to back off.

"Fine have it your way. Go in the other room and I'll make you your dinner," said Abby. She was in no way giving up. Abby knew when to call the battle done.

"Fine," said Will. He picked up his teacup and exited the kitchen without giving his daughter a second look.

* * * * *

CHAPTER 16

On that long restless night the Bellen family came together again. Abby found herself in the lake room peering out the bay window at the darkness and the glowing grey blanket of the lake hovering within. There were no phantoms floating in the mist before Abby yet her mind was clouded with the ghost of what Will had said. Of course, he would have told her brother the many things needed to carry the Bellen legacy and had the cancer not taken her mother there would have been so much more her mother could have shared with her.

A father has his son and a mother has her daughter, or so was their family dynamic. Will loved his daughter, the Bellen family was full of love, Abby however was under Emily's wing. Will and Abby did not know how to be alone with each other. Abby was never daddy's little girl. Abby was in her teens when her mother passed and was in college when Michael was killed. Will and Abby had essentially lived separate lives.

Abby felt she knew why.

Outside the window, Abby could not help notice, large in the dim lit sky, the silhouette of her mother's weeping willow haunting the horizon. Her eyes fixed upon the tree and thought went to the time Abby spent with her mother before she died. Abby knew that Emily would not want Will to continue on his downward spiral. She knew not just because her mother had instilled in her the same compassion and gentleness that her mother held within herself. Abby knew because of a promise that was made that had already been broken once with Michael. As the cancer ate away at Emily, she asked Abby to watch over her brother and father. After Emily passed, Abby took the unrealistic request seriously. The request was not taken so seriously by her brother, he thought the need ridiculous, or by her father, distancing himself from Abby because she reminded him of her late mother. The request was the essence of Emily reflecting the glue that held the family together, the concern for each other's well being. Michael and Will had rejected that compassionate concern. Abby felt she failed Michael and now was not sure how deep she would have to go for further compassion if Will rejected what she had available for him.

Gradually the sky above the horizon began to illuminate with the first glow of the coming day. Outside of the bay window, some shadows dissipated while others took form. In the height of the tree, the branches of the willow were now clearly etched in the horizon, and at the base of the tree, the first morning light revealed a figure on the split log bench. A man sat with his arms wrapped around himself rubbing his sides. Abby had not seen Will go out of the house yet she knew he was the man on the bench. "He could have been out there half the night," she thought. Abby continued watching Will through the bay window as the morning brought more light. With the morning light Abby was able to see Will clearly. Will was talking to the tree.

Abby was not sure how long she had watched her father down by the frozen lake. Some time had passed and the sun had fully risen to a vibrant day. The golden light refracting from the morning sun created shimmering diamonds on the icy snow and small animals and winter birds were moving around. Abby stood up and stretched her arms from her sides. She decided that she needed to go out and speak to her father. Abby did not get dressed. She put her coat and boots on, wrapped a blanket around herself, and tromped out to the lake.

"Good morning," said Abby.

"Oh, Good morning."

"I saw you out here."

"I was here, here I am."

"I mean I couldn't sleep either. I watched the sun come up from the house and saw you were out here, early," said Abby.

"Oh yea, well you know, you get old, you're up early."

"I saw you talking to the her willow."

"I'm a crazy old man. I mumble I guess."

"I came out here to ask you something, if it's alright?"

"Ask away."

Abby turned to her father and then toward the lake and asked, "What do you talk to her about?"

Will looked at Abby then toward to the lake. He pulled out his pack of cigarettes.

"You want to know what I tell her." Will paused and lit a cigarette. "I know you probably think I tell her that I am mad that she is gone, that Michael is gone, that I should be gone instead of the both of them. I don't tell her that. I used to, years ago but not anymore."

"What do you tell her then?" Abby looked back at Will.

Will turned his head so that their eyes met, "The same thing I've been telling her for forty years. The answer to the one question she'd ask me every morning. Hell, the one thing I know she wants to know, that she ever cared to know. What are the colors of the sunrise as I see them?" Will shifted his eyes back to where the sun had risen as if the sun were rising once more, "And today the colors were green, cyan really, with streaks of vermilion and magenta."

Abby followed her father's eyes to where the sunrise had

been. With Will, Abby saw a sunrise that existed only for them. "She'd want to know that," said Abby.

"Every morning for forty years," said Will dropping his head. Will lifted his head and gazed out onto the lake one final time and then turned and took a step toward the house.

"You know," said Abby. Will stopped, their backs to each other, Abby was beginning to tear, "she'd want you to tell her tomorrow." Without turning around, Will reached back and placed his hand on his daughters shoulder. He held her for a silent moment and then started into the house. Abby stood in the snow with the blanket held tight around her shoulders, holding still as long as she could before her watering eyes washed the invisible sunrise away.

* * * * *

CHAPTER 17

Caroline made her way to the sofa and let herself sink back into the soft white pillows. The children had been fed and sent off to school, the first wave of office calls were already finished, and Brian was out on errands. Now came the time she had been anticipating. Caroline dialed the Bellen house. As the phone rang, she kicked off her slippers and put her feet up.

Abby picked up the phone, "Hello."

"Hi, Dear."

"Hi, good morning. You're up early enough."

"Early, half the day has gone by already. Wait until you have kids," said Caroline.

"I'm sure," said Abby, "I was up quite early myself."

"Will?"

"Him and the universe."

"Oh, so how was your day yesterday?"

"What do you mean?"

"What do you mean, what do I mean? Don't be coy. I already talked to Mitch this morning," said Caroline.

Abby was on the cordless phone, relaxing with a tea, and still gazing out onto the lake as she had been since early this morning. Upon hearing Mitch's name, Abby's voice went up a pitch and she curled her legs up under her.

"Really? So, what did he have to say?" asked Abby.

"Well, he said that he was happy you came by, and that he enjoyed showing you the house, and that you two had an interesting conversation."

"What else did he say?"

"Not much, except that he would like to see you again."

"He did not," Abby straightened her neck from the current angled position.

"Well, not directly, but when I said the kids and I were going to go watch Mitch and Brian's hockey game later he asked if you were coming."

"He did, eh?" asked Abby.

"He sure did," said Caroline.

"What's this hockey game all about?"

"A bunch of the guys get together every week and play hockey, it's just an excuse for them to drink beer. A lot of us go and cheer them on. It's a lot of fun. You'll enjoy it."

"Sounds like fun."

"Well I already told him you're coming."

"Sure, when?"

"This afternoon, after family skate, after the kids get out of school. You can go to that too."

Though Caroline and Abby made plans to meet later in the day Caroline could not wait to hear every detail of Abby's visit to the Johansson house. Abby repeatedly complimented Caroline on the work underway and Caroline in turn repeatedly shifted the conversation back to Mitch.

"There is something else I wanted to talk about," said Abby.

"Uncle Will," asked Caroline.

"I told him I am bringing someone in to take care of him and he went cold."

"Well I can't say that I'm surprised."

"Me neither, actually the whole thing went better than I thought. I backed down before I got too much of a rise," said Abby.

"With the way Uncle Will's been recently there was a real risk that he may have gone on a bender," said Caroline.

"I may have reeled him in when I asked what mother would think of his self destruction. He was definitely contemplative this morning."

Caroline got up from the sofa, "What do you intend to do next? You certainly can't go back to the city so soon. Will needs help on a daily basis. This is obvious to everybody except Will. I'm concerned that if you leave so soon there would be no helping Will adjust. There needs to be some transition time between family and a caregiver."

Abby's chest tightened and she began to speak at an accelerated pace, "Whether I am here or not does not make a difference. He does not listen to me. He does not want me here." Abby paused. "I'm afraid I'm coming off as though I am trying to dump my father on you."

"I don't think like that," said Caroline.

The more Abby talked through Will's predicament the more she convinced herself that he needed family around to help him. The more Abby was convinced Will needed family to help him the more she was convinced that she wanted, needed, to get back to the city. By the time Abby was finished making her case, the only thing she had convinced herself of was that she needed to get somebody into Will's house so that she could get out.

Caroline had heard something very different, "It sounds like you might need to stay longer. As much for your sake as for his."

"I just told you I need to get back to the city," said Abby. She stood up and began to pace. Abby thought she had made a riveting case for her exit. A case that convinced her, at least, that she could get out of this.

"You need to calm down dear. My god, listen to yourself, and not just your words but also your heart," said Caroline.

"What is it you're trying to tell me?"

"You shouldn't be running from your father, you should

be running to him."

"Run to him? I ran all the way from the city for him."

"It's a metaphor," said Caroline. "You haven't caught him yet."

* * * * *

CHAPTER 18

Mitch stood outside the cabin door with three brown paper bags labeled Willow Lake IGA. He had a bag in each arm and a third was cradled between the two, covering his face. Mitch was singing 'you cannot hide from love' as he entered the cabin. His leather work-boot poked into the open doorway to check the path, then one, two, three steps and the two bottom grocery bags were at rest on the Formica table. With a pause to sing the songs chorus, Mitch placed the crowning bag on the counter next to the dish rack that still held his plate and coffee cup from the morning's breakfast. Inside the bag were bunches of grapes and he reached in and plucked several then popped some into his mouth.

Mitch continued to hum while he voraciously chewed the sweet grapes and then he shut the door and went over to the wood stove to see if any remnants of the morning fire were still burning, popping more grapes into his mouth along the way. Mitch had natural gas for heat however as a rule, he kept the thermostat low and used the wood stove to keep an even temperature. Inside the wood stove, a charred log brightly glowed. When Mitch opened the door to the stove the log ignited with a little yellow and orange flame.

Mitch did not need to relight the log. Mitch put in a few small pieces of wood that he had split earlier in the week then shut the stove up tight.

Mitch then took off his brown canvas coat and unlaced his boots. The rest of the day was going to be light, a good day. The day started out good already. Mitch had gone up to the job site at the Johansson house, swung by Brian and Caroline's for coffee, and spent the rest of the morning shopping at the IGA. Mitch was going to take care of the few chores he had around the cabin and then hockey with the fellas this afternoon. He was glad to hear Caroline mention that Abby was going to be at the rink. Indeed this was going to be a good day.

Mitch emptied out the groceries onto the table. The contents were staples to a bachelor's winter. There were the cans for assorted any time eats: tuna, soup, and chili. Pastas and rice for cooking an actual meal at some point as needed. Mitch bought a large steak that appealed to him as a breakfast steak though he could see now that the steak was easily large enough for two dinners. He debated whether the steak should be eaten soon or frozen. There were the necessary breakfast foods: eggs, bacon, and orange juice in addition to assorted vegetables and fruits: broccoli, carrots, apples, and grapes. To wash all of the food down there was beer and red wine from the liquor store across the street from the IGA.

The kitchen was small yet this much food did not take much space, nor was much time needed to put the food into the vintage white refrigerator or to fill the flower curtained cupboards in the stairwell pantry.

The log cabin was not large, nor rustic, by any means. Over the course of fifty years amenities such as gas, electric, and indoor plumbing had been added. Upstairs there were two rooms that overlooked the lake and an attic room too low for Mitch to stand in. He used one of the lake view rooms for his bed and the other for a study. The main floor was split between the kitchen and bath on one side and a large room that faced the lake. Mitch had filled the room with a large table and a couch near the fireplace. The large screen porch ran the whole front of the cabin and peered over the lake down a tall embankment fifteen feet away.

Mitch had come into possession of the cabin in a rare circumstance. He became caretaker of the cabin soon after he had moved to the lake ten years ago. Within five years, Mitch had renovated the bathroom, finished the two rooms upstairs, and thinned the long neglected overgrown landscape. The aging owner asked Mitch if he would like to buy the place. Mitch wanted to yet he did not have much money or credit. The owner said he would talk to his accountant to see if he could find a way to make things work. Six months later, a letter from the owner came with a deed of ownership. The letter explained the owner was giving Mitch the cabin and surrounding acre of land. Mitch had been a far better custodian of the property then the owner had ever been. In his aging years, the owner saw no reason to wait to die to be the benefactor of the land.

This was the end to what had been a transient existence for Mitch. Apart from college the five years he had spent at the lake was the longest he had ever spent in one place. Now he had put down real roots. Mitch liked Willow Lake, liked the people of Willow Lake, and the people of Willow Lake liked him.

After putting the groceries away, Mitch grabbed some more grapes then went to the living room. He peered out the large window, through the porch, and onto the lake. There were shanties spread across the ice near the cabin. The ice fishing was good on this side of the lake. Mitch stopped humming, put two more grapes in his mouth, and rubbed his nose with his index finger. He thought that fresh trout would be delicious for dinner and wondered if anyone at the Stone Bar may have some for sale. If any quads were out on the ice, he could go out to a visit shanty and see how the catch was going. Mitch picked up the binoculars he kept on the log he used as a table under the window. The only quad he could see belonged to the Lacroux boys. He had just seen the two in the village so Mitch knew they were just now dropping lines. He would have to wait for the evening after the hockey game. Maybe Abby would want to join him for dinner.

Mitch was silent now and had stopped chewing his grapes. He slowly stretched his head from side to side his eyebrows lifting high. "Maybe Abby would want to join him for dinner," he iterated in thought. He resumed chewing and reached down to pickup his black lacquered acoustic guitar then spun to his left, landing on his old quilt covered couch. Eyes fixed to the far corner of the room he put his last two grapes in his mouth, chewed slowly, and then swallowed. Mitch tapped out a beat on his guitar and started to hum. He stopped, plucked three strings, tuned the guitar, and started to hum again. Mitch started to play his guitar, improvising words as he went along until he found a melody he liked.

There was no doubt that Mitch was enamored with Abby. Once Mitch found a melody that fit the late morning, the poetry that followed had the designs of his attentions toward her. Mitch was not writing a song so much as an ode to meeting someone that had inspired him for the first time in quite some time. When Abby talked to him, Mitch did not have to pretend to listen. He honestly wanted to hear what she had to say. Mitch wanted to hear what Abby thought about, where she had been, where she was going, what her interests were, and what she was working on. Mitch had known her for less than a week and in the night, before sleep, the only thing he could think about was Abby.

Mitch sang the melody fast and slow for almost an hour before deciding that he was satisfied he knew the bits well enough to play again. Mitch set the guitar down on the couch, stood up, and stretched his arms toward the ceiling. He put another log into the wood stove and went out onto the screen porch.

Mitch closed the door to the cabin behind him. The unheated porch was sheltered with storm windows so not as cold as the outside, still colder than the cabin interior. Mitch could feel the cold through his grey t-shirt covered yellow thermal and through his cotton socks. He found the brisk sensation revitalizing. Curling his fingers like claws, Mitch scratched his scalp with both hands then dropped them onto his waist and scanned the lake, a recurring ritual that Mitch did several times during the day.

Like most everyone else on these waters, the open expanse attracted Mitch.

To meet Mitch, one might not guess he grew up in the city. Mitch appeared as natural to the lake and woods as any of the hunters and fisherman in Willow Lake and could easily be mistaken for someone raised on trout and by shotgun. Mitch's transition from concrete to woodland appeared seamless because he had embraced the simple life with head and heart in the transcendentalist spirit of Thoreau. He had brought a copy of Walden with him to the lake and that suited him well. Like the house on Walden Pond had been for Thoreau, the cabin was close enough to the village and had just enough of the wilderness to suit Mitch's needs. Of course, eventually Mitch found out that the simple life was not all that simple and that life on the lake went forward like everywhere else. Still Mitch found a place where he could fit in.

The sun was now high above the lake and Mitch thought best to get a few chores done. He went back into the cabin and put his boots and coat on then went out to the log pile to split wood. Mitch had a couple hours before he would be grabbing his hockey gear and heading into the village and wanted to do whatever he could to pass the time quickly.

* * * * *

CHAPTER 19

Caroline and Abby shared many memories on the ice. Their mothers loved to skate and often took Caroline and Abby when they were children. Together the two girls had learned spins, first in place, and then camel spins with one leg high in the air. They helped each other make costumes and laced each other's figure skates. Slung over Abby's shoulder by the long knotted pink laces were worn white figure skates. Abby recalled the late winter day when she first saw them. Each year her mother would drive the kids across the county to Floyd's Skate Swap. Floyd's was an Old Dutch farm in complete disarray. The animals had taken over the premises and roamed freely. Emily would speed most of the way to the swap, determined to get there before they closed at three. Abby, Caroline, and Michael droned the "Sanford and Son" theme song the whole way up the dirt driveway while Emily futilely tried to keep order from the front seat. After lumbering the make shift parking lot to find the driest spot to leave the Volvo, the kids draped last year's wrecks around their necks and set off running toward the field stone skate swap in the bottom of Floyd's barn. As potentially embarrassing as this situation could have been for the teens, all the kids in the county participated in the swap. Hundreds of pairs of exhausted black and white figure skates, a good selection of clunky hockey skates, and dozens of strap-on runners with tattered leather ties crowded what used to be the leather tack end of the stable. They were in every size from toddler to adult. The skates the kids brought with them were turned in to Floyd's freckle faced teenage daughter. Floyd's daughter sat at a table with a clipboard. She rated the incoming skates as used, still in good condition, and recorded them for a credit so the children could quickly scout out a new pair. Michael wore hockey skates so his selection had more to do with getting the right size versus how many socks molded his foot to the skate. He went right to work. The girl's choice was a bit more delicate, to them at least, and they inspected each pair of figure skates with persnickety attention. The kids had come to the skate swap late that year and the skates had already been diligently picked through.

Abby found a bright white pair she liked. The skates appeared barely worn however her mother told Abby they were the wrong size and that there was no way she could squeeze into them. Then Emily brought Abby a pair she had found in the back, a pair that was unique to the other white figure skates because of the trim. All of the other white figure skates had white piping for trim if there was any trim at all. The white skates that Emily held had thin pink piping for trim. Abby's eyes went wide. The skates seemed so new. Emily told her that on the way home, she would replace the dull grey laces with pink ones to match the trim. Though the laces had to be replaced a couple times over the years, the skates still fit. The last skates from the last skate swap Abby had been to with her mother. That was the year Emily was diagnosed with cancer. That was the year Abby's mother had died.

* * * * *

Abby walked over to the green wooden bleachers behind

the Stone bar. Caroline would be there waiting for her. The empty outdoor rink at the edge of the fairgrounds sat next to an indoor arena. A teal Zamboni resurfaced the grey blue ice as children crowded the green carpeted benches surrounding the rink. The children showed their eagerness to get back on the ice by fidgeting their knit caps, mittens, coats, snow pants, and skates.

Caroline sat on the bottom bleacher and zipped up Lilly's purple jacket while Andrew stood on his skates, mitten in his mouth, watching the Zamboni crawl by.

"Thanks for parking the car," said Caroline. "Herding these kids from the back lot is tedious to say the least."

"Not a problem," said Abby. She sat down next to her cousin and removed her boots.

Caroline finished getting Lilly ready and instructed her to stay next to Andrew. He shuffled his skates back and forth ready to go at first sign of release. Abby and Caroline fervently got their skates on to be ready for Andrew to launch. When the Zamboni glided off the back of the rink all of the skaters poured in from the edges in one seemingly orchestrated flow. Abby followed behind Andrew and Lilly onto the ice leaving Caroline to finish lacing her own skates and sort everyone else's belongings. Caroline would catch up with Abby and the twins when they circled around.

To skate on the ice rink felt fantastic. Abby had worked out her creeks and cobwebs by skating on the lake. On the rink, skating was natural. Her feet effortlessly slid over the ice in unison. Lilly in front of her had the same ease, Andrew looked as though he was working very hard. Abby reached for the twins in vane. The twins scurried away, their little legs walking rapidly at times rather than skating.

The weather was warm for a winter day. The sun was out and the sky was clear. Abby and the kids did not take long to circle the rink. Caroline joined them when they neared the bleachers.

"You must be keeping up in the city," said Caroline.

"Not as much as you think," said Abby. "This is great!"

They lapped the rink five times at a leisurely pace before Lilly and Andrew fell back red faced and decided they wanted to hold Abby's hands. As a group, they lasted two more laps before the twins needed a break. Caroline skated to the bench closest to their bleacher to get the backpack. Abby and her junior entourage, ready to receive apple juice and water, slid in behind her.

Caroline fixed the children's scarves and hats as they sucked away at the straws of their juice boxes. She arched her eyebrow at Abby, "So did you think about what I said this morning?"

"Listening to my heart, that?" asked Abby.

"Yea that," said Caroline.

"Actually I have," said Abby, " and something occurred to me. Will is holding back on something."

"Why do you say that?" asked Caroline.

"Because this morning when I saw him talking to mom, he told me he did not have that much to say to her. But, he has been having conversations with that tree everyday since I've been here. And he told her a lot more this morning than he is letting on to anyone else."

"So you think there is something going on, beyond his drinking, because you see him talking to a tree?" asked Caroline.

"Yes, I do, maybe even causing his drinking," said Abby.

"You know you sound ridiculous."

"You think it's ridiculous to think he is confiding in my mother?" asked Abby.

"Not when you put it that way," Caroline buttoned up Andrew's top button. "It's the talking to the tree bit that makes you sound a little paranoid."

"I see your point," said Abby, "but there has to be more there."

"Why does there have to be so much more? He's old, he's alone, he drinks," said Caroline.

"But why start now? Michael has been gone for ten years, Mom for twenty. It doesn't make sense for him to start drinking heavy now," said Abby.

"Who said he just started?"

"But Will was never a big drinker. Neither was Mom or your parents," said Abby.

"Well there is one way to find out," said Caroline. Caroline shifted her eyes toward the liquor store across the street. To simply go into the only village liquor store and ask them how often Will came in had not occurred to Abby. She could only see the back of the store from the bleachers. Abby imagined walking into the front and hearing something that she did not want to hear.

"We're overreacting, blowing this all out of proportion," said Abby. The comment was not really meant for Caroline. Abby was talking herself out of the possibility that she could have missed years of alcohol abuse, denying that any problem could exist with her father.

"You do remember why I called you to begin with?" asked Caroline.

Abby did remember why Caroline had called her in the city asking her to come back to Willow Lake. Will had launched into a tirade with representatives from his hotel account when one of them mentioned that they might change some of the custom work on the new commission. Fortunately, they put Will's behavior down to he being a passionate artist yet after they left he did not stop. Will went into the Stone bar and tried to stir up a fight. Of course no one would ever fight old Will or for that matter serve him in that state yet he was still too drunk to drive out of there and would not let any one help him. After Bob Jensen took his keys, Will insisted on staying in his truck, and that was when the police had come by. Bob talked the police into calling Caroline to come down to the bar. Bob knew Caroline could keep Will calm and get him home. That pushed Caroline to call Abby to come home. Until then, Caroline too denied the signs that her uncle was ill.

Abby was no longer interested in going back on the ice. Caroline encouraged her to remove her skates, go to the liquor store across the street, and ask about Will. "It will only take you five minutes," said Caroline. Abby did just that, unlaced her skates, and laced up her boots. Abby sent Caroline and the kids back out on the rink and headed across the street.

* * * * *

CHAPTER 20

The little bell announced Abby as she left the sunlit street and entered the shadows of the village liquor store. Though Abby had been in this store many times before today her stomach was knotted and the store had an odor that tasted bad on the back of her throat. Dennis was working the register today. He sat on a stool doing a crossword puzzle. A little black and white TV sitting at the end of the counter was turned to an old movie, or the movie was black and white and the TV was color, Abby was not sure. Either way Dennis's eyes did not leave the puzzle. Like any good counter worker though Dennis was well aware that Abby had come into the store.

"I heard you were back," said Dennis. "Your Dad said you're here for a visit."

"He did, did he? Yea, I'm here for a week or two. Has he been in today?"

"Not yet, I expect him round supper."

Abby wanted to look like she had come in with a purpose. She paused and looked around the store. She took her hands out of her pockets and picked up a bottle of brandy near the end of the aisle.

"That's not the one," said Dennis.

"Excuse me." Abby looked up at Dennis. His eyes were still fixed on his crossword.

"That's not the one. That's not the elixir," said Dennis. "It's the one next to it."

"The elixir?" asked Abby.

"That what he call's it, but that's not the one, he likes the brand next to it." Dennis pointed the eraser of his pencil to the row of ginger brandy.

"Oh right," said Abby picking up a bottle of ginger brandy, "here it is, his elixir." She walked toward the counter examining the bottle.

"I'll save you some time and grab his wines for you so you don't have to search them out," said Dennis. He set down his puzzle and circled around the counter.

"Thanks," said Abby. This struck her as peculiar that Will had a particular flavor that Dennis would know to grab and wines as well. Then she remembered, 'drug of choice'.

"How often do you see my Dad?"

"I work six days a week here now," said Dennis while he pulled down the wine, "so I guess I see him in here most every day. A couple times a week at least."

Abby faced away from Dennis when he said this and good thing because her eyes went wide. As Dennis came back around the counter Abby composed herself. "So you see him every day, how long has that been going on?" Abby smiled as if to insinuate that the fellas had been hanging out together.

"Well, lets see," Dennis paused briefly, Abby thought she might have a date as to when this started, "I started here almost nine years ago, so I guess it's been at least nine years. Almost every day."

Abby tasted acid in her mouth, "So you're old friends?"

"I guess you could say that," said Dennis, "anything else?"

"No thanks, that's it," said Abby, "oh, I almost forgot, don't tell him that I was in here. I'm making a surprise dinner for him and wanted to make sure I had everything he liked."

"Our secret," said Dennis. "It's nice to see ya."

Abby could not wait to get out of there. She paid Dennis for the wine and brandy then took the bottles out of the store. Abby stood for a moment on the corner. Surely, Dennis had been exaggerating about Will going in there every day. The wine and brandy could not be consumed that quickly. Maybe Dennis meant every other day, or twice a week, neither mattered. Besides, Abby often had more than a few glasses after work and had effortlessly polished off a bottle in the museum late at night after hours while doing research. That was not an everyday occasion though. Actually last time Abby drank a bottle of wine alone had been quite a while ago. Abby asked herself if Will could really be drinking this much every day.

Abby looked down at the bag in her arms, she was not going to take this back to the ice rink. She checked to see if she still had Caroline's keys in her pocket then turned up the road toward the parking lot. When Abby got to Caroline's Subaru, she opened the back hatch then put the bag into the car beneath a blanket.

Caroline saw Abby returning to the bleachers and exited the rink to join her. The children had just gotten back out on the ice and would be good for a few more laps. Caroline noticed Abby's eyes moving from the sky, over to the rink and then beyond to the fairgrounds. Caroline wondered if Abby was searching for something or someone. Abby was a few feet away and intently staring past Caroline when Caroline realized Abby's head was somewhere else.

"I take it you found some answers," said Caroline.

Abby turned to her cousin. Abby focused her eyes on Caroline. Caroline took her by the arm and the two sat down.

"More like questions. Apparently Dad has been making trips to the liquor store on a daily basis for quite some time."

"Well honey, I'm sad to say I'm not surprised. This has

to have been going on for a least the last year."

"A lot longer than that. According to Dennis over at the liquor store Will's been making regular purchases since he started working there nine years ago. About a case of wine and half a dozen bottles of brandy a week, nine years Caroline."

Caroline's hazel eyes grew large. "That is surprising," said Caroline. "How could we not have known that?"

"How would you have known?" asked Abby. "There was no one in the house to watch him. I bet this has been going on since Michael died."

"Well, we have to put a stop to this. Did you tell Dennis not to sell to him anymore?"

"I didn't even think of it."

"I'll grab the kids, lets go tell him now. What was he thinking anyways?" said Caroline. Caroline stood up and raised her hand to get the twins attention. Abby grabbed Caroline's arm and eased her back down to the bleacher. "There's no point banning him from the liquor store, at least not until I talk to him. He'll just get pissed off. Besides he'll probably just drive the twenty miles to Fremont to get what he wants anyway."

"You have a point," said Caroline, and then she asked the question spinning in Abby's head, "So what are we going to do?"

"It's time for me to do what you suggested this morning," said Abby, her blue eyes welling with water and her cheeks turning flush, "listen to my heart."

* * * * *

CHAPTER 21

Mitch and Brian walked up to the ice rink bleachers carrying their hockey sticks and large duffel bags full of gear. Caroline had her arm wrapped around Abby. Abby's head rested on Caroline's shoulder. Caroline consoled Abby, still the fellas could see that both had been crying. When the girls saw the two helpless men watching them, they both started to laugh.

"We look that bad, do we?" asked Abby.

"You look like two beauties," said Mitch.

"I take it we missed something?" asked Brian.

"I'll fill you in later," said Caroline.

Abby sat up and wiped her eyes with her gloves.

"Here," said Mitch, he offered the girls a small package of Kleenex that he had in his pocket, "these should help."

"Thanks," said Abby, she wiped her eyes and nose. "I must look ridiculous."

"Not at all," said Mitch.

"You know, you fellas are early. No fair sneaking up on us," said Caroline.

"We thought we could get some practice in inside before everyone shows up," said Brian.

"Uh uh," said Caroline, " there's a price to be paid, you

will help me get the twins together, and Mitch, you're going to take Abby for a coffee."

"Brilliant," said Mitch, "I can't argue with that."

"That would be nice," said Abby. "Let me get my things together."

"I'll get your skates," said Caroline. "You go on and we'll see you when you get back."

"You can just put them with my stuff, I have to drop it inside," said Mitch.

Abby got up and gave Caroline and then Brian a hug. Mitch gestured toward the indoor arena with a turn of his head and Abby stepped up, waving to the twins as they came off the ice.

Mitch looked good to Abby in the bright sunlight. Mitch smiled at the children and though the sun reflected on everything around them, his face still managed to stay in the shade. His unconventional handsome face looked more boyish outdoors. Like a dark haired cherub, Mitch's cheeks puffed like a babies when he squinted in the light, giving him a completely new dimension than his inside look. Abby also liked the sporty black jacket Mitch was wearing over his jersey. The jacket gave Abby a different perspective than the canvas coat she had seen Mitch in that last couple of times they were together.

Perhaps the vulnerability that Mitch sensed in Abby with her eyes red and cheeks puffy, another dark haired cherub, gave him the urge to nurture her. Mitch put his hockey stick in his hand with the duffel leaving the arm closest to Abby free to put around her shoulder, which he did. Abby reached up with her outside arm and touched Mitch's hand. Thinking Abby was going to remove his arm Mitch relaxed to let her. Abby did not push his arm away. She moved close to him, walked in step, and pulled his arm tighter around her shoulder.

Abby and Mitch walked silently to the arena and once inside she let go of his hand so he could set down his duffel. Abby motioned to the large ice rink with the Plexiglas towering above the removable sidewalls.

"This place makes me feel so nostalgic," said Abby.

"You and Caroline came here to learn how to skate?" asked Mitch.

Abby's cherub cheeks spread wide with a toothy smile, "And later as young teens to meet boys."

"I see."

"I think they are still playing the same music."

"Some things don't change."

The music that played low through the sound system was the same as twenty some years before. How ironic that now Abby was with a boy she liked inside the arena while Caroline was with her fella outside. She felt good in a giddy way. If anything, Abby had needed a distraction and what better distraction than Mitch.

Pleased as Mitch was that Abby had come to the fairgrounds he did not like seeing her so upset.

"Would you like to go over to the Lakeside for a tea?" asked Mitch.

"Yes, the Lakeside Diner would be lovely," said Abby.

Mitch and Abby exited the arena and made their way across the fairgrounds toward the village corners and the Lakeside Diner. Mitch made small talk to help Abby to relax.

"Can you believe how sunny and warm the weather is?" asked Mitch.

Abby smiled, the enthusiasm she had mustered in the arena already passed.

As they came upon the ice road leading out into the lake from the corners Mitch pointed to the edge of the shore. "Would you look at that, the edge of the lake is melting. If the warm weather holds, the winter carnival coming up will be more of a slush fest." Abby giggled at the thought of ice and snow sculptures, with the bright colors sprayed on them, turning into slurpees before the eyes of all of the people attending the festival. Seeing he had Abby's attention again, Mitch scrunched his face causing her to laugh out loud.

* * * * *

CHAPTER 22

The diner was an old Silk City prefab with lots of stainless steel and pink neon in the windows. The diner had been built in the early sixties when the summer business first started to boom by the lake. Today the diner was out of place next to the older IGA and an outright anachronism to the old Stone tavern. Though initially seasonal, the diner was now open year round and many of the locals often ate there, including Mitch.

Abby and Mitch took a booth near the door.

"I don't recognize anyone in here," said Abby.

"Really?"

"You know I can still tell who everyone is."

"What do you mean?"

"Well, there have always been three different types of patron in the diner," said Abby.

"Seriously?" asked Mitch.

"Sure, there are three classes of customer in here. You see the year round locals are dressed in comfortable clothes and sit nonchalantly amongst the other patrons," her fingers waved across the counter. "The weekenders and vacation home set, also nonchalant. They however wear newer fashions and brands not custom to the lake. Now those

99

kids over there," she gestured to a loud group in a corner booth, "just stopping in on their way to or from the ski lodge on Mount Frisia."

"Well that's easy," said Mitch.

"Ok, ok. That table over there, the people are overdressed for the season, their clothes, jackets, and hats. What really spells it out is their chattiness with each other and how quickly they're consumed by the time it takes to either get, eat, or pay for their orders."

"Very good," said Mitch, "I can tell the same thing by their shoes alone."

"No way."

"Sure, the locals have proper winter shoes and boots that are at least slightly worn. The weekender residents have brand new shoes or loafers for travel from the house, to the car, to the diner and back."

"Ah," said Abby, "I see it."

"And the skiers for the most part have sneakers on, and if they do have boots, it's one of the few times they have ever wore them."

Abby looked at the feet of the diner's patrons and began to laugh.

"You just made that all up," said Abby.

"Right this minute," said Mitch.

Abby thought the diner quaint to city restaurants and liked the relaxing way the waitress eased over with the coffee pitcher already in hand to fill their cups, though Abby still ordered tea.

Mitch wanted to ask Abby about Will, he knew that must be what was bothering her, yet he did not want to upset her again now that she had returned to her jubilant self. He continued with small talk and that was fine with Abby. Mitch told her about his day, his shopping trip, and his morning playing guitar. He did not tell her of the Ode to Abby, he thought that would have been creepy.

"Would you look at that," said Abby. She had noticed something outside the window of the diner.

"What?" asked Mitch. He had missed whatever she had seen.

"I just saw a white mink, or weasel scurry up that pine right outside the window. That's rare."

"You never see them around people," said Mitch.

"I think I have only seen one ever with a white winter coat."

"You know I had one for a pet when I was in school," said Mitch.

"You had a mink, or a weasel, or whatever that was?"

"Well a cousin. I had a ferret named Podo after the ferret in the movie 'The Beast Master'."

"A ferret? Really?"

"Ya, I adopted Podo from some girl off campus. She didn't know how to raise the animal and she gave him the cliché name. Podo was almost starved when I adopted him. The girl had been feeding him rabbit food so I had really rescued Podo."

"Rescued? How so?" asked Abby.

"Well ferrets are not omnivores they are carnivores, they cannot digest rabbit food, much easier for them to digest rabbits, though cat food worked just fine to bring Podo back to health," said Mitch.

"Oh that is so sweet. You rescued the little meat eater and the food chain."

"Ha ha, sarcasm, nice," said Mitch.

"I'm sorry," said Abby. "You were sweet. You are sweet. What ever happened to the little guy?"

"I left Podo with a girl when I left school one summer for a job and while I was away she gave Podo away and went off to Europe."

"Ouch," said Abby.

"Ya, ouch," said Mitch.

"Were you and the girl still together when she left for Europe?"

"Yes, we were together, sort of. I mean there had been a mutual break up because the girl had graduated so…"

"I see," said Abby.

"Ya, she was the first love of my life and I thought I was mature enough to handle the separation and ended up heartbroken. I continued writing letters throughout the next school year and eventually followed her to Europe only to finally realize the relationship was over. Then I went to Prague to drink away the sorrow of love lost in the most romantic city in Europe, if anywhere."

"Prague, how beautiful," said Abby.

"If you are ever a young adult just out of college and want to go somewhere to forget your problems, Prague is, or was the place to go," said Mitch.

"I wish I had known that when I finished school," said Abby, "I could have used a place to forget about the loss of my brother."

"You know I formed a band in high school that only knew three chords?" said Mitch.

"Three chords eh?" Abby lifted her brow. She knew what Mitch was doing.

"We played a lot of parties then ended up breaking up because I only wanted to write ballads."

"I so want to hear a sample. Lyrics please," said Abby.

"I assure you that they are all long forgotten and that if I did remember any I am pretty sure they all sounded the same, some corny rhyme scheme pertaining to topics of the teenage mind."

"That sounds appropriate for high school. Not good at all?"

"Well mostly they were rip-offs of other ballads I had heard."

"My troubadour," said Abby, genuinely impressed, "how are your rhyme schemes now?"

Mitch leaned back in his side of the booth, straightening his torso, "I am proud to say that after high school I moved away from the ballads to political songs in college. Then on to poetry for a while, the kind that you needed a decoder ring for. That all gave way to the study of English and

Philosophy, which involved so much of my time that everything else just got pushed to the back." This was not the truth exactly. Mitch always played his guitar and sang what was on his mind however at risk of being exposed, he stuck to his story.

"You have to share some of those old poems with me some time," said Abby.

"I would like that," said Mitch, and he was sincere. The idea of sharing with Abby anything from his heart made the very moment more intimate, "and one day I will."

"Promise me troubadour," said Abby.

"That's a promise," said Mitch.

Some time had passed since they had left Brian and Caroline so they decided to head back. As they walked to the fairgrounds Abby took Mitch's hand.

"Will you be attending the Winter Slush Fest this year," asked Abby.

Mitch squeezed Abby's hand, "Wouldn't miss it."

* * * * *

CHAPTER 23

When Mitch and Abby entered the arena Brian and some of the other players were already maneuvering out on the ice by passing the puck indiscriminately to each other. The music was louder then earlier, AC/DC's 'You Shook Me All Night Long' echoed out of the huge speakers surrounding the pavilion. Abby used to think AC/DC was a hard rock band when she was young, outside the edge of tolerable listening by adult standards. Now AC/DC sounded to her like a blues band, hard blues, yet a blues band all the same. Mitch picked up his gear and headed into the locker room to change.

"Thanks," said Abby.

"For what?"

"I appreciate you taking the time to... well, thanks." Abby swung her hands to her front and clasped them together.

"No problem, I'll see you in a few minutes," said Mitch. Abby scoured the sporadically filled bleachers that circled the rink and found Caroline across from where she stood feeding the twins out of a white paper sack. They had not seen her and Mitch come in so Abby took the moment to look again out onto the rink. She did not miss the irony of her past. She had just sent a boy into the locker room and was about to go sit next to Caroline to watch the fellas play hockey. Her lungs felt fuller when she breathed in and her legs weightless, a warm breeze moved through the arena past her toward the opening doors behind. So many things changed since they were kids in school, yet in her stomach was that old familiar pain, and as she made her way around to the end of the rink, she thought of how she liked the way Mitch had firmly held her hand walking over, how she still felt like he was holding her hand.

Abby made her way up the bleachers past other spectators to Caroline and sat next to Andrew. Caroline offered her a paper sack full of French Fries, and Abby gladly accepted. She had not eaten any thing since this morning and she thought that could be contributing to her emotional day.

"There doesn't seem to be more than one team on the ice," said Abby.

"It's actually a pickup game tonight. They all play together. The real contest comes at the winter carnival when other teams come in," said Caroline.

"Is that so?"

"The boys say these ongoing games are preparation."

"Preparation for what exactly?"

"Defending the honor of Willow Lake when the festival rolls around."

"Have there been any hockey wins like when we were kids?"

"Despite some of the older fellas out there, Willow Lake still manages to hold its own," said Caroline.

Mitch entered the rink with high fives from some of the nearest skaters. The thirty-seven year old boy glided into the middle of the other players and immediately fell into play. What happened next was choosing of sides and three periods of action that involved no high sticking, little checking, and quite a bit of cycling of the players to keep them fresh. Abby had seen many practice games that had more vigor. The players tried to hold their youth yet when the steel hit the ice, their age was revealed. To say that the players were kind to each other would be an overstatement, though they certainly were respectful. The puck did get a lot of movement though and no one stayed still for long. Brian and Mitch played against each other and the end score tallied two to one, and not due to lack of play. Neither side had allowed the other to score, regardless of attempts on the net.

Caroline and Abby, as well as other watching family members and friends, enjoyed the game. After the last period was finished, the girls and twins went down to the boards to see the fellas and to compliment them on a good game. Brian and Mitch glistened with sweat and each had a hand towel to wipe their face and dripping brow. Caroline raised both hands, cheered, and clapped as she had throughout the game. Caroline was possibly their biggest fan next to Lilly, cheering the whole time as well. The boys smiled and waved as they went to the locker room to clean up and get their gear together before heading over to the Stone Tavern.

Caroline was not surprised when Abby told her that she wanted to stay in the village to have a beer with the boys at the tavern. She asked Abby if she needed anything before she went then gave her cousin a hug and a kiss on the cheek. Abby reminded Caroline that there was wine in the back of the car. Caroline told her that she would take care of the wine and then opened the doors of the pavilion into the new dark night.

While Abby waited for the boys to finish in the locker room, she sat on the bottom bleacher and leaned back against the seats behind her with both hands in her pockets. The teal Zamboni was rounding the rink and Journey played on the sound system. She thought that when fifty years should pass the ice rink would still be playing Journey. She closed her eyes and thought about a boy she knew in junior high school that danced with her to a Journey song so many years ago. His name was Bobby Haremon. Bobby was skinny, shorter than her, with dark hair, and dark eyes. He was funny, and cute as a button. To dance then was to hold each other close, a loose hug really, and move slowly in a circle. Thinking back, the dance was not so spectacular, however Journey and the right boy, was the recipe to swoon in his arms. Though she wanted him to, she did not let Bobby kiss her, that was not some thing she did in junior high. There were other boys and other dances and there was always Journey, "perhaps that was the formula," she thought.

* * * * *

CHAPTER 24

Abby continued to daydream until she heard the players start to exit the locker room. Mitch was happy to see that Abby had stayed behind. He walked over to greet her and make sure that she was on board for a beer. Abby took the hockey stick from him and the two went out into the night, first to stow Mitch's gear in his truck and then to meet everyone else inside the tavern.

The amber lamps outside the pavilion held back the satin black sky just above them. The outside humidity and the temperature were still up creating the sweet odor of fresh melt in the air. The two walked around the crowded outdoor rink toward the parking lot. The same music that had been playing indoors was playing outside.

"Did you always play hockey?" asked Abby.

"Out of the womb, I guess," said Mitch, "did it at the boys club. My dad was into pushing athletics. I haven't seen you on your skates yet."

"You haven't?" Abby paused, "I guess not."

"I hear you're a pretty good skater."

"I used to be, ok," said Abby, "why?"

Mitch set down his gear bag next to the bleachers, reached in, and pulled out Abby's skates.

"Want to show me?" asked Mitch.

"You're on," said Abby, she took the skates from Mitch and put them on as he put on his hockey skates.

The two entered the rink holding hands and skated in pace with each other. Both had cheeky smiles and both firmly pressed each other's hands.

After circling the rink twice, Abby skated around in front of Mitch so that she was still holding his hand yet skating backwards. He took her other hand and the two locked eyes, their pace a natural rhythm.

"So you can skate," said Mitch.

"I told you," said Abby, " a bit rusty, but I can skate. How about you."

"Whadda ya mean? You saw me playing hockey all night, I got moves."

"The moves of a lumberjack."

"Ouch," said Mitch, "ok, watch this."

Abby turned and lined up along side Mitch as he launched forward, and then turned backward. He held up his hands for acknowledgements and Abby clapped, and then Mitch held up one finger, looked back for a second for clearance, and then lowered himself. He bent his skating knee down to the ice and extended his other leg, the whole time gliding, a backward shoot-the-duck. Abby clapped again, and right then Mitch fell backward on his bottom. She skated over and pulled him up as he brushed away the ice.

"Not bad with hockey skates," said Abby.

"I can do more."

"Just skate next to me," said Abby, and Mitch did.

They held hands once more and continued to circle the rink oblivious to the other couples and older children that were out on the ice with them. They skated until the whistle blew for the ice to clear and circled one last time holding hands firmly all the while.

When Abby exited the ice, she could have easily left her skates on all night not bothering her in the slightest. She was floating on air. When Mitch and Abby did sit down on the bleachers to take their skates off, she complimented him on his skating prowess, and he returned the compliment adding that she must be getting some time skating in the city.

"Not like this," said Abby. Abby was not sure if the difference was the ice rink or the company she was keeping while on the ice. Abby was swooning.

"I suppose not," said Mitch his eyes moving out to the ice, up at the black satin blanket with the amber lamps blocking the stars, and then over to Abby. He thought she was referring to the place. She was not.

Mitch put his skates in his duffel bag.

"Why don't you give me yours as well," said Mitch.

"Are you sure?"

"No problem," said Mitch, the corners of his mouth rising with a grin.

"What's so funny?"

"Nothing, you can get them tomorrow."

Mitch and Abby held each other by the waist walking to the road and then to the back parking lot of the fairgrounds where his truck was parked.

Once Mitch and Abby were away from the lamps of the rink and the streetlights of the village were to their backs the sky opened up a myriad of stars.

"This is some thing you don't get in the city," said Mitch.

Abby stretched her arms, smiled, paused, and then said, "This is something I do miss. You know, on a clear night we have at least three stars in the city."

"Ha, ha," said Mitch. "Ha, ha," said Abby.

While Mitch and Abby walked, they tried to identify constellations even though neither knew more than the big dipper. The truck was in the center of the parking lot and no one drove through while they walked. Abby leaned back on the tailgate and put both hands in her pockets. Mitch put his gear into the box of the pickup and then turned around and leaned on the back of the tailgate next to her with his hands in his pockets.

"Oh the hell with it," said Mitch, and he turned to the front of Abby, took his hands from his pockets to firmly hold her waist and placed his lips on hers. Abby put her arms around his shoulders and pulled his neck close, putting more pressure on their kiss. The kiss was long and after their lips had touched, they gently placed each other's foreheads against one another and let their eyes meet. They both smiled.

"Well this is the best thing that's happened in a long time," said Mitch.

Abby could not agree more. She brought one hand down to his side. She let her other hand caress his cheek. "I don't think that's happened in a long time," said Abby.

He lifted his forehead from hers and then kissed her lips again. Abby eagerly returned the kiss she had been waiting for.

When Mitch and Abby went into the bar to join the others, truly feeling as though she was back in school, Abby debated for a moment as whether or not they should enter separately and they would have had Mitch not convinced her that was not necessary.

* * * * *

CHAPTER 25

Abby pulled the pickup into the driveway as the mid afternoon winter sun prepared to set behind her. She had spent most of the day thinking about Mitch and still felt like a schoolgirl. Since their first kiss the night before, every moment had become more intense, more enjoyable.

The entire day was not all thoughts of Mitch, Abby knew at some point she would need to tell Will that Nathan was coming to dinner tomorrow night. She told herself that she could just wait until dinner and have Nathan show up. That would not be fair to Will, besides, she needed Will to cooperate. She decided that instead of waiting until dinner she would go talk to Will now. She needed to talk to him. She walked into the lit up house and called for her dad. There was no answer so she headed for the studio. Walking through the lake room, she looked out the bay window and saw Will sitting on the split log bench talking with the willow again.

Will looked across the lake at the approaching night sky and pulled his hand out of his coat pocket to scratch the bottom of his chin.

Abby walked up behind him and touched his arm, "You got any of that 'elixir' dad?"

Will looked at her, "What?"

"The brandy you keep in your pocket," said Abby.

"Uh, sure," Will unzipped his coat a third and reached into his inside pocket. He fiddled for a moment and then pulled out the half-pint of ginger brandy then handed the bottle to Abby. Abby pulled her hands out of her pockets opened the bottle and took a long sip.

"Ooooh," Abby put the palm of her hand to her lips, "it burns." With a hint of a laugh she said, "Wow, you drink that stuff." Abby handed the bottle to Will and put both of her hands into her coat pockets and let her back go straight to somehow push the warmth of the alcohol through her faster.

Will himself took a nip and shook his head, "It's got a bite."

"Elixir, eh?"

Will offered Abby back the bottle and she put up her hand, "Maybe in a bit."

"It's an acquired taste," said Will. He put the bottle back into his pocket and zipped up his coat.

"What you thinking about out here old man?"

"Just that, getting old. That's what old men think about," said Will. He smiled at his daughter. "Would you look at that sky," Will gestured up through the branches of the giant willow next to them toward the billowy clouds above being slowly pulled across the lake to the new night sky, "no moon behind those clouds yet, the moon rises in an hour and their edges are going to light up like quicksilver."

"I remember you used to tell me that the Quicksilver was a Pegasus that came from behind moonlit clouds, and that when the clouds raced across the sky it was because Quicksilver and all of the other Pegasus' were moving them," said Abby.

"Yea," said Will, "you used to creep out of bed at night and grab the binoculars by the bay window and try to see if you could see a Pegasus. Except you called them Begsus when you were, I don't know four, five."

"Really binoculars?" Abby was laughing.

"Really, I would come out to see what was going on and you'd say 'I lookin' for kiksilva daddy. I'm lookin' for Begsus'," both laughed at the idea. "I'd have to chase you to get those binoculars from you and your mother would have to calm you down. I don't know what she promised you."

"She promised me that if I was a good girl, you would get me a ride on a Pegasus," said Abby.

"And you bought it."

"And I bought it," said Abby, "she told me that you were secretly a King and I was a Princess and that if you called Quicksilver he would have to come to take me through the clouds. But first, I had to go to sleep. She could tell me anything."

"Me too, hon."

"I saw you from the window looking at the tree."

"Looking at the tree. Looking at the sky. Thinking old man thoughts."

"Yea, I miss her too," said Abby.

"Of course you do," said Will, "the temperature is going to drop. We should be going in."

"I wanted to ask you, are you sure about those cables up there?" Abby was referring to the two cables that went from high in the tree to the studio and the house.

"Oh ya, this summer Connie Zeller brought over his cherry picker and we made sure they were fastened up good. They'll hold," said Will.

"You really think the tree is going to fall into the lake?"

"Well you can see how close the lake is getting. I don't want to take any chances. She's good and anchored now."

"Well ok. I got the house in shape," Abby was changing the topic. "Fixed everything back up the way you like it, got all of the laundry done, old mail sorted out, everything dusted."

"You've been a big help Abby, you have, but you didn't have to do all of that."

"Dad, you had clothes growing together, and I don't know what was living in the refrigerator."

"Nothing that would have stood a fighting chance," Will was trying to cute his way out of the conversation.

"You got to promise me you will keep it up though," said Abby.

"Well, sure I'll do my best."

"You promise?"

Will now detected a ruse yet was not quite sure what that would be.

"Ok, I promise," Will's voice quickened, "now can we go in?"

"In a minute," said Abby sweetly. " I don' think you can keep that promise by yourself."

"Now hold on just a minute --," said Will however he was too late, he had fallen into Abby's trap.

"There's no way you an take care of this whole place by yourself anymore."

"I have been just fine for pert near seventy years and am just fine now. I told you before I don't need any one messing around here. I'll shoot whoever shows up."

"You will not Will Bellen. Your assistant Nathan will be here tomorrow."

"My assistant?" asked Will. He had not been thinking of a man at all, certainly not an assistant.

"Yes your assistant, be ready to tell him what to do. He can help in the studio too."

"He can stay out of my studio," said Will, one last stand.

"At first," said Abby.

"I guess I won't shoot him."

"That would be nice, we do have to pay him either way," said Abby and she bent over and kissed her father on the cheek.

Will took the bottle out of his coat again and offered the brandy to Abby. She took the bottle and took another nip, "Whoo," said Abby, "and very shortly we're going to be talking about this too."

"I told you it's an acquired taste."

Abby handed the brandy back to her father, as he grabbed for the bottle she held the glass tightly for a second before releasing, "That's not what I mean." She then bent over and kissed her fathers forehead.

Will kept his gaze forward into the coming darkness of the new night sky. He took another sip of elixir, put the bottle away, then zipped up his coat, and put his hands in his pockets.

* * * * *

CHAPTER 26

The following evening was uncharacteristically warm for the season and the expected snowfall fell in large wet flakes. Will built a fire in the lake room and stoked the coals on the bottom until they burned bright orange. The room was toasty and both reading lamps were on giving the impression that the bay window was a painting of the grey outside if not for the large wet chunks of snow running down the pane.

Will yelled into the kitchen, "The roads are going to be impossible you know."

Abby yelled back, "He called. He's still coming."

"Well, if he makes it here. I don't know if I'll be able to get him if he gets stuck somewhere."

Abby ignored his last comment and continued creaming the sugar and the butter in the large clay-mixing bowl. She decided to make a cake for their guest, or maybe for Mitch, or maybe to relax her and she knew that this evening had the potential to be a disaster. Abby never considered herself a great baker or cook yet when things became stressful she did a fare share of both. She had heard on a food show that a favorite around the set was pistachio-cardamom cake so she had the recipe. That recipe ranked easy on the simplicity scale, always put her in a good mood, and turned out to be one of her favorites. The cake could have been pistachio cake if the IGA had not had cardamom or chocolate cake if they had no pistachios. Baking any cake would have sufficed to ease the stress.

* * * * *

Their guest tonight, Nathan Albright, had just moved to the other side of the lake from Fremont. Nathan decided to move to Willow Lake for a more relaxed pace than he found working in Fremont and had been seeking a position while Abby was searching for someone to help Will out. He had been commuting to his old job. This job would give him the chance to work locally in a more intimate setting and he was looking forward to meeting Will. Abby had warned Nathan that Will did not look forward to meeting him.

Nathan drove his jeep a constant twenty-five miles per hour down the bends and turns around Mount Frisia and South Point and then up to the Bellen's. Having been there already once before to talk to Abby he was comfortable in his way, despite the quickly falling snow.

* * * * *

Abby had mixed in the ground pistachios with the egg, cardamom, and flour batter and poured the mix into a pan to put in the oven. The raw batter was delicious and Abby was sure she could eat the whole batch if she allowed herself.

After putting the cake in the oven, she checked that everything else was ready for dinner. She had moved the lasagna from the oven to the microwave to keep warm. The string beans and butter were essentially finished in the saucepan and would just need heat. The risotto would need some final preparation, yet was simmering fine. She checked the place settings on the table to be sure they were in order and determined that if anything went wrong in the next few hours the food would not.

This meeting would have the same outcome no matter what Will's response. He had always been sweet, cordial to everyone in the past, and for the most part still behaved that way, regardless Abby rightly considered him unpredictable now, on this topic in particular. Since the news of the dinner guest had been delivered, Will had appeared to be unaffected. Sure, he had made a couple of slight comments that could have been interpreted as aggressive yet they were not outright hostile. That had always been his way at his worst, to whittle away and badger by comment until he gained some sort of satisfaction or repose. Whether he had any ill intentions was hard for her to tell. Her guard up, Abby did the best she could with what was under her control and prepared a good dinner. The rest she would have to take in course.

Twenty minutes later headlights filled the window of the kitchen door. Nathan had arrived. Abby gave Will a thirty-second warning and told him that if he was counting on any surprises to forget about them altogether. Ignoring her comment, he came into the kitchen to greet their guest.

Nathan made his way to the door in a quick jog with his head bent, his long sandy blonde hair covering his face, and his sneakers splashing through the slush accumulating in the driveway. Abby held the door for him as he entered. Will stood behind her not quite sure of what he was seeing. Abby had not described to Will the guest coming to dinner. Will just knew the guest was supposed to be someone to turn his life upside down. Will's forehead furrowed and a pleasant smile crossed his face. This was not somebody's old wet nurse at the door. Nathan was just a kid not even thirty and Will would have no problem driving him out.

The first thing Nathan did as he walked in the door was hand Abby a bouquet of mixed ranunculus and anemones. "These flowers were the best I could find at the florist," said Nathan. " I was lucky. I didn't know they closed so early. I was the last customer of the day."

Abby took the flowers, "Nathan, they're lovely. These ranunculus are beautiful. Thank you so much." Will could not wait for Abby to finish thanking Nathan, he stepped up and introduced himself, "Hi, I'm Will, can I take your coat?"

"Sure," Nathan started to remove his denim jacket and hooded sweatshirt beneath it, "I'm Nathan, pleased to meet you." Nathan's thin-framed glasses began to fog over.

"Let me help you with that," said Abby in a low tone as she took the back of Nathan's jacket with her free hand so he could remove the coat easily. She decided she needed to distract Will before he could do any damage by unsettling Nathan. "Will, I think the beans might be burning. Can you check them please?" The beans were fine of course yet now Will was subdued. Abby added, "And could you take a peek at the risotto too while your there? I'm afraid it's drying out."

"Risotto, that sounds real good," said Nathan.

"I hope you like lasagna too," said Abby.

"Sure do."

* * * * *

CHAPTER 27

Once in the kitchen Abby offered Nathan a seat at the table, put the bouquet of ranunculus and anemones in the sink, and then went to the refrigerator. Will figured he would make another start "So, Nath--,"

"That risotto does look like it's getting dry," Abby handed him a box of chicken stock, "here, add three tablespoons of this once every minute, no better be every forty-five seconds, and keep stirring, don't stop stirring."

"Uh, ok," said Will.

"Oh, you have to keep the lid on the whole time," scolded Abby.

"The lid, but how can I?"

"Like this," Abby showed him how to leave just the side open to stir.

"Now don't stop stirring," said Abby. "Got it," said Will.

"Three tablespoons every forty-five seconds," said Abby. Will nodded his head.

This would keep him occupied for ten minutes.

Abby went back to the sink and winked at Nathan. She would not let Will get the best of Nathan, though the price so far may be risotto soup.

"Nathan can you reach that yellow vase on top of the cupboard?" asked Abby.

"Sure," said Nathan as he rose to help her.

"How was the drive over here?"

"It's all going to turn to ice," said Will. "Keep stirring," said Abby.

"It wasn't so bad. My Jeep's four wheel drive made me feel pretty safe, and I keep it under thirty miles an hour if the weather is at all questionable," said Nathan.

Will so much wanted to comment yet he had to keep count to forty-five. "What a complicated recipe," he thought.

"Let's see," Abby scanned the kitchen and counted with her hands, tapping each finger on her thumb. "Nathan can you help me with the bread?"

"No problem," said Nathan.

Abby sliced the French loaf procured earlier that day from the IGA then Nathan spread the garlic butter she had prepared onto each piece, placing them on a sheet pan so they would be ready for the oven when the cake came out. They talked about Nathan's new apartment while he laid out the bread and Will listened. The new development had just been built on the lake on the south edge of the village next to the small boat docks. The development had three buildings each three floors high as well as a pool, game room, and gym. The whole complex could be seen almost directly across the lake from the Bellen studio. Will wanted so much to say something about this too.

"They're an eyesore," said Will.

"Will," said Abby.

"Well they are. Right there next to the village," Will shook his head, "have to look at 'em."

"They actually blend in nicely, and they are a lot better than that mill that used to be there when I was a kid," said Abby. She was right, the development was put in place of an abandoned lumber mill.

"That old mill was just a big rusted metal building with

those ugly beltways leading to nowhere while the new buildings are designed to blend with new trees and boulders. You have to admit that they landscaped the grounds beautifully," said Abby. "Keep stirring."

"Hmm," said Will.

"Ok, It's time for the cake to come out," said Abby.

Abby let Will step away from the stove then turned the heat off the risotto and the beans. She removed the cake then put the bread in the oven. She started to corral the men to the table so that she could begin bringing the food over. Will took the opportunity to excuse Nathan and himself to wash their hands.

Five minutes later, the bread was out of the oven, the food was on the table, and the men had not returned. Abby became suspicious. She could not hear them talking. She thought for a moment, "would Will do anything radical, of course not." She walked into the lake room and no one was there. Out the side window, she could see the studio lights were on. "That could be ok," she thought. "He's not going to put him in a kiln. It's just the standard tour."

* * * * *

CHAPTER 28

The Bellen tour was a studio standard that Abby had heard many times before. She helped Michael learn the tour when they were children. The studio at first glance was haphazard yet might as well have been a museum display. Every piece or tool could be referenced at any point during the tour or made a prop as if planned all along. School children from fifty miles away had come on field trips to the studio to see the Bellen urns and to learn how over the years the pottery had found homes around the world. In the foyer of the studio, there was a wall of fame that featured photographs of Bellen pottery on display in the cities of Paris, London, Vienna, and of course the Bellen urns of the White House. Through out the studio was every tool a potter or ceramic artist might want to use: feathering tools, drill tools, fettling knives, fluid writers, and on and on. For each tool an example of the finished work or a work in progress. There were manual kick wheels, electric kick wheels, small kilns, of course the large kilns. There was the urn assembly line, though the process was never referenced like that, which would be explained in detail with examples along the way. In addition, in every tour the pedigree was discussed, there had always been a Bellen, from this father's father to that father's father back to northern Italy.

Abby slipped on a pair of large green rubber boots that she kept by the back door, grabbed a jacket off a hook, and tromped out into the wet snow with the jacket over her head. When she got to the studio she stomped her feet on the concrete floor to get the sticky snow off the boots. Sure enough, she could hear Will in the big room talking about when his grandfather built the studio. She walked in and smiled, Will and Nathan were holding paper cups and a bottle of wine sat uncorked on the worktable. Naturally he would have wine in the studio, "there had always been drinking hadn't there?" she asked herself. "There certainly was when Michael died," a voice inside her head echoed that did not seem to be her own. They were all artists, they all drank, and she asked herself what made her father any different, what was different now?

Will stopped talking about the pedigree, "Hey there Abby. Nathan and I were just getting to know one another."

"You two disappeared on me," said Abby. Just getting to know one another, her father was a very charming man and she was a bit scared for Nathan.

"Your father was just telling me all about the studio and how your great-grandfather built it," said Nathan. His voice sounded confident, just as charming she thought. Good, he was not going to let himself be sucked in.

Will tilted his head back and let his chest pump out, "Did you know Nathan has been to the Bellen installation at the Fremont museum? They still have it there."

Will was quite proud of the museum installation and the stories about his grandfather. Bellen pottery was renowned in his grandfather's own generation making him a local celebrity.

"You don't still go every year to check on it?" asked Abby.

"Not like I used too," said Will.

"I'm glad the two of you are talking, but dinner is on the

table," said Abby.

"Oh my risotto," said Will, "don't want it to dry out."

"Might as well bring the wine while you're at it," said Abby.

The three went back into the house and sat at the table, Will across from Nathan. Abby was quite pleased that Will and Nathan were getting along, which essentially meant that Will did not hate Nathan. She watched Will as he picked up his fork and Nathan bowed his head. "This could be bad," she thought.

"Do you say grace?" asked Will.

Nathan raised his head, looked across the table to Will with an impish smile, "Yes Will, I do. I take it you don't."

"Not normally."

"Would you like to join me?"

"Um, sure," Will bowed his head. Abby also bowed her head, leery of any outburst that may come from Will concerning grace.

Will was not an atheist, or even agnostic. He believed in God all right, he just had some issues with him. Issues in particular concerning the death of his wife and son.

Nathan bowed his head again, closed his eyes behind his glasses, and spoke slowly and solemnly,

"We thank thee, O Lord, for this food,

And for the health of those here to share it today."

Good thought Abby, brief and to the point.

Nathan went on,

"May we use it to nourish our bodies,

And thee, O Lord, to nourish our souls."

Abby peeked over at Will, his head was bowed, a good sign.

"Make us ever more mindful of the needs of others,

And the needs of our planet.

For we have the benefits they do not,

And we have you, O Lord."

Abby could tell Will was rubbing his teeth with his tongue by the way his cheeks and lips were being pushed from his gums. Nathan had more prayer to share,

"May we be ever thankful,

And forget not those benefits.

Through Christ Our Lord, Amen."

"Amen," said Abby.

"Amen," said Will in a slightly enthusiastic voice, "Covered the world on that one too, good job. Now let's enjoy this dinner," Will paused, tilted his head to the side and made an ear to ear grin, "before this risotto dries out."

Abby portioned the lasagna and served Will and Nathan while all three talked about how everything on the table looked so good. The subject of grace and God had passed and Abby, relieved at that, decided to move forward with her task.

"Nathan tell us about what you were doing in Fremont before moving to the village," said Abby.

"I was a caregiver," said Nathan.

"What does that mean – caregiver?" asked Will.

"Well the shared home where I worked was the residence of six people ranging from around my age to the mid-fifties. Two of the residents were not ambulatory, the other four were, and all had health conditions that necessitated either twenty-four hour care or basic help. I performed various activities from mowing the lawn to monitoring people while they slept, which basically meant just being at the house a couple nights a week in case anyone needed anything."

"So you were a babysitter?" asked Will.

"Will, he was not a babysitter," said Abby.

"Actually," said Nathan, "I kinda was, in a lot of ways. Maybe not a babysitter exactly, but I was around if anybody needed anything. And stuff needed to get done, the shopping, the laundry, the cleaning."

"There ya see," said Will.

Abby weighed Will's comment, not sure whether he was patronizing Nathan. Will had appeared to like Nathan yet maybe that was a ploy.

"I can certainly use some help like that around here," said Will. Abby did not have any words for a moment.

"Abby tells me I can't seem to keep up with anything anymore. I guess she's right. Besides, I'm back ordered in the studio and some help would free up my time."

"This was too easy," thought Abby, "Will could not be giving in without a fight." She was certain that Nathan would find Will capricious by his next actions, yet they did not come.

"Yes," said Abby, "as we discussed, there are a lot of things that need to be done around here once I get back to the city."

"Great, let's go over them after dinner," said Nathan. "Will, tell me more about the Bellen studio." Abby thought this genius of Nathan to change the subject and to one of Will's favorites. With pride, Will continued to discuss the aspects of firing pottery passed down through the Bellen pedigree in detail.

After Will and Nathan each had two servings of lasagna, Will excused himself from the table.

"I thought we might go over some of the tasks that you have in mind for Nathan before he starts," said Abby.

"You go right ahead," said Will, " I'm going into the other room to stoke the fire and rest for a moment. You two should join me when you're done."

Abby let Will leave the room without saying another word to him. She had decided that he was going to accept Nathan coming on board peacefully enough and this was better than she had hoped for.

"That didn't go so bad," Abby said to Nathan after Will had stepped out of the room. Nathan picked up the near empty bottle of wine and poured the remainder into Abby's glass. "That's because he was drunk. I could have lit the place on fire and he probably wouldn't have minded as long as I was polite about it," said Nathan.

Abby knew that to be true. Abby had surmised that Will had been drinking all day out of her sight.

"It's a start," said Abby.

"Agreed," said Nathan.

Abby got up from the table and began clearing the dinner plates. Nathan stood up and started to help by clearing the serving bowls from the table and putting them on the counter. Abby took the serving bowls from him before he had a chance to set them down.

"Go on into the other room, I'll get some cake for us," said Abby.

"What about the roads? Should I be worried about getting out of here?" asked Nathan.

"Oh, I am pretty sure Will was right. You're staying in the guest room tonight. I already had it freshly made up, just in case," said Abby.

"In for a penny, in for a pound," said Nathan.

"You're in for something, that's for sure," said Abby.

* * * * *

CHAPTER 29

The only vehicle parked outside the garage was Mitch's yellow pickup. The other workers were gone for the day and the Johansson house looked desolate. Maybe because of the size of the house or because no one had lived there for so long, either reason the house had always appeared eerily vacant to Abby any time she looked at the vacuous windows. She parked the truck and went to the kitchen door where she had entered before. Taped on the kitchen door window was a note written in black marker that read, 'GO TO THE FRONT DOOR', in capital letters. Assuming work was probably being done on the floors of the kitchen, or some adjoining area, Abby walked around the driveway to what Mitch had called the guest entrance. She looked forward to having lunch with Mitch and then maybe spending the afternoon together if he could get away.

They had not seen each other since they had kissed a couple of days before. Their eyes had been locked on each other the rest of the evening and Abby had used all of her strength to not cuddle against him when they went back into the bar. When the time came for Brian to drive her home, she could have easily let herself leave with Mitch. She was glad he had not offered. She only had three beers at the bar still Abby felt that she had little control before she ever arrived. The intoxication came from somewhere else.

Once on the porch Abby saw another note taped to one of the large oak doors that read, 'COME IN TO THE LIBRARY'. Remembering what her father had said about the urns made her smile as she walked past them. In the foyer, she was hit by the smell of popcorn.

The house was warm and Abby did not hesitate to take her jacket off as she entered the library where she found another note hanging on the curtain entrance to the theater that simply read, 'IN HERE'.

"What is this?" asked Abby. The theater lights were an amber hue, the aroma of pine and popcorn made a peculiar combination. On a table between two of the cushioned chairs sat a large bucket of popcorn.

Mitch spoke from behind the back wall, "What's it look like? We're going to test this baby out. Sit down and I'll dim the lights."

"Ok then," said Abby. She took her seat and set her jacket next to her, as she leaned back the chair went into a reclining position and at the bottom of the seat a footrest quickly shot out. "This is nice."

Mitch came out from behind the back wall with a bottle of champagne and two flutes in one hand and a remote control in the other.

"What's back there?" asked Abby.

"A kitchenette and a projection booth. Have some Milk Duds," said Mitch. Mitch revealed a box under the remote control, "and take these if you will," he handed her the two champagne flutes. Out of Mitch's back pocket, he pulled a towel that he wrapped around the neck of the champagne.

"The trick is not to spray this all over the new furniture," said Mitch. He twisted the top of the towel. 'POP', the cork released in his hand and he removed the towel to pour the champagne.

"Well this is class," said Abby.

"The best way to launch," said Mitch. He poured the

two flutes full of champagne and then sat down in the chair opposite the table from Abby. He lifted the flute to her and toasted, "It's magic time."

They tapped their flutes together and Mitch hit the play button on the remote. Immediately the lights of the theater went dark and a projector started behind them. Up in the front of the theater the curtain slid to the side. The screen lit silver, then black, then with trumpets playing the old Warner Brothers shield momentarily filled the screen, backlit in the shades of grey only found in older films. The shield faded and was replaced by a large statue of an ominous black bird.

"You have got to be kidding," said Abby. The title screen rippled onto the screen, 'The Maltese Falcon'.

"No I'm not."

As the rest of the titles faded on and off the screen, Abby started to laugh aloud.

Mitch laughed too, "What?"

"Here's your art history lesson," said Abby, quieting herself as the text of the prologue began scrolling up the screen.

"Oh yea, Knight Templar, Golden Falcon, pirates, got it. No truth to any of it, eh?" asked Mitch.

"Nope."

As Bogart appeared on the screen, they clapped their hands together and cheered through his opening line, "Yea Sweetheart."

Throughout the movie, they shared comments as each of the shady characters entered and exited the screen. In the middle of the movie when Spade took Cairo's gun away from him both reached for their champagne flutes in the center of the table between them, as they did their hands brushed against one another. Neither of them pulled their hand away. Abby reached out and lightly began to caress Mitch's hand. His fingers lightly responded, sending electricity up her arm and into her chest. A couple of times during the film Mitch looked at Abby and thought what a gorgeous woman sat beside him. They let their hands subtly roll within each other until the final scene when Bogart looked at Mary Astor crying in the elevator.

The words 'The End' faded on and then off the silver screen. Mitch lifted the remote and turned off the movie, triggering the curtain to close, and the lights to brighten to the amber setting that washed the room before the film.

"Isn't that a great film?" said Abby.

"All class," said Mitch, picking up the bottle of champagne to pour, only to see that they had emptied it. "This went quick too."

Impressed with Mitch, Abby looked into his deep eyes. She lifted her feet up from the footrest and pulled her shins close to her. Mitch thought she looked beautiful crouched in the big cushion chair. Her chestnut hair radiated in the amber light and her eyes were sultry. He realized now that the flaw in the theater was that the big cushion chairs were separated by the coffee tables. She was so very far from him that to make any subtle move in her direction would be impossible. Mitch thought that he saw in her eyes an invitation. He was right. Abby wanted him to kiss her again. Mitch lightly sighed and stood up.

"I should pick this stuff up," said Mitch. He picked up the two flutes, put them in the hand already holding the neck of the champagne bottle, and then reached for the popcorn bowl. Abby reached over and grabbed his wrist. If Mitch was not going to make the next move than she would.

"Put those down," said Abby. As soon as Mitch set the flutes aside, Abby pulled him around to the front of her and then slid her arms up around his neck. "This was so sweet of you."

In Mitch's eyes, Abby glowed and now he had permission to recapture the sensation of the other night. He put his arms around her and leaned down, lightly pressing his lips to hers. Abby had been waiting for him and pulled him tight to her as she gently kissed him. He tasted sweet from the champagne and she felt like devouring him. The longer they kissed, the more intense they pressed their lips together.

Abby's whole body filled with adrenaline. She had to have him closer. She attempted to bring him into the chair. He could feel adrenaline rushing through him as well. This was not why he had asked her here yet he was compelled to lean forward by her unsaid invitation. Abby locked her eyes to his. His fingers caressed her forearms, his hands moving into hers. He knelt on the floor and eased her off the chair. She knelt beside him and they drew together in a tight embrace. Abby's body shivered as Mitch ran his fingers down the center of her back. He then kissed her ear and the nape of her neck, sucking gently with several soft kisses down to her shoulder. With these wonderful kisses, Abby tilted her head back and closed her eyes. She clasped tightly to his upper back where she could feel the muscles below his shoulder blades moving in unison with the massaging of his hand upon her breast. To him she felt delicate and to her he felt so strong. She grabbed his head with both of her hands and let her fingers work through his hair. She pulled her face across his lips, letting him cover her in kisses, until her lips were upon his. They eased down to the carpeted floor and went with their passions.

* * * * *

CHAPTER 30

"Let me get this place straightened up and we can get out of here," said Mitch. Abby thought he sounded like he was apologizing. Abby said nothing, relaxed her hands, and let Mitch's hands slip away. He raised his eyebrows before he looked away, an unspoken request for understanding.

Mitch took the bottle and popcorn bowl back to the kitchenette. Abby stretched her arms high above her head. The movement of blood through her body had sobered, cooled from the moment before. She rose to the cushioned chair and stretched again.

"I was thinking we could walk off some of this popcorn," said Mitch from the back room. "Sounds great," said Abby. She was glad he had brought up the idea. Their time together had her reeling inside and she needed to displace the energy trapped inside of her.

The two cleaned up silently, afraid to ignite more sparks while still inside. After shutting down the theater, they stepped out the foyer to the double oak doors then into the crispness of the winter afternoon. Mitch suggested a walk down to the lake so Abby took the lead down the driveway. They each had both hands in their coat pockets.

There was no discernible sun. Bright white cumulous

clouds filled the sky trading light with the snow-covered ground. When they rounded the bend of the driveway they could see across the lake. Cars moved along the ice road and the lake was dotted with quad runners and snowmobiles.

At the bottom of the drive, they crossed Willow Lake road and Mitch launched himself over the snow bank onto a large rock among the field of rocks on the waters edge of South Cove. Once there he reached down to Abby and helped her up. They walked on the rocks, hopping from one to the other, skirting the shore as they went. When they came to a boulder that jutted out into the ice like a cliff edge they walked to the end and stood.

They had been silent on their trek over the rocks and were silent now. Mitch looked across the lake at the shanties and snowmobiles scurrying between them and then over to Abby. She too peered out in the direction of the lake yet he could tell that whatever she was seeing was not on the ice, or anywhere in front of her, at least not now.

"What do you see?" asked Mitch.

"It really doesn't change," said Abby.

"I suppose not," Mitch assumed Abby referred to the vista. "People have been doing the same things out here for years."

"Not that," said Abby, "the cove itself."

"What do you mean?"

"I have imagined this cove a lot over the years. Sometimes this place is lit up, most of the time it's menacing, ugly," Abby lowered her chin and looked down at the boulder they were standing on. "When I think of this place, there are a lot of ghosts. Now that I am standing out here, it's the same as it ever was. Like nothing has ever taken place out here. There are no ghosts."

"Ghosts are only where we put them," said Mitch. He now remembered, "Your brother, Michael, this is where he had his accident, where he died."

"Twelve years ago Michael's jeep hit a tree over there

somewhere," Abby pointed across the road, "and then into the rocks." Her hand dropped an inch as her voice trailed off.

"I'm sorry," said Mitch.

"Don't be, he was drunk. It was a long time ago," said Abby. "It's ironic though."

"What is?" asked Mitch.

"We had a lot of good times out here when we were kids. We played on this very spot."

"Right here, eh?"

"Yea," Abby lifted her foot and stepped back down on the boulder, "My brother and I used to fish down here. The fishing isn't bad by the rocks."

"I can't quite picture you fishing."

"Oh yea. I was a bit of a tomboy, and quite a fisherman. This was our secret fishing spot."

"Well it can't be that secret. I'm sure everyone on the lake knows about it."

"Don't be so sure," said Abby. "If word got out, South Cove could be overrun."

"Well, your secret is safe with me."

"How do I know that?" Abby felt playful, "How do I know you won't go marching into the village and tell everyone? Or worse, if word got to the city."

"Well, you can rest assured that I won't be going to the city. That's the last place I need to be."

"What do you mean, the last place? That's the second time you said that. I didn't think you were serious before when you said you never went to the city. Are you hiding out or something?"

"Deep cover."

"Like witness protection?"

"Something like that."

"How very interesting," said Abby. "You are going to at least come visit me aren't you?"

"The farthest I go from the village is Fremont, I like it out here where it's peaceful."

"I thought maybe we would meet up at O'Malley's after a day in the museum. You said you liked that bar."

"I do, I mean I did... I do," Mitch was confusing Abby. Mitch suddenly was serious. "I just don't do the city anymore. There is a reason I am out here," said Mitch, "your cousin did me a big favor bringing me here. At a time when I didn't have anywhere else to go."

"I know the two of you knew each other from college. You weren't a couple, I would have known."

"No, nothing like that. But we were close. And when I needed some help, after college, she was there."

"What kind of help?" Abby could tell that Mitch was trying to say something and the words were not coming.

Two birds flew overhead, one chasing the other. Mitch had both hands in his pockets again. He turned toward the lake, toward the trees away from Abby, and then back again.

"After college," said Mitch, "I spread myself a little thin. I told you about going to Prague. Well, I never really got my head together when I came back. I went to work in the city at a job that I couldn't stand. Had an apartment and did all of the stuff you're supposed to, but nothing was adding up."

"That sounds like a lot of people," said Abby.

"I suppose. Maybe I was just going out too much, but it all started falling apart. That's when Caroline told me to come out here. After that, everything fell into place. I just don't have a need to go back to the city. To complicate my life any more than it needs to be."

Mitch had calmness when he spoke that told Abby he believed that things were simpler here. She certainly did not. Perhaps Mitch needed an excuse to push everyone away, to push her away.

"Give me the city," said Abby. "Willow Lake is a neat little package for you, for me it's a large piece of luggage."

"That's fair," said Mitch, "if it's true, but maybe it's not Willow Lake that has all of that weight."

Abby put her hand on Mitch's shoulder and said,

"Maybe it's not the city that you are hiding from out here."

"Who says I'm hiding?" said Mitch.

"Well, if what you're saying is places are what you make them, then you have made this an oasis for yourself and that's great. The world is still out there though. I'm not hiding from it. I'm avoiding it. It's different."

"Avoiding it, or running away from it?" asked Mitch.

"Semantics," said Abby as she turned back toward the house. "I'm getting cold and I need to get back. Will needs his truck this afternoon."

They silently made their way back over the rocks and across Willow Lake road. When they started back up the drive, both had their hands free and Mitch reached over to take Abby's. She let her fingers slip into his. For a few moments she had been annoyed with Mitch yet as soon as she felt his thumb caress the back of her hand she melted. A warm sensation cycled through her body.

Abby felt that her body betrayed her by wanting to be with Mitch. She was not sure as to why he had more than once pointed out his distaste for the city. She wondered if there was more to why he had come out to the lake. She needed to sort out her feelings for Mitch and why his situation bothered her so much. Caroline would tell her what Mitch would not.

When they got back to the pickup truck, Mitch opened the door for Abby and she pulled her hand away. Where speaking had come easy before now things seemed awkward. They searched for words to fill the space where simply saying goodbye would do. Abby wanted to kiss him and pull him into the truck. At the same time, she wanted to just go. She felt that if she could just separate herself from him the building urges would calm.

Mitch wanted to say something grand or poetic. He wanted to reach out to Abby and hold her. Subconsciously he defeated himself, not even able to utter a word much less anything that would reflect the significance of his feelings.

The two were like school children, neither knew what to

say, and the urges did not seem right no matter how strong. So Mitch just said he would see Abby later, and she said, "ok." Mitch stood in the drive as Abby turned the truck around and they politely waved to each other before she drove away.

* * * * *

CHAPTER 31

The light of the afternoon sun filtered through the pines and maples along the road. The truck was old yet the heater had a strong fan that blew out toasty heat and the FM radio worked well. A woman singing filled the truck with a song about someone treating her wrong, yet the words were lost on Abby. She tapped to the music as her mind raced from Mitch to Will. Abby had decided to take her time to get to the village. She drove around Mount Frisia before heading north around the lake.

The awkwardness of Abby's departure from Mitch was not lost on her and the thought crossed her mind that maybe she should take this as a sign and cool her urges a bit. She had been spending a lot of time thinking about Mitch lately and perhaps subconsciously she was sublimating her actions with Mitch in preference to dealing with Will. Perhaps she should not be thinking about Mitch at all. A list of questions went through her head. What point was there to thinking about Mitch? If he did not want to go to the city, ever, and she did not want to stay out here, how could they ever make anything work? Was there an anything? Abby asked herself if she had been reading too much into their time together. If so, how was she defining that time? How was she defining that relationship? Those were really the cards on the table after all. They were each holding a hand at the same table in the same game. There was a relationship between them and the more she thought the less she could deny. A relationship was not something she was looking for yet she had found one just the same. Now she was unsure of what that relationship was.

The afternoon with Mitch went so well then ended so awkwardly. The movie was fun and what followed was passionate. Then things started to become not quite right. Mitch had certainly been into her. By the lake, Abby felt Mitch had become distant. Did he become distant because of her? Abby replayed the events in her mind. Was she pushing him away? Why had he been making advances and then, well then nothing. He had put together the movie with popcorn and champagne. Champagne, Abby thought that must mean something. The signals that Mitch sent to her were now confusing her the more she thought about them.

Abby picked up her cell phone to call Caroline so that she could unload all of the thoughts racing around her head. The cell had hardly any battery because Abby had not thought to charge the phone since she had been on the lake. Unsure the signal would be strong enough to let her dial out while she was driving, Abby pulled the truck over to the side of the road and dialed. Caroline picked up and Abby told her that she needed to see her. She could not say much more because the phone connection was weak. Once Abby told Caroline that she wanted to speak about Mitch, Caroline said to come right over. Abby told her that she was literally on the other side of the lake. So, the two decided to meet at the Stone tavern.

Abby felt relieved simply knowing she would have her cousin Caroline, her friend since childhood, to listen to her. She pulled the truck back onto the road and drove to the village. She focused on what to say to Caroline, and what to ask her.

* * * * *

CHAPTER 32

"So I don't get the problem," said Caroline. She sipped her white wine then continued, "You wanted to meet someone, a great guy, and hit it off and from what you describe, it sounds like you found that in Mitch. What are you complaining about?"

The tavern was empty apart from the cousins. They sat at a table with a window that looked out toward the lake. The outside was the only light to the interior. Abby's Chardonnay tasted smoky yet warm so she dropped in an ice cube from her water glass that melted without cooling the wine.

As much as Abby did not like what Caroline said she knew the words to be the truth. Mitch did exhibit all signs of the suitor she was looking for. Mitch was a great guy and they sure got along, this afternoon proved that in some intimate ways. Abby did not think a relationship could be that simple though. She had peered into Mitch's eyes at the lake and saw turmoil.

"Maybe he is falling for you?" said Caroline, "That's not the worst thing in the world."

"He talks about the city like it will kill him if he returns there. I know there is something that he is not telling me, and I am pretty sure it's something you know," said Abby.

Caroline's forehead wrinkled at the socially awkward accusation. She would have liked to dismiss the comment with a statement to Abby's overreacting then decided that would not be best. Abby looked at her and waited for a reply.

"I thought enough time had passed since I brought him out here."

"Why did you bring him out here? What kind of baggage are we talking about?"

"Well, where do I start?"

"Start with how you know Mitch, then how he ended up in Willow Lake," said Abby. Abby began to wonder if her cousin purposely withheld some piece of history, another 'surprise'.

"What did he tell you?" asked Caroline, unsure whether Mitch had shared too much.

"He told me he had a job in the city and that things weren't working out so you brought him out here."

"Did he tell you about anything before that?"

"Uh, yea, that he never really came back from Prague... Oh, don't tell me that this is all about this old girl friend floating around somewhere."

"Nah, that was years ago. What all did he tell you about her anyway?"

"That they had split up and that he had thought he could deal with it, but ended up chasing after her. Only to find in the end that it was over 'in the most romantic city in the world' as he put it," said Abby. "I should have known he was still hung up. How long were they together?"

"Couple of years," said Caroline.

"And?"

The conversation had turned to a direction that Caroline could exploit, so she continued, "Mitch, Marcy, and I went to school together. We were tight. The short of it is that Marcy decided overnight that she was too young to be tied down and needed to see the world so she headed to Europe.

She asked Mitch to respect it, which he did at first, yet it wasn't too long that he was heartbroken. I mean it was sad to watch." Caroline took a sip of her wine, "so, he finally went chasing after her and caught up with her and her girlfriend in Dublin, followed her through London, Paris and Prague, where she cut him loose. She told him he needed to go. He was devastated and stayed in Prague drunk for a season. When he finally got back to the States he found out Marcy was living with some guy somewhere in Morocco. He tried to get back on track and, well I think you know the rest. He essentially had a breakdown in the city. It broke my heart to see him tear himself apart, so Brian and I brought him out here."

"Caroline, what am I supposed to say. That is so sad," said Abby. "When you say broke down what do you mean?"

"Helpless."

"What about his family?"

"There's no family, he's somehow the last of his people. He never knew his mom and his dad disappeared when we were in school."

"I gotta say I'm touched but c'mon Caroline." Abby felt insulted. "You think I remind him of this Marcy. That's just wrong."

"I don't think it's so, it's been years," said Caroline, she could see that Abby had been caught in the allure of the story. "He knows you're going back to the city and that probably just freaks him out in general. I mean if there is really something going on between you two that would make sense."

Abby put her finger to her temple and fixed her eyes to Caroline.

"And what's this thing about the city?" asked Abby.

"Mitch grew up in the city, simple as that I think."

"Ghosts are only where we put them," said Abby.

"What?"

"Something Mitch said to me that makes more sense

now," said Abby as she picked up her Chardonnay and took a drink. "He literally keeps his ghosts in the city, that way Willow Lake is free and clear. As long as he avoids the city he's fine."

"Sounds familiar doesn't it."

Abby smirked at Caroline's reversal. "There aren't just ghosts in Willow Lake, Deary. There are plenty of ghoulies too."

"I suppose there is at least one at the studio."

"Tromping around in the darkness," said Abby. They both laughed and then there was a silence. Caroline looked out the window.

"So what do you plan to do?" asked Caroline

"What I planned to do, I am going back to the city."

Caroline looked out toward the lake and back at Abby, "You didn't tell Mitch when you plan to leave did you."

Abby turned her head down to her wine glass, "I didn't see any point in complicating things."

* * * * *

CHAPTER 33

The large acrylic brush coated the two-foot urn with a now soft green viscous glaze. After seasoning in the kiln, the glaze would become a clear thick lacquer. Nathan had four urns to glaze and this was his second. Will hovered above coaching him not to be afraid to 'glop' large amounts of glaze onto the urn. Will had his glasses on so he could see exactly what was happening. His energy was up today and he had been working at a good pace.

Abby was surprised to see Nathan glazing. "Didn't take long to find Nathan something to do other than just sweeping up," said Abby.

Will lifted the corner of his top lip. Abby was sure a biting comment would follow, and then he eased back. "Eh," said Will, "If I'm going to keep up on the current orders Nathan will have to do something around here that can help me out. It's a job I give to most interns."

Nathan appreciated Will's hidden compliments in their banter. Nathan smiled when Abby winked at him. Helping in the studio had been one of the enticing draws to the position.

Abby leaned over Nathan's shoulder, "Everything working out so far?"

147

"Will's a gem," said Nathan, and then added softly and quickly, "We're getting along fine. I've found my way around the house and the studio easily enough. Will has not stepped in front of my duties and in the short time that I've been here, I've been able to move through the bedrooms to do the laundry, through the kitchen for cooking and shopping, and freely through each room to keep the place tidy. And Will has been really great to get along with, I think Will is delighted in having assistance around the house."

Nathan added, "Oh and as you suspected, Will has replenished the not so well hidden bottles of brandy around the house that you had thrown out. I have also seen Will drinking brandy several times when he thought I wasn't looking and he openly drinks wine around me throughout the day when you're not around."

Abby walked over to the large bay window. The icicle-laden eave of the studio cast a shadow on the sill. She had spoken with Nathan to set her comfort level enough to head back to the city. Her plan was to get a good night's rest and leave in the morning. Abby had come to tell her father yet as she gazed upon the lake a thought occurred to her. Seeing her father today reminded her of how he used to be. Maybe she was rushing off too soon. Perhaps if she spent more time with her father things would change between them. Perhaps she could fulfill her mother's promise. All he needed was someone to take care of him.

Abby looked at her father and was filled with new compassion. How handsome he appeared standing with his hands behind his back walking around his studio as the master craftsman. She thought for a moment how lucky she was to have a father that was such a craftsman, an artist, and a true one in a million. How precious their time really was together. With that, she decided that the museum could wait a little longer. Maybe she would take an early sabbatical. In a moment of spontaneity, Abby asked Will to come over to the window.

Abby had long thought about working in the studio with her father even if only in the back of her mind. Will had a large number of special orders and backorders for his regular clients. Abby knew her father could use her help. She knew the standard Bellen designs and could surely help with the backorders. The criteria for the Bellen mark was that they were made by Bellen hands, she had those. She quickly rationalized that if ever there was a time to offer up help, she should now, Will needed help and he would be happy for this chance for his daughter to work with him. Abby's mind flashed to throwing clay high into urns and tending kilns until dawn. She saw images of her and her father doing detail work in the studio together late into the evening. This would be the way she would reach out to him. She determined to offer to do so.

Will stepped over to the window next to Abby and looked out onto lake with his hands behind has back and a grin upon his face. He glanced back at Nathan and then at Abby and said, "You know you had a good idea here. I like this fella, spies on me a bit though."

Abby glanced back at Nathan, he had heard Will, and then with a smile to Will, "Does he?"

"Not all the time, but he sure is curious every time I have a nip."

"I'll bet."

"Prays a lot too. Not just at meals, all day. That's ok though, I like 'em."

"Good... So, Dad, I'm pretty much ready to head back to the city. The house is in order. You're saying that Nathan is working out. But I was thinking..."

"What's that you're thinking about dear?"

"Well I was thinking, the museum doesn't need me back right away, and you have so many orders, I was thinking the studio maybe could use another Bellen for a few days, or longer. Whadda ya think?"

Will's smile went away from his face and his hands slipped from behind his back to his front pockets. He dropped his head and clenched his jaw, grinding his teeth a little. Though not long at all, to Abby the pause lasted for some time. She tried to keep smiling then her eyes began to fail. Abby could see that Will's head was going through some elaborate deliberation process. She wondered why would he have to do that. That there would be a chance he would say no had not occurred to her a few minutes before. She no longer smiled.

Will said nothing. He was not deliberating at all, caught off guard he was in some type of shock. Whatever had manifested as new compassion toward her father washed away with his solemn rejection. He could not even humor her to look her in the eyes. He knew that their relationship was diminishing and still he could not help himself. He was overtaken by a void and there were no words he could share with her. Will was engulfed with the thought that the only recent Bellen to work in the studio beside him was Michael. Abby had triggered some kept emotion that he knew too well yet had not felt in some time.

Abby could not believe that Will had gone catatonic on her offer to help in the studio. The thought that to have her work beside him bothered him so badly and not give a reason, not even a response, infuriated her.

"I guess that's a no," said Abby. She waited for a reply. Abby had to give him one more opportunity, not out of compassion this time, rather to verify that what he was truly doing was emotionally shunning her, shutting her out, and not the first time. The response did not come. After the pause Abby said, "I'll be packing in the house," and then she turned and walked away.

Will stayed in the position he was in with his head turned down. He was unaware that Abby had said anything or that she had even walked away. Will was away in his own little world.

Abby left the studio and walked the newly shoveled path to the house. Her eyes did not well with tears yet her cheeks were flush and her jaw was tight. Once in the house, she went into her bedroom and shut her door. Abby began frantically removing clothes from the bureau and closet and placing them on the bed. The morning would be too long to wait to leave this house.

* * * * *

CHAPTER 34

A soft knock came upon Abby's bedroom door, yet Abby continued going through her closet. The knock came again accompanied by Will pleading, "C'mon let me in." She took the clothes in her hands from the closet and moved them to the bed with her back to the door.

"I'm sorry, open the door," said Will.

Abby went on sorting clothes.

"Hey listen, I'm sorry, for whatever I did, I'm sorry," said Will.

Abby stood straight from organizing the clothes on the bed with some still in hand.

"Whatever you did, you're sorry?" asked Abby.

"Yes," said Will, thinking this a quick end to his plea, "now open the door."

Abby threw her arms straight down, still holding the blouse she was folding, and turned to the door, "You don't know what you did?"

"Well maybe. Open the door, let me explain," said Will, realizing he had been overconfident.

The door flew open in front of Will and Abby marched out passed him, "Let you explain. Explain what?"

"Why I didn't answer."

Abby turned back to Will. "Is that all you think you did," said Abby and then kept going down the hall, leaving Will standing in the doorway.

"You just caught me off guard," said Will. Will began to follow Abby. He caught up to her in the lake room, " I hadn't thought about --."

Abby cut him off, "—Another Bellen besides Michael?"

Abby kept going into the kitchen. She had processed what had happened in the studio. The question was not of Will deliberating whether or not she should stay and help. Abby realized that he was spinning again about her brother. To Abby, the issue with Will was always her brother.

"Now hold on," said Will walking across the lake room. "Now what exactly is that supposed to mean?"

"You know."

"There you go," said Will. He stopped at the kitchen doorway. Abby was at the sink shuffling dishes around with her back to him.

"Whadda ya mean there I go?"

"There you go again. I'm supposed to know what you mean, and, you bringing up Michael," Will raised his voice, "Christ your brother's dead!"

Abby stopped shuffling the dishes, raised her head, and with out turning asked, "Is he? Is he the one that's been dead for the last twelve years?"

"What kind of damn question is that?" Will raised and placed his hand on the back of his neck.

Abby turned toward him, "How about the last twenty?"

"Last twenty?"

Abby looked as deeply as she could into her father's eyes, "Yea, Daddy," said Abby, "twenty years ago when Mom passed away and you started pretending I wasn't there. You think I didn't notice. Oh, but Michael. You embraced Michael. It was always Michael."

Abby raised her voice, "I was right here Daddy!"

Abby took a breath. Calmly she added, "I was hurting too. And when Michael died..." Abby nodded her head, "I was hurting then too. And we could have had each other then, but no, you pretended like you were the last member of the family, like you were alone. He was the last of the 'Bellen Line', isn't that what you said at his funeral? Do you know how that made me feel? You made me feel alone. You make me feel alone."

Will did remember saying that at Michael's funeral. He of course had been devastated by Michael's death, had he really excluded his daughter? He couldn't honestly remember much, everything was dark when he thought back to then, and he did not ever try to think back to then.

"Abby that's not at all true. I didn't know what I was saying, my son died --,"

"—It's all true. You knew what you were saying, the 'Last of the Bellen Line', I offered to help in the studio today and you couldn't even look me in the face! I'm not Michael, Daddy, but I'm a Bellen and I can make pots and urns better than most anybody, I can work with clay and detail better than Michael ever could."

Will lifted his chin and his voice, "That's no way to talk about your dead brother." His hand on his neck began to rub back and forth.

"Still defending him, he's not even here."

Will backed up against the doorway, "That's just about enough, I loved you both. You just don't understand." Will put his hands on his face, "I just... with you... after your mother died." Will tried to form a thought and his brow wavered up and down, then he dropped his hand's to his sides and looked up toward Abby with surrender, "Hon, I love you, I appreciate everything you've done, but this is not the place for you."

"Don't understand. Not the place for me. That's just beautiful." Abby looked up in the air and raised her hands, "You hear that Mom, he pretends I don't exist for twenty years and then says I don't understand." She dropped her hands and looked back at Will, "Make me understand. Make me understand why, when I keep reaching out to you,

you keep pushing me away. Why are you pining away waiting for his return when your daughter is right here to help you? Make me understand cuz I don't. I don't understand. I don't understand why you won't let me, your daughter, help you. More important I don't understand why you're killing yourself in the process. Make me understand."

"You wanna know?" said Will, his eyes lighting up, his back straightening from a slump.

Abby startled at his reaction, "Yea."

"You want to know?"

"Yes, I want to know," said Abby, unsure now if she really did now that he had offered up an answer.

"Which question do you want an answer to? What's with Michael? What's with me? Whadda ya wanna know?"

Abby was surprised by his frankness. The discourse was emotional and she was confused. She decided to walk over to the table and sit down. She placed her elbows on the table, clasped her hands together, and looked up at her father, "I don't know. Either, both."

"Well," said Will. He approached the table to sit down beside Abby, " the answer is the same."

* * * * *

CHAPTER 35

Abby flashed her eyes to Will and softly said, "This is no time for games, Dad."

"It's no game," said Will, "The answer is: I deserve it."

"You deserve it."

"That's the answer. I deserve it."

"Ok," Abby was tiring, "why do you think you deserve it?"

"I deserve it because of what I did. I can't sleep. I'm haunted knowing what I did. I've told your Mother I'm sorry a thousand times but it doesn't make me feel any better."

"What you did, what did you do? You're right, I don't understand. What are you talking about? What did you do?"

"Those boys, Michael and Thomas, I might as well have been driving the jeep myself," said Will.

Abby rested her hands flat on the table, her jaw dropped open. Was Will sincere or could he be trying to frustrate her. Abby had heard her father voice this frustration after her brother's death. To blame ones self was an understandable part of the grieving process, still Will was going too far. She spoke deadpan, "Really? That's the best you have to offer."

"Really," said Will surprised.

"Michael was drunk. He hit a tree. He died Dad. You get it. You didn't put him in the car," Abby was becoming disgusted with her father.

"You're wrong, I did."

"You did," said Abby.

"To get beer," said Will. Abby looked at him and said nothing, "to get beer," Will repeated.

"What?"

"To get beer." Will threw up his hands, "I sent the boys to get beer."

Abby furrowed her brow, "Really Dad?"

Michael and Will had been drinking buddies long before that night. To hear him speak now as if there were something that never occurred was hypocrisy and Abby knew as well.

Still Will was serious. His cool blue eyes deepened as he subtly leaned toward his daughter. His unwavering voice aged ten years, "We were tending the kilns the whole night and all day. The Lee boy was there to help Michael out by moving stuff around out in the old kiln and chopping wood. And we were drinking, drinking whiskey and beer. The beer ran out. I threw Michael his keys and told 'em that we needed more beer. I knew he was drunk. We were all drunk. But he was happy to go. Said he'd be right back. But he wasn't."

Abby tried to understand her father. "Don't you think I knew that?" she asked. She realized her eyes were watering again at the thought of her brother.

"I guess I knew you did, but I was ashamed."

Abby put her hands in her face and sighed, "So this is what you're doing to yourself? Making amends by punishing yourself and me?"

"I don't think I'm punishing anybody."

"Of course not," said Abby, "but you have to see yourself. You need to let it go."

"I just can't."

"Not the way you're going about it. I should've put two and two together a long time ago. Stop blaming yourself. Michael knew better. He was a grown man, you need to stop taking all the credit for him being an idiot." Abby pulled her head up straight and wiped her eyes with the back of her hands.

"It's not that easy," said Will.

"It is," said Abby, she felt as if she were speaking to a child, "I'm here for you, if you let me. I always have been."

"I know, I'm sorry I pushed you away."

"Then why did you?"

"You were always with your mother. You look like her; you talk like her, hell you even argue like her. After she died, I saw her every time I looked into your eyes. And it hurt, I miss her so much."

"I miss her too," said Abby, "but you didn't have to ignore me. I needed you."

"You didn't need me like you thought you did. You're strong like your Mother. Michael, he needed me. He was lost. He could never go out in the world like you did. He barely made it through high school. You—well look at you—fancy job at one of the best museums in the world. You've traveled places your mother and I never made it to. You've seen things your mother never lived to see, things that I'll never live to see. You're doing the things your mother would have wanted you to do." Will's eyes were blue pools of water, "Don't you think I know you can throw a pot better than anyone? I can teach any lummox to do what I do over time. Your brother was always going to make a career here because he never could do anything else. Your Mother nurtured you because you could do anything since you were small… like her."

Abby's eyes too were wet again. She had not expected Will to say anything like that. She put a soft smile across her face, "You never told me any of that before. That you felt like that."

"Well that's how it is."

"That's how it is," said Abby. "I see then, you don't need my help after all. I better finish packing and get out of here."

"I don't want you rushing out of here like this. I tell you what, why don't you stay for a few more days. In the mean time, if you don't mind, you can help me catch up in the studio."

Abby's heart filled with the idea that Will had just extended an olive branch. "I appreciate that, but you're right, there are things I need to get back to. I'll pack up tonight and you can take me to Fremont in the morning."

* * * * *

CHAPTER 36

Mitch raised his hand above his right ear and then let his arm fly forward, releasing the dart too early. The steel tip planted into the green cork above the twenty, the second to miss the board in a row. He had been throwing darts for the last hour. Playing cricket against himself and not faring so well. On most occasions, his precision was spot on however Mitch was not really paying much attention to the board. His thoughts were where they had been most of the week, with the girl with the chestnut hair. He thought about how she smelled. He thought about how she talked. He thought about how she smiled, laughed, and tasted.

Mitch thought about the way that Abby Bellen made him feel. Certainly she made him feel good, there was that, she was a pleasure to be around, and there was more than that too. She made him physically feel something in the pit of his stomach. He felt a flutter, an ache, and nausea all at once. Maybe he was coming down with something, whatever that something was felt stronger when she was near. He threw another dart scoring not on the twenty rather the eighteen.

Mitch did not like the way things had left off yesterday when he last saw Abby. He had tried calling the Bellen house today and no one had answered. He was not exactly sure what he wanted to say to Abby. What was his next move? Dinner he supposed, though that seemed so formal. He reasoned they had already had a date at the theater, definitely a date, so why not ask her out for another.

Mitch walked to the dartboard and pulled a dart from the board and two from the wall, prying one that had sunk deep. He marked an eighteen on the chalkboard and then walked back to throw badly again.

Mitch asked himself where to have dinner. Of course, he could cook himself, would that be too presumptuous? He could take her to the South Point Inn for a gourmet meal. Then again, he did not want to come off as too overbearing. Perhaps to just try to call her again would be best and see where things went from there. He dialed her cell this time rather than the house and the call went right to voice mail. Stammering Mitch left a quick message for Abby to give him a call back. Putting his phone back into his pocket he sighed to himself then sat down at the table, poured a beer from his pitcher, and then took a drink.

* * * * *

CHAPTER 37

Abby flipped through a copy of the City News that someone had left on the train with little interest. Will had taken her to the station in Fremont midmorning after a stop at the cemetery to wipe the snow away from her mother and brother's stones.

As the train came through the next populated area Abby's cell phone chimed. She saw a new message in her voicemail inbox. She put the phone to her ear and struggled to hear the message. She could not entirely decipher what was being said. She could hear Mitch's deep voice through the static and did get the four words that mattered, "give me a call." She placed the phone on her lap realizing that she may have blundered. Abby could have at least stopped by to say good-bye yet had decided that she did not want to complicate things, that she had was obvious to her now. Opening her cell phone, she could see that the chance to call back would have to wait until she returned to the city. That would be for the better because that would give her a chance to call Caroline.

* * * * *

CHAPTER 38

Will offered to help Nathan clean the dishes after their late lunch. Nathan told him that washing dishes was his responsibility and that Will should feel free to take care of the work he had piled up in the studio. Will headed out to the studio yet he did not feel free at all, despite what Nathan had told him. As he crossed the walkway to the studio he looked out across the lake, paused, and then turned to walk toward the birch bench. His walk to the bench, slow and determined, carried him through the same steps he had taken too many times to count since his youth. On the bench, he pulled out his camels and took one from the pack. He thought to himself that he smoked more lately. He cuffed the cigarette when he lit the end and glanced up at the willow towering next to the bench then out to the lake. He looked up at the tree again as he exhaled. As Will peered at the willow he thought that there were things, such as what was bothering him now, which could not be hidden. Still he took a posture away from the tree by resting both of his hands by his sides on the edge of the bench and leaned forward into them, peering out across the lake. He slowly rocked back and forth occasionally sucking on his cigarette and then peeking up at the tree before turning his head back out to the lake. When Will finally gathered enough courage, he lifted his eyes high into the tree and spoke. "Sorry," was all he said. Emily and Will shared a love deep and dear. Will felt Emily could hear him talking to her as closely as when they were young. Will did not feel right about what he had done. Abby got on the train congenially yet he knew things were still not right between them.

Though the words seemed foreign to him when spoken the night before, Will could not pretend to himself that there had not been an issue all of these years past. He had chosen to deny the gulf between him and his daughter like all of those other things in his life that had not made sense since Emily had gotten ill. Abby even now embodied Emily in his eyes. After last night, he could not be sure if the rift would ever be closed.

Will peered deeply into the weave of willow branches towering above him in search of solace. Emily would not have been pleased with him all of this time. She would not have been pleased with him last night and Abby was right that Emily would not be pleased as to how he was taking care of himself.

* * * * *

CHAPTER 39

Caroline had just put the twins to bed when her phone rang. The call was expected. Brian had gone over to the studio earlier in the day to check on part of the order and spoke to Nathan. Nathan told him that Will had taken Abby to Fremont to catch the train. Caroline had asked Brian not to mention to Mitch that Abby had gone until she had a chance to speak to her. Brian told Caroline that Mitch would want to know why Abby had left so abruptly. She was expected to stay through the week. Caroline assured Brian that Abby leaving must have something to do with Will. Abby's issues always had something to do with Will.

By fortune, Brian did not have to mention anything to Mitch as Mitch had made himself scarce for the day. Caroline had waited for the call that she knew would come.

Leaving Willow Lake quickly was typical of Abby, not saying goodbye was not, especially to Caroline and the twins. When Caroline picked up the phone apologies for the quick exit came first.

"I'm really sorry," said Abby. "I just had to get out of there."

"I understand completely," said Caroline, "if you needed to get away from Will then that is what you had to do."

"I'm not sure what to think now. He really caught me off guard."

"You just need some time to process."

"You think?"

"I do." Caroline set Abby at ease then quickly changed the topic, "But it wasn't right to leave Mitch hanging like that no matter what the circumstances. It's not only unfair to Mitch to leave without saying goodbye, but unfair to you too."

"Why do you say that?"

"You just let a great guy, the right guy, slip through your fingers. Besides, it's just cruel of you not reaching out to him and letting him know that you were going back to the city. I mean... He is so sweet."

"Well, I feel a bit better about Will. But I gotta say, you know how to pour on the guilt."

Of course Abby would need to call Mitch, yet what to say? "Sorry and thanks for the good time," she thought. How many times in her life had she let a man put her in that position? Now the shoe somehow ended up on the other foot and did not fit her well.

"What are the words?" asked Abby. Caroline was her best friend since childhood, Abby should have known better.

"You will have to find your own and you had better think of them quick because this can't be put off until tomorrow, that would be childish beyond cruel," said Caroline. That Caroline was always right usually assured Abby yet this time she felt as though she had been a child caught doing something wrong.

"Ok, ok. I'll call Mitch as soon as we get off the phone."

* * * * *

CHAPTER 40

Mitch had left two messages on Abby's phone. He called again then hung up when her voicemail began. He was afraid of sounding like a stalker. He was convinced that her cell phone battery had died and did not want to be the guy that had left fifteen messages. By trying to call back periodically he was confident that he would catch the phone recharging. By afternoon he stopped calling all together because he decided that if she had heard his messages and had chosen not to call him, he would still come off as a stalker. All he could do was wait.

Mitch took his guitar in hand and sat on the couch. He let his hand lightly brush up and down the strings as he searched for a chord. The fireplace was lit and the flame shown on the side of his face. He began to play a wandering melody that soon formed into a softer and sweeter version of the Ode to Abby melody he had composed earlier. He closed his eyes and thought about the theater. Abby's kisses so soft and intent, her body so nimble, and her passion so giving. Mitch pushed the ache he was creating from his chest out to his fingers adding lightly defined notes to the warm melody. His inside warmed with the images of Abby and the room warmed by the music she inspired. He felt less lonely and only now realized he had ever been lonely at all.

When the phone rang Mitch almost did not hear. Mitch awoke from his daze. The guitar stopped and a sobering silence took place of the warm music. Mitch almost tripped over himself getting across the room to answer the phone.

"Hello," said Mitch.

"Mitch," came the voice on the other line.

"Hello, Hello."

"It's Abby."

"Yea, I mean Hi," said Mitch. Mitch now stood straight composing himself.

"I can't hear you that well."

"Just a second, I'll go near the porch." Mitch walked quickly onto his screen porch, grabbing a jacket by the door to pull over his t-shirt.

"I tried to call you," said Mitch. "Earlier."

"Yea, my phone didn't have any reception." Abby had planned a drawn out explanation, as was her nature she went direct, "I was on the train."

"I see," said Mitch. His voice had lowered then he quickly recovered, "I didn't realize you needed to get back so soon."

Relieved at Mitch's response Abby quickly said the first thing that came to mind, "Well, something came up this morning and I didn't really have time to get things in order at the lake. I'm really sorry." She asked herself if that sounded as bad as she thought.

"No don't worry about it, things come up," said Mitch, his heart pounding.

"I plan to get back to the lake again soon though."

"That would be great!"

"Yea," said Abby.

"So, you're probably tired of traveling all day?"

"Yea. I better get some rest." This was to be a quick call.

"Well, ok then, thanks for calling." Mitch could not get

off the phone fast enough. He felt like he was fourteen.

"Well all right, see you when I get up to the lake," said Abby.

"See you then," said Mitch.

And that was all.

Mitch looked into the phone in disbelief. His heart sunk deep into his chest. The porch was cold. He had only socks on his feet and his whole body was numb. He had known that things had been left awkward with Abby yet this had struck him by surprise. What had he done, what had he said that scared her off. Mitch looked up to the screen facing the lake and could see only darkness behind. He shook his head, turned back into his cabin, and sat back on the couch. His guitar sat at the other end where he had just put the instrument while stumbling to the phone. Mitch raised his brow, reached for his guitar, and began to play where he thought he had left off. The melody still sounded passionate and sweet and now also a touch melancholy.

* * * * *

CHAPTER 41

Abby put down the phone and rest back on her bed. The pitch in Mitch's voice was one she had heard from herself more than once. The voice that said 'Don't worry about me'. She now knew for sure that he felt the same way about her as she did about him. Abby really did not doubt that before. She ran her fingers through her hair and then sat up letting out a sound of frustration. She stood up and took off her shirt and pants and in her panties walked to the bathroom to turn on the shower. Once in the bathroom, she decided to draw a hot bath instead with bubbles and salts. To be back in her apartment among her things felt good and after travelling a bath would relax her. She could sort out the discussion with her father, the phone call with Mitch, or just forget everything altogether.

When the bath was ready, the whole room smelled like lilac and rose. Abby dimmed the lights and slipped into the tub. She let herself ease into the hot soapy water slowly. The bubbles tingled on her skin as she slid through them. The hot water held her. At the back of the bath, Abby had rolled soft terry towels, and she let her head rest against them. The bath was silent, warm, and enveloping.

Abby rested in the steamy bath and let the world wash

away. She began to drift and let herself relax in both body and mind. As her mind relaxed, images of Mitch began to return. Memories of the phone call had been put aside. Passing through her mind now were the images of the intimacy they had shared. She imagined the contours of Mitch's chest, muscular and firm, and how she had pressed her head against him and held his back with her hands spread open to pull all of him to her. Abby could see Mitch's deep brown eyes peering into hers and could feel his breath on her neck. Her stomach had been unsettled all day because of the emotional evening the night before. Her insides yearned the recognizable ache that comes from wanting to be close to someone, to be close to someone that you care about and cares about you. She caressed herself for comfort, imagining that the touch, soft, gentle, and tender was Mitch's. Abby's eyes began to lightly tear as she let her self go with her imagination.

* * * * *

When Abby felt the water cold around her, she was unsure how long she had let herself relax. Sleep must have overtaken her. The day had been long. She removed herself from the bath and felt a cool chill, the room no longer warmed by the heat of the water. She dressed in her robe and then toweled off her hair. Leaving the dim light of the bathroom on she went directly to her bedroom. If Abby went to bed sleep would still be close. Sleep was close. Sometime later, she awoke abruptly in her dark room overwhelmed that she had made a dreadful mistake.

* * * * *

CHAPTER 42

Will sat on the edge of his bed. He knew he would not be sleeping. He started to take a cigarette out of the pack he had put on the nightstand and stopped. A promise had been made to Abby that he would not smoke in the house. He had never smoked in the house when Emily was alive. He tried to remember if he smoked that often back then. Cigarettes used to be a nickel. He was not sure if he even smoked then. His mind was wandering on nonsense.

Will pulled his trousers on and walked to the back door where he slipped on his boots and jacket. He let the door slam as he exited the house then urgently pushed through the studio door. He flipped on the lights and heat as he marched into the room. He tossed his jacket on the bench by the window then went to get two fists of clay. He carried the clay to a wheel, plopped the blob down, and then got two fists more. His jaw firm, his blue eyes bright, his white hair disheveled, he looked vibrant, possessed, ten, fifteen years junior. He brought some water to the wheel then began the spin by powering the pedal. Clay slid through his hands. The clay enveloped them, competed with them. The clay resisted changing form, fought to keep shape. Will's hands were steady and his eyes fixed. He had thrown the clay on the wheel in such a way that now he was breaking a stallion. The sides that wanted to break free he kept to the middle. Not by shifting his hands back and forth to adjust and shift, no, Will's hands were steady and his eyes fixed. Will's cool blue eyes were peeking deep inside of the clay, soothing the clay, and the clay soothed, the clay mellowed, until a perfect half sphere spun on the wheel.

Will relaxed his shoulders and his brow. He smiled. "There," said Will. When Will was with the clay nothing else could cloud him. This interlude had chased away the thoughts he could not otherwise escape. He considered himself a good person. Emily would not have married him otherwise. How he could hurt anyone, he could not fathom. He literally could not fathom. There was a lot of clay, and there were many orders. All he had to do was keep busy. That would not be hard from here on out.

Will began to caress the sides of the clay. To start the dance this way had not been necessary still the dance had begun.

* * * * *

Nathan had gone home after dinner. Will had told Nathan he was going to want to stop early. The day had been long. Though Will had put on his usual good face Nathan knew that he was bothered. He had only been with the Bellens' for a few days yet he could see that hidden in their family there was much pain. When Nathan got home to his apartment overlooking Willow Lake, he looked back at the Bellen Studio across the water. He could see the lights of the studio shining out into the night. There would be no rest for Will tonight and Nathan felt that in the city there would surely be no rest for Abby. Nathan went to his bedside and knelt down. He clasped his hands together and said a prayer in the Lord's name for the Bellen family.

* * * * *

CHAPTER 43

Mitch grabbed the kettle with his bare hand then instantly released. He curled his knuckles to free the slight tinge then reached again, this time with a towel, and pulled the boiling water from the stove. He poured the hot water into a cup then shoveled in instant coffee. Oatmeal bubbled in a saucepan. Mitch was not thinking clearly. His head was cloudy from lack of sleep. He was awake in bed most of the night and had been up periodically, compelled with thirst or the urge to leave the inside of the cabin and walk out onto the lake. At one point in the late evening, or early morning, he wrapped a blanket around himself and sat out on the porch. He sat until he was numb from the cold and then sat a while longer before sauntering back to bed. The air on the porch had been refreshing and he thought that might help him rest better. Rather the fresh air revitalized his restlessness.

The coffee went down before the oatmeal finished cooking. The coffee was acrid still he was invigorated. Mitch may have lost a night's sleep, yet he was still a fit man that could be jolted by a cup of caffeine.

By the time Mitch went outside to start his truck he had begun to feel confident about the day ahead of him. As he waited for the engine of the truck to warm, he looked up through his windshield to the tops of the maples and pines that surrounded his yard. The sky was a bright blue and the morning sun shown golden on the highest branches of the trees. He looked at the small Japanese maple that grew just in front of the cabin with branches still covered in morning frost that lightly glistened whatever light could reach the shadowy hiding place.

Mitch reflected on the strong, constant, and majestic trees. Whether he was going to be out in his truck this morning to catch their splendor did not matter, they were still going to be there. No matter what was said or done today, the sun would shine on the tallest pines, and the Japanese maple would be pleased with whatever light was received. Since there was no breeze, they would stand silent today as they did this morning. He watched the trees until he heard the truck's engine change tone, signaling the vehicle was warm enough to drive. He switched on the heater and pulled out of the driveway.

Mitch's mind was no longer cloudy. He felt refreshed and clear while he drove the pickup along Willow Lake road with the sun through the trees and the radio off. Inevitably his mind began to wander. He wondered what Abby was doing in the city.

* * * * *

CHAPTER 44

Abby had thought about going back to work first thing then realized that she needed to take a day to get things sorted. One more day was not a big deal, as she was not expected back any way. She called Olivia at the museum to check in. Olivia asked about lunch and went on to describe how unbelievably tired the pregnancy had made her. Abby was no more up for lunch than she was for going into the museum. To catch up on all of the latest gossip was fun though. The five-minute phone call easily turned into forty-five minutes. The best part of the forty-five minutes was that Abby did not have to bring up anything concerning Willow Lake. When Olivia did ask how her father was, Abby replied that her father was fine and that was the end of that, refreshing. There was plenty of talk about coworkers and Henry, Olivia's partner, and an event that Abby had missed. All were fun topics and Abby enjoyed the conversation. When Abby finally put down the phone and the reality of being back in her apartment struck, she no longer needed affirmation as to whether coming back to the city had been the right thing to do. Her doubts rested with how she could have done anything differently.

Abby decided that she needed to keep herself busy. She

got up from her comfy couch and started to clean up from the night before. Now was the time for the cleansers to come out. The apartment needed a scrub down anyway. Cleaning the bath and kitchen took up the rest of the morning. Then she made a list of errands. The problem was that the list was short. Abby had taken care of most everything before she left. There was dry cleaning to drop off and she could stop by the market on the way back from whatever she did. She grabbed the dry cleaning and scurried out of the apartment to the elevator.

Once on the street Abby stretched her legs and moved with purpose. She dropped the dry cleaning off and then kept going in the direction away from the apartment with no particular destination in mind. The sidewalks and streets appeared clean with the snow freshly melted from the midmorning sun. People were out on their lunch breaks, running errands or in the city just to shop. The smells of the restaurants, their lunch crowds chattering as she walked by, did not appeal to her. Abby had coffee and a muffin this morning and nothing since, yet was not really hungry.

Abby thought going to a movie would be a good distraction yet when she turned the corner to the small neighborhood theater she hesitated, reminiscing of a few days prior. The memory warmed her, yet she still did not want to think about that day too much. Going into the theater would be fine, and silly not to.

Abby approached the ticket counter to see what was playing on the three screens. Her lucky day, she thought, a date movie, and a romantic foreign film, both she had been waiting to see and a lousy action movie about a robot blowing everything to pieces. This was a no brainer for Abby. She bought a ticket for the action movie.

* * * * *

CHAPTER 45

The Bellen assembly line had not seen this much production in years. Anyone walking into the studio would have been surprised to learn that. Will had been at the electric wheel all night and on the worktables he already amassed several pieces for the ornamentation: leaves, ivy, birds all created with the clay leavings from the wheel. Other worktables were covered with light mossy green ceramics glazed earlier in the week. The only area of the studio that did not smell like clay was over by the dingy plastic coffee maker with the pot, cracked on the rim and burnt on the bottom, sitting half full on a stained burner. Each time Will poured a cup of coffee some would leak out onto the burner and the alkaloid smell would fill that section of the room. Will kept a fresh cup beside him throughout the night to help maintain a whirlwind around the studio. Now one sat on the worktable where Will just finished aligning and organizing the pieces in rows across the top, staging them for the next step in the line. He leaned back against the worktable his eyes fixed on the door to the adjoining kiln rooms, and started to think about firing up one of the kilns. His elbow in one hand, Will plied his Zippo in his other near his chin, his thumb maneuvering the lighter so that the lid would begin to lift on the spring and then force back closed against his finger. He did this again and again, making a clicking noise every time the lighter snapped shut. The math did not take up much of his mind. He knew which pieces would need to go into electric kilns and which would need to go into the gas. There were two small electric kilns by the door that could be filled with the smaller pieces from the table, they were ornamental pieces, and for a uniform result would be electric fired for the oxidation. The large pots and urns had to go into the gas kiln to get a proper firing, he did not mind the subtle differences of reduction firing caused by the gas. He dwelled on whether he wanted to fire the gas giants up now, after being up all night, or wait until he had slept. The electric kilns were like little space capsules and were as easy to run as a microwave oven. The gas kilns would have to be watched with a keen eye. Will was not ready to throw in the towel and head to sleep quite yet, though he certainly did not want to babysit the kiln. Then an epiphany, Nathan was supposed to be his babysitter, and Will could tell him to babysit the kiln. All Nathan would have to do was to let Will know if anything went wrong. Will would come in and do the temperature regulation himself. That would give Will time to continue at the wheel and, if he needed to sleep, Nathan could grab him.

Will curled his lip up on one side having satisfied himself and slipped his Zippo into the front pocket of his pants.

Traditional craftsmanship was honored above all else in the Bellen studio yet the utilization of the best tools available was an expenditure that Will kept up on. So in reliance to auto-magic Will loaded the squat silos of the electric kilns with some of the smaller pieces he had put together midmorning and with some of the pieces Nathan had glazed that needed oxidation. When the electric kilns were loaded he switched them on and went back to his wheel, getting another cup of coffee along the way.

* * * * *

CHAPTER 46

Caroline parked her Subaru in the back circle drive of the Johansson house. The morning was late and the sun was high in the sky. The light reflecting off the snow made her eyes tighten when she slipped off her sunglasses. Brian had been here earlier in the day and when he returned home, he mentioned that the carpenters had run to Fremont for supplies leaving Mitch alone at the house. Caroline had wanted to speak to Mitch so she told Brian that she had errands to run and drove directly to the worksite.

Caroline tapped her sunglasses on the steering wheel a couple of times then took a key fastened with a green bread tie from the console and opened the door of the Subaru. The key unlocked the large wooden doors to the foyer. She could hear hammering coming from the front of the house. Saying nothing as she entered, Caroline removed her gloves and scanned for signs of progress on work since her last visit a few weeks ago. Her face revealed no reflection as to what her thoughts were on the matter. A person of expectation, Caroline would only respond if anything were out of sorts from predicted. Things in the Johansson house were as she expected them to be.

The furnace was on and the foyer was quite cozy.

Caroline removed then folded her coat over the banister of the front stairwell and then ran her thumbs along her waist adjusting her pencil skirt before walking into the next room.

When Caroline entered the hearth room Mitch did not appear to notice. He was kneeling on a piece of cardboard in the fireplace with his head awkwardly cocked up toward the flue. The hammering sound was coming from a piece of wood Mitch was knocking against something up inside. She stood silent in the door and watched. In just a t-shirt, Mitch's muscles appeared contorted as he bent forward and twisted his torso up to his side.

"What brings you up here, Caroline?" Mitch asked without turning his head toward her.

Caroline smiled at his apparent sixth sense, "Did you see me pull up the drive?"

"It's that floral perfume you're wearing, China Flower," said Mitch.

Caroline chuckled lightly, "It's China Rose, but that's good." She stepped toward the window so that she was standing near him. Crossing her arms across her chest, she peered out over the lake. Mitch continued to bang the inside of the flue a few more times before maneuvering himself out of his awkward physical position and setting down the small section of two by four he had been using next to him.

"What are you doing?" asked Caroline.

Mitch spun around and sat on the floor, he responded by reaching into the fireplace and moving the handle of the flue back and forth. From inside the chimney came a series of squeaks and thugs.

"There," said Mitch, "the handle was a little loose. All set now."

Arms still crossed, Caroline shifted her gaze down from the window to Mitch and raised her eyebrows. "That's great," said Caroline.

"Well it's ok, good at best," said Mitch. If he had a sixth sense then he was now sensing that Caroline had something else on her mind that was making her slightly pensive and that he was about to find out what that was. Mitch would not have to wait long to see if he was correct.

"You are here alone today," said Caroline. Her feet began to tap one to the other.

"Yea, the fellas went to get some things from town," said Mitch. He peeled off his heavy leather gloves and rested his arms on his knees.

"Brian said they would be gone for the rest of the day."

"So you knew I was up here alone?"

"I confess," said Caroline.

"So what's on your mind?" asked Mitch.

"I just thought it has been a while since we talked."

"So what would you like to talk about?" asked Mitch.

"Have you talked to Abby?"

"Yes."

"So what are you going to do?"

"Do, what do you mean? She left for the city. There is no 'do' to be done."

Mitch sounded rather matter of fact when he said this yet Caroline was not buying. She had asked what Mitch's intentions were though what she really wanted to know is what they had been from the beginning.

Caroline let her eyes meld into Mitch's. Her face lost expression, her mouth opened to speak then abruptly Caroline shifted her gaze back toward the window in hesitation.

"What is it?" asked Mitch.

"How could you let this happen?"

"Let happen, she decided to go back to the city."

"That's not what I mean," said Caroline. "I mean you and Abby, what were you thinking?"

Mitch raised himself off the floor and started to walk to the next room. "We aren't going to get into this."

"Get into it?" Caroline dropped her arms to her side, "She is my cousin."

Mitch kept walking toward the kitchen and Caroline

followed him. "So what if she is, what's your point?"

"My point is that she is my cousin and it matters to me how you feel about her."

Mitch opened the refrigerator door when he reached the kitchen and took out a bottle of water.

"Abby is nice," said Mitch.

"You know if she is that important to you, you should go to her," said Caroline.

"I don't think she wants to see me," said Mitch. Mitch had considered that he had put off Abby.

"Don't be silly," said Caroline, walking passed Mitch. She leaned over to him, "Who wouldn't want a cute fella like you?" said Caroline. She gave him a quick peck on the cheek.

Caroline walked back toward the front of the house, speaking loudly as she went about the project and what was looking well. Mitch welcomed the change in topic yet did not follow Caroline, he was happy to let their conversation echo through the house.

* * * * *

CHAPTER 47

The movie was not so bad. The hero somehow reminded Abby of Mitch, as did the villain because of his eyes. The theater conjured up a sense memory of Mitch's embrace, though she liked that. When the movie ended, she sat in her seat until the credits had rolled and the lights had come up. Then with her empty soda cup in hand Abby exited to the aisle and slowly strode up to the waiting daylight.

Abby's plan had been to walk out of the theater refreshed with some new insight. This of course was not the case. The pit of her stomach felt bitter. Abby turned on her cell phone anticipating a list of messages, any message, any distraction. There were none.

Abby started to walk, again away from her apartment. The people on the street were now wisps in the corner of her eye.

Abby's thoughts circled back to Mitch and the call from the night before. The more she thought about the night the more she ached. Abby realized she had not really eaten anything and decided she better get something in her stomach. Surely some food would settle her emotional state.

Abby stopped for a slice at a pizza joint. Through the window a young Latino man spun a disc of dough between his hands with his fingers spread open, his hands coming together and then going apart, again, and again in a fluid motion. The whole time he spun the dough he chatted and laughed with a younger squat teen behind the register. In mid-conversation and without warning the pizza maker did a twirl with his hands and the dough disc spun high in the air floating above him only to come down where he caught the dough again and continued spinning the disc. Abby smiled and paused to watch him do this three more times before going in. He never blinked or stopped his conversation with his young friend. The dough was merely an extension of the young man and his actions were automatic, requiring no thought. If she were to try that, Abby thought, there would be dough spread across the kitchen. The key was that the young man was not trying so hard. He was just doing. There was no focus, just action and if she didn't over think things, life would still ebb and flow. Abby knew what she needed to do if she wanted some normalcy back as soon as possible. She needed to get back to work.

* * * * *

CHAPTER 48

Will had opened every drawer in the studio searching for the small clay item. He was certain he had seen what he was trying to find behind or under something in the back or on the side. There were so many small clay items around the shop that his mind easily played tricks on him when he saw glimpses of objects close in size. Will needed to find this one piece though, because this one was going to be the model for a new line. When he found the little piece of clay, the object appeared a little marred yet was recognizable. He took the item from the drawer and years of stasis then held small piece tight in his hand close to his lips. The tiny piece was something Michael had created as a boy. More than that, something the family worked on together.

When Michael was a small boy Will wanted to teach him how creating something could be magical. Michael's father did this with a simple method just as his father taught him. Will set up a play area in a well-lit corner of the studio, not far from the wheel where he himself often worked, and filled the area with clay.

Michael's mornings and afternoons were spent playing with the clay. Music played through the studio and Michael was comfortable in his own little area. Michael built castles out of pinecones, thistle, grasses, and twine. Army columns were created from sticks and clay. He would lump in sand, gravel, and dirt into the clay for color and texture on the sides of the castle walls during battles. Nothing was disallowed. In doing this, Michael had an easier and easier time making the shapes that had at first challenged him. The clay mixed with filler began to be cumbersome and slow compared to the clay alone. Before too long Michael would reach for the pile of clay to shape what was needed. As his father watched, over the course of days, the odds and ends worked their way out of the clay and to the side of the play area. Michael had learned to do everything he needed to with the clay alone.

Michael's most successful pieces were his clay soldiers. The soldiers were very detailed with rifles and helmets. Michael's favorite, the General, even had a handgun.

One day before Michael went to dinner Will asked him to gather up all of his favorite soldiers. Michael gathered up the horses and the carts, the rifleman and the grenadiers and lined them all up on the worktable on a big sheet of white paper his father had laid out for him. From the days of work there were now over two hundred figures. Standing in front of all of the men and horses was the General.

Will told Michael that the soldiers were magnificent and that he should leave them there and go off to dinner.

The next morning after breakfast, Michael was ready to go right back out to the studio again. "You need to help me shop in the village this morning," Emily told Michael. The little boy's shoulders shrugged in defeat, he so wanted to be out in the studio with his Father. Michael felt that was where his place was to be, so much so that he shared the sentiment with his mother.

"I'm supposed to be in the studio Mommy," said Michael.

"Well, that may be the case most days," said Emily. "But, today you're supposed to be at the supermarket."

Without any further fuss, Michael and Emily were off to

the market while Abby stayed behind with Will.

Mother and son shopped at the IGA where Michael was allowed to push the cart and reach for groceries as Emily called them off the list. Then at the check out Michael helped put the groceries on the electric belt and with the bagging.

Emily and Michael returned home early afternoon. Michael helped his mother bring in the groceries. He wanted to start to put them away as he often did. This time his mother suggested they go out to the studio and bring Will and Abby some sodas because the day was so hot. Emily opened two bottles of soda and handed them to Michael and off he ran for the screen door with Emily after him to slow down.

When Michael entered the studio he yelled, "Surprise!" Abby yelled back at her brother, "No, you Surprise!"

This confused Michael. He examined Abby in her paint smock covered in splotches of green and black paint then over her shoulder to the worktable. On the table, lined up in formation, were all of Michaels soldiers, the General standing in front of them. The General's hand, gun, and boots were black and his uniform was blue, even his little face was painted peach. All of the little figures were painted, even the horses.

"So what do you think?" asked Will.

"They're incredible, can I touch them?" asked Michael.

"Sure they're yours, you made them," said Emily.

"We just helped with the finishing touches," said Will. "They had to be fired to be made hard. Pick one up, you'll see."

Michael picked up the General turned the tiny soldier in his hands, across the shoulder was painted a gold braid, and on his chest was a tiny red ribbon. The arm that reached out and above him now appeared properly commanding with his sword painted silver.

Michael then picked up a horse and marveled at that as well. After setting the horse down, he picked up a soldier.

The soldier was in a green uniform like all of the others. All the while he held onto the General.

As Will remembered, Michael held onto the General most of that summer and into the winter.

This taught Michael the magic of creating, and Michael worked in the studio ever since, learning everything to learn about the studio.

Now Will held the General in his hand. He inspected the little commander closely. The General did not have a face or fingers, however the little body was proportionately close for a figurine. The sword had broken off long ago still the General's arm was still raised in the air to lead his troops.

Will took the General over to the table and set him down next to some tools and clay he already put out. Then Will slipped on his glasses and went to work. "Well, Sir. We're going to build you some friends," said Will and started forming figurines.

* * * * *

CHAPTER 49

When Nathan arrived at the Bellen's after lunch and walked into the studio he did not know what to say to Will. Every light in the studio was on and the music was blaring. The temperature was high because Will had kilns firing away. Urns were set up on the worktable near the kiln room ready to be fired and at the table in front of the big bay window with his back to the lake was Will, serene in the midst of a storm.

"Hi there Will," Nathan yelled. Will did not hear him. Nathan leaned forward so that Will could see him and yelled again, "Hey there!" This time Will peered up over his glasses and yelled toward Nathan, "Can you turn the music down?! I can't hear you!"

Nathan went to the stereo and turned the volume down to a tolerable level. "There," said Will, "Now I can hear you. What were you yellen' about any way."

"No wonder you didn't answer the phone," said Nathan.

"Phone? Couldn't have heard it, the music was on."

Will tilted his head back down and continued working on the soldiers.

"I just was calling to check in on you and to let you know that I was doing the shopping," said Nathan. He now

190

noticed that Will was working on figurines, he also noticed a lot had been done since he had left the night before. "So, you've been up all night."

"Yep."

"I didn't know you did that kind of work," said Nathan, curiously leaning into the table and slipping his hands into his pockets.

"I didn't," said Will, then he shifted his cool blue eyes at Nathan and grinned, "but I do now." Will then bent his head back down. "Have a seat, you make me uncomfortable when you hover."

"No, I have to put away the groceries."

"Ok, then." Will continued with his work with out shifting his focus.

"Ok, then," said Nathan. He started walking to the door.

"Nathan," said Will with a pitch in his voice. Nathan turned initially not sure what Will wanted. Will gestured to the stereo. "Oh right," said Nathan as he walked over to the stereo and turned the volume back up.

* * * * *

CHAPTER 50

Abby reached into her pocket for the two crumpled dollar bills put aside for the coffee and poppy seed muffin. The two young women waiting in line behind her were talking rapidly about a date one had gone on the night before while they simultaneously texted on their phones, the conversation was the same Abby had heard herself have many times before. The fella seemed nice enough still all in all the date was a dud. She did not have to listen hard for the details because dates like these were universal. Thoughts of work had filled her mind since she awoke this morning, by the time she reached the coffee window she was thinking of Mitch again. The reprieve had been short and her stomach quickly sank.

The morning commute was going to consist of a detour through the park then Abby decided to take the avenue. At a crosswalk she watched a street vendor set up his table for the day. His wares were sunglasses and as he pulled out each pair to place on the table, he polished each lens. She had seen him do this often and was impressed with the special care that he took wiping each lens, then holding the frame to the light, the pride that he had for his product. Each morning on the short walk to work there were always familiar faces and so many more she had never seen before. Abby could easily pass a hundred people she had never seen in her life, all of them on there way somewhere.

When Abby rounded the corner to the museum, she was pleased to see the majestic steps of the façade. Some people she knew that worked at other landmarks in the city told her that going to work was just like any other job. Abby however did not know anybody at the museum that did not feel some form of reverence for the grandeur of the place. Employees of the museum may have found their day-to-day duties mundane, yet if asked they would tell you that they felt privileged to perform those duties there.

When Abby entered the side entrance Louis, the security officer, welcomed her back. They exchanged greetings as he passed her bag through the metal detector and she walked through one herself. The detectors for employees were a necessary insurance formality that was mirrored by a quick bag check at the end of the day.

Abby made her way in to the recesses of the building toward the unadorned offices and let herself become consumed with thoughts of the responsibilities that would once again be hers. She opened the main office door and made her way to her work area, an unkempt desk under a corner window with a flat panel monitor resting on an old stained blotter. Stacks of oddly shaped envelopes, brochures, and trade magazines over-flowed her corner inbox. Abby sank into her comfortable and familiar chair and set her coffee and muffin on the desk. She contemplated whether to go through the pile of papers in her inbox or to turn on her computer, and then decided how nice to clean a little before the occupants of the other two desks, Olivia and Jules, arrived and took her day for a turn.

Abby reached for several of the envelopes at once. She grabbed too many and some slipped out of her hands spilling coffee on the edge of her desk and across the cover of a book on renaissance period artists. She quickly opened her bottom drawer to find the paper towel roll she kept there and soaked up the small spill. No damage done though as she finished mopping up the mess she saw a note that she had scribbled on her desktop shortly before leaving for the lake. The note read 'patch all things up with Dad—you love him'. Abby held the wet paper in her hand while she read the note and thought about her state of mind when the letter had been written. The note was written not that long after speaking with Caroline. Caroline had her half convinced that Will had one foot in the grave. That may or not have been true, yet the essence of the note was that she really wanted to remedy whatever rift was between them.

Abby's hand made a final pass over the desk and she tossed the paper towel into the basket at the side. Abby had thought about Will on the train ride back to the city and had been consumed with distracting herself since. Had she remedied whatever rift was between them? Hardly, still Abby thought she had finally identified what the rift was. Abby decided she would give Nathan a call later and check in and then speak to Will himself. Maybe she would call Mitch too. Abby caught herself sorting through the mail now and not even seeing what was in front of her. Hours away by train, Willow Lake once again was with her.

* * * * *

CHAPTER 51

"I figured it wouldn't be long until you showed up," said Will. Will peeked over his glasses at Caroline approaching the worktable. "What's the weather like sunshine?"

"Partly cloudy, storm's a comin'," said Caroline, taking a seat across from him.

Will continued painting the little soldier he had in his hand with the focus of a master. The painting of his soldiers, like the ornamentations on the urns, was intricate, the tools and brushes he used were fine and commanded a high degree of attention. Yet, from years of using these tools, he easily split focus to his niece, "Like a tag team, the two of you," said Will.

"You love the attention uncle Will."

"Never said I didn't."

"Where's Nathan, you didn't scare him off already did you?"

"Oh no, he was complaining I wasn't eating enough so I sent him to the diner to get some meatloaf."

"I thought you hated meatloaf?"

"I don't like him nagging neither."

"I see," Caroline nodded her head. She knew better than to goad her uncle any further, particularly if she wanted to get him to discuss what she came to discuss, her absent cousin Abby.

The worktable had half of the surface covered with soldiers waiting to be painted, which appeared to Caroline to be around twenty-five. Will had already finished painting five. Scanning the studio, Caroline saw little legions of clay soldiers on the other worktables and ledges, some fired some not.

"I like these. How many did you make?"

"Well, I suppose, let's see I spent yesterday and last night... Probably have about two hundred by now with the ones in the kiln."

"And each one is different?"

"Yea, well, not really, but yea." Will still did not raise his head from the soldier he was painting.

Caroline reached over and picked up a little green and khaki rifleman, "Didn't Michael have a set of these when we were kids?"

Will peeked over his glasses and smiled, "Yea."

Caroline set the soldier down on the surface of the table, still holding the delicate soldier with her fingertips, imagining playing with the little form yet not letting herself dare to do so.

Now absently gazing down at the table, Caroline said nonchalantly, "When I spoke to Abby the other day I was under the impression she was going to stay a bit longer. She left kind of sudden."

"Did she?"

"Well, I thought she would at least be here until next week."

"I guess you don't know," said Will. He set the soldier on the table and peered intently at Caroline, "I asked her to stay."

"What happened between you two?"

Will set the brush down, took off his glasses and stood up from the table. He rubbed his eyes with his forefinger and thumb. "I guess you could say that we had a few words the night before she left."

"What does that mean?"

Will chuckled, he was still rubbing his eyes, "You're asking me what it means? I haven't been asleep in three days because I don't know what it means." Will dropped his head and turned toward the window. "Maybe it means I was a bad father, a bad husband. Maybe it means I was asleep at the wheel. It means I missed every clue for everything in my life that has been going on since Emily died..."

Will fixed his gaze on something out the window to the side of the studio, Caroline could not see at what. "Hell, I don't know if I ever had a clue before that."

"Wow, I guess you did have a few words. Sounds like you two went at it. Are you ok?"

"Yea, it was just about time for me to start thinking a little bit I guess."

"Ok," Caroline had expected there had been some type of quarrel yet Will was usually flippant about such matters, "so what are you thinking about?"

"I don't know yet." Will pulled his hand over his face and abruptly changed the subject, "I have some of your order about finished, and at this rate it will be done in plenty of time for me to get the other urns out on schedule."

Caroline studied her uncle. His silhouette in the window amplified his stature. Changing the topic amplified his confidence. Caroline pressed him, "So that's your plan, to work in the studio and hope every thing takes care of itself? You might want to rethink that."

Will distanced his gaze out onto the lake, "What you suppose I should be doing?"

"Well how's Abby? Have you talked to her?"

"She was ok when she left," said Will.

"I know she was ok, I spoke to her and she sounded ok, but how are things with you and her?"

Will tipped his head down and let his eyes close. He had not slept in three days for more than a few hours in a stretch. His head swam with a rush of thoughts that he had been holding back, all of which were about losing his daughter. Teardrops formed fast in pools on his closed eyes and his lip began to tremble. Caroline realized she had triggered a repression to break free and went to him. She had paid her uncle a visit because she knew that the situation between Abby and him certainly would be amiss and she wanted to be sure of his well-being. Still Caroline was taken back by Will's sudden turn to tears, she thought the visit would be a vane attempt to convince him to patch up whatever had been broken with Abby, rather the time had now turned to her nurturing her Uncle's exhausted emotional state. She embraced him to calm him. Will felt Caroline's head press against his back and her arms reach around him. "It's all right," said Caroline softly as Will let out soft intermittent sighs. Will's exhaustion had driven his emotional state to a place he would not have gone.

"I've driven her away," said Will.

"You just need to call her," said Caroline. "Abby isn't that far away."

"I don't mean now, I mean…"

"I know what you mean. Give her a chance, she's given you plenty."

"Yea, I guess she has."

Caroline moved to Will's side, "You really haven't eaten anything have you?"

"No, I pretty much have been runnin' on coffee and cigarettes."

"Lets go in the house so I can make you something."

Will walked with Caroline out of the studio toward the house. "You should knock some of the ice off those cables," said Caroline. She Gestured up to the cable jutting from the studio to the willow tree. "At least over the walkway."

"Yea, I suppose," said Will.

Will surprised Caroline once again with his quick compliance. Most times he would have found a reason to not touch the cables for the sake of putting off the suggestion.

Caroline walked with him into the house and sat him at the kitchen table. The refrigerator had been stocked well since Nathan's arrival and inside she found the eggs, milk, and cheese to make a quick omelet. Something with protein that Will could get down quickly to curb the state that had come over him when she had brought up Abby. She removed her jacket and went right to work while Will sat patiently. She changed the subject to the Johansson order to alleviate him and that helped immediately. Will sighed and struggled at first to put his thoughts around the order and then embraced the conversation. Soon Will was fervently speaking of the pieces that had been put together over the last couple of days. Caroline put a pan on high heat and whisked the eggs and milk together. After pouring the eggs, she put the kettle on. Deciding that Will had enough coffee in him for the time being, Caroline searched through the teas for something that would be soothing and relaxing to her uncle. Will commented that he liked the Black Breakfast tea and Caroline told him that she could do better. He nodded his head and continued to discuss the order.

When the eggs were done and the stove had warmed the kitchen, the breakfast aroma alone made Will's shoulders melt into his chair. He had not realized how tense he had become. Caroline placed the omelet on a plate before him. Will wanted to tell her that she should not have bothered however when he raised his head to see the concerned expression on his niece's face he thought best to simply smile and say thank you. Pleased that her uncle was feeling pleasant, Caroline smiled in return.

When Will finished eating, Caroline talked him into building a fire in the lake room so that the two of them could relax and talk. Will happily accommodated her and once the fire was going, he took a seat in his cushioned recliner. She spoke to him from the kitchen and he replied a few times. When she entered the room with a tray of tea and cookies he had already faded off to sleep. Caroline took the crocheted afghan from the couch and placed the blanket over his chest. She took the tray back into the kitchen to wait for Nathan.

When Nathan returned from the village, he parked behind Will's truck so as not to block the Subaru in the driveway. He had not seen the Subaru at the house before and did not know the owner. The car was a typical for someone around the lake, though less likely to be one of Will's cronies that dropped by on occasion.

When Nathan came into the kitchen, he was pleasantly surprised to find Caroline sitting at the table drinking tea and reading a magazine. Nathan recognized Caroline by description and had been anticipating meeting her as a manner of changing of the guard from Abby. Caroline stood and he quickly and politely introduced himself, setting down one of the two bags he was carrying to shake her hand.

"Hello, I'm Nathan. You must be Caroline," said Nathan.

"Yes, finally, nice to meet you. Let me help you with the groceries."

"Thank you. Where's Will?"

"Oh," Caroline made a snicker, "He had a bit of a melt down. I fed him an omelet and tucked him in by the fire."

"I'm not surprised," said Nathan. "He has been showing signs of exhaustion."

"Has he really been up for three days?"

"It's not just that," said Nathan. "He hasn't had a drink for a couple days."

"Are you sure?"

"Pretty sure. He's been making up for it working around the clock."

"Huh."

The bags were empty with the last two items being some type of hot Italian meal in tin foil with a plastic top that

Caroline could not decipher, "This isn't meatloaf," said Caroline.

"Chicken Parm, he hates meatloaf," said Nathan.

* * * * *

CHAPTER 52

No one would accuse Abby Bellen of being low energy, however when she walked along the avenue with Jules, Abby was along for the ride. Jules Stalwart entering the building was never stealth nor a secret to anyone. Before entering any room she could be heard approaching halfway down a hall.

Jules was a tall feisty firecracker of a girl, with bright orange hair and emerald green eyes that lit up her clear complexion. A flash from Jules's eyes said she knew something others did not, and if one were part of her circle, she just might clue them in.

Olivia had left the office early to run some errands for the baby in her belly, so Jules and Abby decided that they would follow suit. Rather Jules decided they needed to slip out to catch up. Before Abby could put up too much resistance, they were on their way out the door to the Lavender Room around the corner.

Typical of older hotel lounges in the area the Lavender Room was sparsely lit. A forest had suffered for the wood paneling covering the wall and the dimly lit mirror behind the bar, stained with an indelible mist, barely reflected anything beyond the row of liquor bottles lining the back.

Per the lavender namesake, the room had a lavender décor from literal lavender blossom table settings to the colored fabric of the booths, napkins, and sashayed curtains that hung strategically through out. The bar even served a Lavender Martini as the house drink yet overall was known for great Appletinis, which Jules adored because they contained a light dash of rum that made them buttery. Abby was certain that Jules also liked the Appletinis because they highlighted Jules green eyes.

The girls chose two lounge chairs at a small table near the door. Not so close to the entrance as to be interrupted with any one walking in and out, yet close enough for Jules not to miss any potential opportunity to make eye contact with the young men that frequented the lounge.

Abby was pleased to be back in the city in the refreshing company of her friend. Jules ran rampant in discussion, unafraid to speak her mind and often unconcerned whether anyone could hear her. Abby enjoyed dishing all of the gossip with her yet there was always a risk that Jules would blurt out something just beyond Abby's taste, usually sexually shocking statements that were not quite vulgar. At times there had been outright propositions to innocent male bystanders. Over the years, Abby had heard a long list of whom Jules would 'Do' and had 'Done', and she always chuckled at Jules's pronouncements.

By Jules second Appletini, she was midstream in bringing Abby up to speed on everything she had missed while she had been gone. Olivia had given Abby a surface spin and now Jules was here with the drill down. Jules went through the checklist of office romances, people they both knew outside of the office, and then onto people that Abby had never met yet had heard about time and again from Jules. Abby punctuated Jules enthusiasm with an occasional "Really," and "You know, I thought so." Even the slightest show of response fueled Jules yet Abby was pretty sure Jules could go on talking with or without her participation.

After they had covered everyone that Jules knew came

time to discuss Jules herself. Jules had been seeing a guy when Abby went out of town yet now that was in the past.

"What did he do," asked Abby.

"It's what he didn't do. He didn't excite me," said Jules.

"What made him so boring?"

Jules raised her brow, "He didn't excite me."

Abby sighed briefly taken back, remembering she was talking to Jules.

"That's a shame," said Abby. Abby sipped her drink afraid for the next few minutes of conversation. Fortunately Jules eased off and said something to surprise Abby.

"It is a shame," said Jules. "I really liked him."

Abby saw a glimmer of sadness in Jules eyes which drew her back to missing Mitch. With the few Appletinis consumed, the thought of Mitch hit Abby with an alcohol driven nostalgic sensation. Ironically, at that moment Jules decided that Abby's turn had come to talk about her time away.

"Did you hook up with any lake men up there in those woods?" asked Jules.

Abby hesitated, daring herself to answer, thus unleashing Jules on a whole new area of exploration. However Abby could not and did not want to keep to herself. With a blank stare, Abby fixated on Jules.

"Yes," said Abby, and then nodded her head slowly, "Yes Jules, I hooked up with a great guy."

Elated by the discovery that Abby had conjured up some form of romance on her sojourn, Jules fortified and furrowed her red brows, "So tell me. Who is he? What happened?"

"What happened, where do I start?"

"At the beginning preferably," said Jules.

Abby gave Jules the run down on how she met, spent time with, and essentially ditched Mitch Carlson.

"So that's it, you're just not going to see this guy again?" asked Jules.

"Well I kind of messed it up."

"You haven't messed anything up yet, only if you let this go."

"I suppose you're right, I should give him a call," said Abby.

"When?"

"Later I guess."

"Now that's messing up. Let me see your phone," said Jules

"You can't be serious."

"Do or die honey, pull out your phone."

Abby picked up her bag and began sifting through it, "I don't know."

"Listen, you'll thank me for this," said Jules.

Abby set down her purse, she had her cell phone in hand, "So what am I supposed to say to him?"

Jules stood up, "I don't know. Tell him you miss him. If he's everything you think he is, he'll respond."

"And where are you going?"

"I'm just going to step away for a minute, you can handle this on your own."

Abby glanced down at her cell phone as Jules walked away. Abby suspected that Jules was going to slip outside and have a cigarette, having been a chronic quitter Jules could not resist a smoke after a few drinks. Abby did not have to search through the phones contact list. Mitch's number was listed as recent under outgoing calls. She hesitated only for an instant before letting her thumb tap down on the send button. Holding the phone to her ear Abby heard the phone ring once, twice, and then Mitch's voicemail picked up and his recorded voice asked her to leave her name and number. Not anticipating voicemail, Abby scrambled as to what to say, she started with "Um," and quickly recovered, "Mitch, this is Abby. I was just calling," she quickly ran through a list of reasons in her mind, "cause I was thinking about you and--," her phone chirped loudly in her ear. Abby drew the phone away to see Mitch's name blinking across the screen. Abby pulled the phone back to her ear, "—You're on the other line. Just a second." Abby held the phone away again, maneuvered a couple of quick gestures with her thumb and pulled the phone back to her ear. "Hello," said Abby, "I was just leaving a message."

"Yea, I guess that's it right there," said Mitch, referring to a beeping sound only he could hear. "So how are you?" asked Mitch.

"Oh great, yea everything is great here. It's good to be back. You know," said Abby.

"Well, I'm glad to hear that."

"Yea."

"So what's up?"

"What's up?"

"Yea you called."

"I called? Yea, of course I called. Well I was out with a friend. I am out with a friend. Jules, I told you about her. I think. She's not here right now. Well any way, I was thinking about you." Abby could not believe herself and was sure that she sounded like a fool.

"I've been thinking about you too," said Mitch.

"Really?"

"Yea, I have."

"I like that," said Abby, and then thought to herself that she once again was sounding foolish. "I mean that's nice."

Abby then went on to tell Mitch about her day back at work and how her day was the day before. She began to tell him how sad she was that she left so quickly, that her father had upset her, and that she was still not sure how to handle that whole situation. Mitch listened on his cell as she peppered the conversation with information about people he knew nothing about from her conversations with Jules earlier. To Abby all of these conversational elements were contextual and to Mitch they were mostly all foreign. Most of all though Mitch was truly pleased to hear Abby's voice and he did not mind listening to her rambling about the day's events. That is until he could tell that she was working herself up emotionally and he thought best to ease things off. Mitch was satisfied to know that Abby had not left Willow Lake on his account.

"Abby?"

"Yea, Mitch?"

"Are you and your friend having cocktails?"

"A couple. Why do you ask?"

"No reason," said Mitch, "but maybe it would be better if we talked a little later. Do you think that would be alright?"

"I would like that," said Abby. "How about if you call me tonight, before you go to bed."

"Ok, I'll do that," said Mitch. "Bye, now."

"Bye," said Abby.

Jules had returned to her seat wide-eyed. She echoed Abby "Bye," and then chuckled. "See, now aren't you glad you made that call."

Abby felt warm and bubbly. She raised her Appletini to her friend. "You were right. I didn't mess up."

* * * * *

CHAPTER 53

When Abby woke the following morning, her face pressed onto her pillow, her scalp felt tight on her skull, and her tongue swelled in her mouth. Opening her dry eyes, she searched for the bottle of seltzer usually kept on the wooden nightstand. Abby perked up as she consumed most of the bottle. In spending time with Jules, she had let herself become dehydrated. This morning Abby would surely suffer from the carelessness of not balancing last night's alcohol consumption with food and water.

The cordless phone sat eye level on the pillow next to Abby. She recalled she had been talking to Mitch before drifting off to sleep. He had called her cell just as promised and she dialed him back on the cordless to hear him better.

How long Abby had been on the phone with Mitch, Abby could not be sure. She did not remember finishing the call and tried to piece together the conversation thinking that she might have fallen asleep on the phone. The last moments before sleep were cloudy at best yet she did remember saying goodbye. All was coming to her now. She remembered saying many things that she probably would not have if she had not gone out with Jules. How much she said for sure though she was not certain and the more she thought about the conversation the more she began to worry that she had come off as a foolish schoolgirl. As she brushed her teeth, she recalled discussing her father with Mitch. In the shower, she remembered ranting about how her father had made her feel over the years. While she dressed, she remembered that the majority of the conversation had been her explaining why she had to leave and Mitch sweetly listening to her. She decided that the call was not as bad as she had first thought when she awoke this morning and though she could not remember where they had left off, she would call him later in the day to thank him for being so considerate. Today was Friday and combined with yesterday the workweek overall would be short.

* * * * *

CHAPTER 54

The kilns had all cooled and Nathan was in the process of emptying the electric kiln when Will entered the studio. Will gave Nathan a look that Nathan took as a sneer.

"I hope it's alright. I was just checking to see if everything went all right with the kiln. It was still going when you went to sleep yesterday," said Nathan.

"That fine. You can't mess up that kiln. It's automatic. The gas is another story."

Nathan stood motionless with a piece of ceramic in each hand. If now was ok to empty the kiln, Nathan wondered, then why had Will sneered at him. "What's wrong then? Why are you looking at me like that?"

"I'm judging your reaction," said Will.

"To the way you're looking at me? I don't like it."

"No," said Will. "You got to relax kid. I wanted to see what you thought of those pieces your taking out of the kiln there. They're the ones you helped with you know?"

Nathan grinned and examined the two ceramic birds in his hands, a hummingbird, and a cardinal. Each had a subtle shine from the glaze that Nathan had applied. "God performs such miracles with his creations," said Nathan.

"I'll give you that," said Will. He walked over to Nathan

and took the humming bird from him, "But I think the help you gave him turned out pretty good."

"Yea, I guess it did. Do you really think so?"

"Sure," said Will. He lifted the piece eye level and lightly brushed his finger across the surface, "You see the evenness of the glaze. This is good. The way the glaze covers the paint on the hummingbird makes every detail accentuated not dulled down. You wouldn't get this iridescent effect where the colors meld between the feathers without the light glaze here, here, and here. This is quality work." Will held the piece up to the light then offered the hummingbird back to Nathan. "You keep this one."

Nathan held the piece up inspecting the details that Will had just pointed out. "Thanks," said Nathan.

"You made it," said Will. "But you don't get to keep everything you make. This is a business. That's your first, so take it home."

"I take it you slept well."

"Slept fine," said Will and then added before Nathan would question, "and I already raided the fridge this morning. So let's get to work."

Nathan put the birds on the worktable where he had been placing the items from the kiln and went back to empty the rest of the items still inside.

"Put the soldiers over here," said Will as he sat down at the station he had set up for painting. "I'm going to work on the boys. I have some more glazing for you to do, maybe some painting today too."

"The boys? The toy soldiers you mean."

"Call 'em what you will," said Will as he put on his glasses and started to sort through his jars of paint.

"I was meaning to ask you about them. I sorted the orders on the board like you asked me. I didn't see any orders for these."

"These aren't for any clients."

"You just decided to build a bunch of toys."

"Something like that, I'm building an army."

Nathan watched Will for a moment. He had another question for Will on his lips. Will had steady hands for such small detailed work, steady hands that had not shown signs of tremors over the last few days, and his breath lacked the usual sweet scent of wine. Nathan chose to go on working. If Will needed an army Nathan thought he understood why.

* * * * *

CHAPTER 55

The train ride had been scenic and peaceful. Mitch had spent most of the ride in the dining car with his notebook. He enjoyed trains and thought the trip was relaxing despite the mounting commuter crowd that had boarded as he approached the city. When he arrived at the station, all sense of calmness went away. Upon exiting the train, he was caught up in the whirlwind that was the city's mass transit center. Mitch had not been to the city in two years and the bustle caught him by surprise. This was mid-afternoon and hardly a busy time by any means, still people whisked past him to get to where they needed to be.

Mitch took in a deep breath, lifted his duffel to his shoulder, and made his way to the street. Still too early to meet up with Abby he did not have an immediate plan. Mitch decided that his time would best be served at a diner and decided to find one nearby.

Out on the street the snow was falling in large fluffy flakes that were building up a layer of slush on the sidewalk. He paused outside of the doors of the station momentarily to get his bearings and was almost knocked down by a large man in a black overcoat carrying a briefcase. Mitch turned to say, "Excuse me," and the man was already down the sidewalk. On the street people were in just as much of a hurry as they had been in the station. Mitch decided he needed to start walking just to not be taken down. He wanted to stretch his legs anyway, he thought, and if he came upon a place to stop he would.

The snow continued to fall and people pressed between cars in traffic with their shoulders hunched up to ward off the wet snow. Taxi's honked their horns at the slow moving trucks in front of them. The vendors along the avenue stood vigil over card tables covered with plastic sheets, the same Mitch bought in bulk for job sites.

After walking several blocks, Mitch could feel the snow starting to cake into his hair and melt down the side of his face. Not wanting to get too wet he stepped into the next diner he saw and took a seat at the counter, placing his duffel on the floor next to him. A large Mediterranean man behind the counter approached him and handed Mitch a menu.

"Coffee?"

"A coffee would be fine," said Mitch.

The man produced a cup and a coffee pitcher in two swift motions, before Mitch's jacket was off his shoulders.

Mitch removed his canvas jacket and before he could set the coat down he heard his cell phone ring inside. He reached his hand to the inside pocket and pulled out his phone to see if Abby was calling. Abby was.

* * * * *

CHAPTER 56

Olivia had left the office early again, leaving Abby responsible for Jules. The two were peers yet Jules defined 'when the cat's away' behavior. Olivia had not been gone for more than twenty minutes before Jules was deep into questioning about Mitch. Abby had made the mistake of telling Jules that Mitch was to call in the evening and Abby had been delinquent to report. Jules had not mentioned a report through the day as Abby was still catching up. Now that the last hour of Friday afternoon was upon them there would be no more slack. So Abby filled Jules in on what she remembered of the conversation. She did not really mind doing so. Having a man to discuss was a bit of an upswing for a change, something positive. The talk did remind Abby that she wanted to call Mitch though so she told Jules to let her go for a moment and Jules did so happily.

Abby tapped Mitch's name on her cell and the phone dialed.

"Hello," said Mitch.

"Hi," said Abby. "How are you?"

"Great. A little wet. The snow is really starting to come down."

"That's funny, it is here too," said Abby glancing out the window at the large flakes floating past.

"Well, I should think so. I'm only about three or four blocks from the museum."

Silence. A pause. "Hello?" asked Mitch.

"Where are you?" asked Abby.

"I think I'm about three blocks over. At a place called the Moon diner. It's on--,"

"—Yea, I know where it is. What are you doing there?"

"I had to step in from the snow. I was getting soaked."

"What are you doing in the city?"

"Oh," said Mitch, "This was a mistake. You don't remember do you? I told you, you wouldn't remember."

"Remember what?"

"On the phone last night."

Abby went back to the night before and rewound the conversation. Abby had said she was sorry she left, she had left because of her father, and she had talked about her father. What else was there that was missing? In a rush, an epiphany came to Abby. She had told Mitch that if he came this weekend she would smooth things over. She had told him to come. Mitch had said no and Abby dared him to come, had talked him into coming.

"Of course, on the phone," said Abby. "Hang on a second."

Abby turned to Jules and whispered frantically, "I invited him to the city last night, and it's all your fault."

Jules did not miss a beat, "So ask him why he hasn't called you?"

Calmly Abby asked, "So why haven't you called me? I mean what are you doing in the city already and you haven't called me?"

"Oh, well I thought you'd be working. You're working right?"

Abby whispered to Jules, "He thought I'd be working."

"Well, tell him we can meet him when we get off," said Jules.

Abby turned back into the phone. "We can meet you when we get off," said Abby.

"We?"

"We, yea, you and me I mean," said Abby. Abby rolled her eyes at Jules.

"Ok," said Mitch.

"Ok," said Abby, "How about O'Malley's, say an hour?"

"Sure. I'll see you then."

Abby put her cell phone down on her desk then let out a guttural sound.

"That doesn't sound nice honey," said Jules. She pulled a compact mirror with face powder out of her bag, opened the clamshell, and applied a soft amount of powder to her cheeks.

"This is horrible," said Abby.

"Is it?" asked Jules. " Now why is that?"

"Because he is here."

"This is going to be fun, I like country boys. I don't think I've met a lake boy either."

"Cut it out," said Abby, " besides, he's from here. He just lives out there now."

"Now there's a thought. He was smart enough to get away from it all. You may have yourself a genius."

"I said cut it out," said Abby.

"Ok, ok. I tell you what. Why don't we head over there now and get a head start. That way you can prepare."

"Well, I'm not going to get anymore work done today. That's for sure."

"Now you're talking."

* * * * *

CHAPTER 57

"I'll have a Guinness and a shot of Jameson and so will she," Jules said to the young waiter at their booth.

"I will not," said Abby. Jules locked her green eyes on Abby and arched her red brows. Abby changed her order, "Ok, I guess I will."

"Sure thing," the waiter said as he turned away, only moderately impressed with the two young women ordering shots.

Jules took note of his cavalier reaction, "I wonder what I have to do to impress him?"

Abby quickly picked up, "Nothing," said Abby. "And this will be it for the shots. The last thing I need is to lose my head."

"I promise," said Jules, "no more shots." When the waiter came back with their beer, she immediately ordered two more. The girls toasted to late night phone calls and drank their shot of Jameson. Both of them snickered their noses at the sharpness of the whiskey.

O'Malley's was large for a bar in the city. Upon entering there was a large recessed floor full of tables that was surrounded on the sides by dark wooden booths and above them a second floor of the same. At the back of the room was a stage that had equipment set up for the sound system. Televisions peppered the bar, Abby thought this the only down side of the bar.

"So how do you feel?" asked Jules.

"I feel hardly anything right at this second," said Abby. They both started laughing again. "Seriously," said Abby, "I'm good, this is good. But really, no more shots."

"Ok, ok. Scouts honor. Look over there," Jules gestured across the room to the entrance. "That cute guy has to belong to you. If not he's mine."

At the entrance of the bar stood Mitch in his jeans and canvas jacket, holding his duffel next to him. He saw the girls watching him so he raised his hand to wave.

"He's mine alright," said Abby. She got up from the booth and walked in his direction.

The two met in the middle of the floor and each raised their arms to the others waists. They gave each other a quick kiss and then Abby took Mitch's hand and led him to the table where Jules was waiting for her kiss on the cheek.

"Aren't you lovely?" said Jules.

"You must be Jules," said Mitch.

The girls sat and Mitch took a seat next to Abby after putting his coat on a hook at the end of the booth.

"So here we are," said Jules.

"So here we are," said Mitch. "I suppose I'll get a beer." He gestured to the waiter that had watched him walk over to the table. Mitch glanced at the two shot glasses that Jules had slid to the end of the table. He exchanged glances with the girls. "What were those?" asked Mitch.

"Wanna try one?" asked Jules.

"Forget I asked," said Mitch.

When the waiter came to the table Abby was relieved to see Mitch ordering a bottled beer.

Abby felt like she was showing Mitch off. Jules was chatting away to Mitch and Abby watched how he held his bottle in his hand away from the table. She liked how he kept a half smile on his face and maintained eye contact with

Jules while she spoke to him. He was wearing a cream collar shirt with a dark blue t-shirt underneath that seemed made for the dark motif of the bar. Abby thought that he was charming, as did Jules. He was charming. To be with the two girls so politely fawning over him was not hard.

Mitch thought wise to order some food for the table, and though the girls said that they were not hungry, everyone ate plenty when the fried calamari and potato skins were brought to the table. Mitch too was pleased to be with Abby. He watched her as she nibbled her food and sipped her beer, giggling at Jules' wit.

After the appetizers were finished, Abby suggested they order another round of drinks. That's when Jules excused herself for the evening.

"Why don't we all go then," said Abby. "I am sure you want to change after that train ride, and I'd like to freshen up before dinner."

Mitch agreed and the three paid the tab and made their way for the door. Outside the sidewalk now was covered with an inch of snow and flakes were coming down thick.

"Isn't this beautiful?" said Jules.

"You want to catch a cab with us?" asked Abby.

"No you go ahead, I'll find my own way. See ya!" said Jules. Jules turned and tromped off in the snow.

"Will she be able to catch a cab?" asked Mitch.

"She's not going home yet."

"Oh, I see."

Mitch put his hand up over his brow and peered in through the snow down the darkened street. " I'm not sure we're getting a cab either."

"That's ok, I'm not far. And I have my slicks on."

Mitch saw that Abby had changed her shoes before leaving the bar. She was wearing blue duck shoes.

"Those look comfy," said Mitch.

"They are. C'mon, this way," said Abby.

Abby took his arm above the elbow and pulled him in front of her so that he could lead the way. The night was velvety black and the flakes appeared from nowhere just feet above their heads.

Abby wondered if Mitch realized that she had forgotten that she had invited him to come see her this weekend. She thought about the linguistic gymnastics she had done on the phone earlier and how transparently clumsy they were. Then Abby thought that if Mitch did know, how charming that he had taken everything in stride.

* * * * *

CHAPTER 58

As they walked along the avenue toward her apartment Abby pointed out shops that were attributed to her and why. She used this drycleaner as a tailor, the other for skirts. This soap shop is where she got her soaps and bath oil yet when Mitch asked, certainly not her shampoo, that would be downtown. And when they were within a block of her apartment she pointed out a sweet shop that had the best gelato and biscotti. Mitch asked how their espresso was and Abby replied that she did not know where to get a better cappuccino. They decided they needed to have some then.

The shop was charming as all sweet shops are, done in a Victorian style and with white Christmas lights surrounding the windows. Mitch and Abby sat at a cozy parlor table by the street window, ordered cappuccinos, pistachio gelato, and split what was described on the menu as molten cake. The fluttering feather flakes of snow curtained their side and they leaned into each other so as not to have to talk much more than above a whisper.

"You're making me eat all of this cake," said Abby.

"I don't think that's the case," said Mitch.

"Have you eaten any?"

"I have."

Mitch started to laugh at Abby.

"What's so funny?" asked Abby.

Mitch put his finger to Abby's chin and turned her head toward the window. Abby could see on her reflection, chocolate syrup from the molten cake on her upper lip. Abby tilted her head back toward Mitch, the corners of her mouth upturned, her cheeks full and rosy. Mitch offered her his napkin. She reached her hand passed the napkin and put her hand on the back of his head. She then pulled him close to her so that he could remove the syrup with his kiss. They kissed softly.

Abby then touched her forehead to Mitch's and nuzzled her nose against his. "You think you got it?" she whispered.

"I think I got it," Mitch whispered back.

"Let's get out of here."

"Let's."

They stood at the same time and slid their jackets on without disengaging their gaze, each with an impish grin. Abby picked up her bag and Mitch his duffel and then she reached for his hand and she led him out of the shop into the snowy night. As she pulled him, Mitch playfully pretended at times to resist, causing her to look back, snicker her nose, then extend her arm and tug. Mitch feigned resistance by leaning back, then he shuffled, and they would go forward for a few more steps like a rubber band. They did this all the way through the door of Abby's building where he let her pull him to her and they began to shower each other with kisses as they made their way to her apartment. At Abby's door Mitch dropped his duffel and began to caress her body as she fumbled through her bag for keys. When the two locks were finally undone the intertwined couple almost fell through the threshold. Mitch pushed his duffel in with his foot while Abby pulled the door closed. Abby's other hand was on Mitch's collar, pulling down on his shirt over his arm. Their mouths now locked deep in a long continuing kiss.

Parts of their clothing flew across the living room as they

moved through, Mitch leaning against the arm of the couch, then Abby's back to the wall. All the while they continually caressed each other's bodies and held that long undisturbed kiss.

Abby put her lips to Mitch's neck and pressed her mouth against him, then whispered in his ear, "This way."

Quickly Abby stepped away from him, taking both of his hands, and pulled him to her bedroom. In the dim light of the hallway, her beauty awed Mitch. Her hair now down over her shadowed bare breasts, only her panties remained on. Abby's sultry gaze once again fixed on him as she backed into the bedroom. Seductively she slowly lowered her hands from his and slipped off her bottoms, then backed up and slid into the blankets of the bed. She lifted her soft gaze to Mitch standing in his unzipped jeans. His stomach barely lit in her darkened bedroom, attractive, trim, and muscular. He kept his gaze fixed to hers still, and with one thumb eased the jeans down the trunks of his legs. Slowly Mitch approached the bed and Abby moved over on the sheet to make room for him and opened the blanket to invite him in.

They had been frantic, and now, lying naked on the soft sheets of Abby's bed, they were tender. Mitch leaned forward and kissed her forehead gently. Her eyes closed, a tremor shot threw her body from the faintest of kisses, then another light kiss, and another tremor. Mitch gave her many tender kisses in many places until Abby could handle no more. Then they held each other tightly and fell into the first true sleep for either of them in the past few nights.

* * * * *

CHAPTER 59

Before Mitch opened his eyes, he had a smile on his face. The sweet smell of Abby on the pillow reminded him that he was not in his own bed. There was another great smell looming in the air as he awoke as well, coffee, and something else, pancakes.

"Really?" said Mitch in a voice just loud enough to travel through the apartment.

"You up?" came a reply from the other room.

Mitch stretched his arms and started to get up when Abby entered the bedroom.

"No don't get up," said Abby. Abby was wearing nothing except Mitch's collar shirt and a ponytail and carrying a tray with pancakes and coffee.

Mitch's eyes lit up, Abby was incredibly attractive, and the sight of her like this excited him. "That's amazing."

"It's just coffee and pancakes," said Abby. She held the tray next to the bed.

"Are those blueberry pancakes?"

"Yes they are."

"Put that down."

"They'll get cold."

"They'll have to wait."

Abby set the tray on the floor and as soon as her fingers were free, Mitch pulled her by the waist onto the bed and gave her a kiss. Abby wrapped her arms around him and rolled him on his side. Soon the two were once again beneath the blankets.

After breakfast they decided to go out to the park and go skating at the pond. Mitch told Abby that he had not brought his skates and she told him not to worry since the rink rented skates. Mitch could not argue with that so they bundled up and rolled out of the apartment to go for a walk down to the park.

The snow that blanketed the city the evening before had already turned to pools and slush.

"There aren't that many people on the street," said Mitch.

"There are never as many as on a weekday in this neighborhood. Many people here have country homes and for those that don't Saturday is not a workday," said Abby.

"I guess since I have not lived in the city in a while that had not crossed my mind."

"Don't worry about finding people, I'm sure there will be plenty in the park."

When they got to the park Mitch found that Abby had been correct. The difference between the street outside and the path in the park was night and day. Everyone that was going to venture outside on a Saturday was here.

The pathways in the park had already been cleared and salted and the cement had a soggy odor. Traffic moved at a set pace through the congested maze of paths as people with children crowded the playgrounds while others with dogs of all sizes split off to the dog runs. Part of the congestion was due to the crowd build up at pathway intersections where street performers held court to park denizens and tourists alike. Mitch and Abby veered around these large groups peeking through to see acrobats, a cappella groups, and musicians.

While walking down the wide arcade toward the skating

pond, they stopped to listen to an older Asian woman dressed in dark sweat clothes plucking a long thin lute. Behind her stood one of the mighty elms of the arcade walkway and other small trees in a field of undisturbed snow. A hill rose in the back of the field blocking the view of the pathway behind so that to all of those watching this woman in the middle of the park, in the center of the city, an illusion had been created that she stood alone. The woman started to sing a slow sweet song in her native language. Abby pulled herself close to Mitch and rested her head on his shoulder. She of course could not understand the words yet she understood the song. Abby could tell the woman was singing about love and lovers. By the way the song rose with the lute Abby sensed the love was a new love: so strong, invigorated, perpetual. The woman's voice went soft again. Her song became what Abby thought might be an appeal to love threatened. An appeal that turned in song to defiance, true love is unstoppable.

The last pluck from the lute left the gathered group silent. Abby realized her eyes had gone misty. She lifted her head from Mitch's shoulder and pulled her hands away to clap for the musician with everyone else. Mitch was moved as well. He removed his glove to dig through his pocket to find a dollar bill. Upon digging one out, he walked over and placed the dollar in a small wicker basket at the woman's feet. The woman acknowledged Mitch with a smile and Abby and Mitch both thanked her. When they turned, Abby took Mitch's arm again with both hands and rested her head on his arm as they walked.

The rest of the walk down the arcade toward the skating pond was not as crowded as the rest of the park had been. The sky was still grey yet the daylight was brighter with less people around them. Their stride was slow and their company relaxed, as a couple that had been together for years and not just a short while. Abby was content with Mitch and he was comfortable with her. With Abby, Mitch was having no issue being in the city. Abby had now washed away whatever Mitch was dreading before. Her upbeat attitude and demeanor made him want to be near her.

When they reached the skating pond Mitch gave Abby her skates and he went to stand in the rental line.

On the ice Mitch found that though the skates were not his own, they were not as uncomfortable as he thought they would be. Abby had not been totally correct on the condition of the rental skates yet she was right that Mitch was able to skate effortlessly in them.

Abby and Mitch skated next to each other and glided around the pond under the towers that bordered the end of the park. Their rhythm synchronized on the ice and with each stride, each could feel the others shared action as if they were parts working from the same mechanism. The couple enjoyed the simple attachment, emotional and physical, that was born between them.

* * * * *

CHAPTER 60

Mitch and Abby scanned the departure boards to see if a track had been assigned to the afternoon train that would take Mitch back to Willow Lake. There was still a little while before Mitch would need to board. They had toyed with the idea of Mitch staying until Monday, and then agreed better to keep the trip short. The two nights they had spent together had been the best either of them could have imagined. They had enjoyed the city together, a hockey game the night before, and spent the entire morning and early afternoon in Abby's apartment, never far from each other's arms. Now at the station they made small talk and anxiously scanned the departure boards each time they rattled the updates.

"I can be back soon," said Mitch.

Abby again let her eyes sync deeply into his and smiled bashfully, embarrassed that she might tear up at any moment. Mitch touched her hand and she intertwined her fingers with his. The weekend had gone by too quickly for both of them.

"I'd like that," said Abby. "I'd like that a lot."

The boards made another loud rattle and track numbers shifted behind each of the postings. Mitch's track appeared behind the name of his train and the boarding sign lit up.

"Well, that's me," said Mitch.

"I'll walk you down."

Mitch picked up his duffle and the two walked through the crowd holding each other's hand toward the entrance to the platform. When they reached the stairwell Mitch turned to Abby and said, "I guess this is it until next time."

"All the way," said Abby. Mitch smiled and the two walked down the steps to the platform and stopped next to the train. Mitch set down his duffel and turned to say goodbye to Abby. Before words could escape his mouth she was upon him with a tight embrace, her feet on tip toe, giving him a deep kiss. After Abby kissed Mitch she told him that she felt like a schoolgirl. Mitch pulled her close and held her, "me too," said Mitch. They both giggled.

Abby made Mitch promise to call her when he reached Willow Lake.

When the conductor gave the final call, Mitch boarded the train. Abby watched him make his way through the crowded car until he found an empty seat near where she stood. He smiled at her then stowed his bag in the overhead bin. He sat near the window and the two gazed at each other until the train started to pull away.

As the train left from the platform Abby's stomach fluttered. She watched the window until she could not see Mitch any longer then slowly turned and went up the stairs to the crowded station. There were hundreds of people roaming through the main lobby as she crossed yet Abby was alone. This was the second time in a week that she had left Mitch, yet the first time she had said goodbye.

When Abby exited the station, she flagged a cab. She had thought of walking home yet now wanted to be as far from where she was at that moment and as soon as possible, for fear of being overcome with emotion.

* * * * *

CHAPTER 61

"Will," said Nathan.

Nathan sat at the next worktable with his head down and his eyes focused on the detail work he was doing. With each of them wearing glasses, over-shirts and smocks, Nathan appeared to be a clone of Will, a young thin clone with long stringy blonde hair, a version of Will that never was.

"How do I get that fade effect again?" asked Nathan.

Will did not shift either. His head like Nathan's was cocked slightly to the right and every once in a while each of them would shift slightly to the left and back to get a better perspective, sometimes in unison.

"Use the straw," said Will.

"Right," said Nathan. "Use the straw."

Nathan meticulously dabbed the small songbird he was holding with his brush one more time and then held the piece away from himself. He set the hummingbird down, scanned the table for the plastic straw Will had given him earlier, and found the straw behind his left arm. He dipped the straw into the Dixie cup that held the paint he wanted to use, and then moved a napkin from the side of the table to the front of him. He removed the straw and gently, without putting his mouth too close, blew at the straw in the direction of the napkin. He then held the napkin up in the air, scowled, and then set the napkin back down to repeat the process.

"Takes a few times to get right," said Will.

"When you showed me it looked easy."

"It's not. Not at first. Just be gentle."

Nathan tried again and again. Then under his breath Will heard him say, "Jesus help me."

"Jesus was a carpenter," said Will.

"What?" Nathan was absorbed in working with his paint and straw.

"As far as I know Jesus didn't make pottery. He was a carpenter. No airbrushing."

"Oh," said Nathan, not at all jarred by Will.

"Now that I think of it. Some say he could have been a stonemason if he built houses. Houses were built from stone back then. Some think of him as a fisherman, too, and a sailor. Others say no. Still, I can't imagine he would have had to do any airbrushing."

"You don't believe in the power of Jesus, Will?"

"Sure, don't think that's going to fix your technique though. Shorter blasts may help. And be gentle."

"You don't believe in God, in eternity?"

"I believe in eternity, in God," said Will. "This clay in my hands, these hands. They're thirteen and a half billion years old, maybe fourteen billion years old. No matter really. And they'll be here most likely for eternity. Probably not eating ham sandwiches or attached to these arms. But this universe isn't going anywhere. Neither is anything in it."

"So you don't believe in heaven or hell?"

"I don't believe anybody's going to be eating ham sandwiches for eternity, that's all."

"What about hell?"

"Every school kid knows the answer to that by the time they're in middle school. Hell can be right here if you let it." Will tilted his head to the left again and then back to the right observing the piece in his hands from different angles. "I think there are a lot of people that make it that way. They like it that way. They don't know how to help themselves."

"Jesus is there to help them with that," said Nathan.

"That he is, saving souls that need saving. But not blowing paint, you need to figure that out for yourself."

Nathan held up the last napkin he had blown into. "What do you think?"

Will shifted his attention toward him and leaned forward so that he could see over his glasses. "That looks good. Give it a shot."

Nathan put some fresh paint into the Dixie cup, positioned the songbird where he wanted and then blew toward the little plastic straw. "Oh man."

Will picked up the jar of white paint from his worktable and extended his arm. "We have plenty of this," said Will.

"I was so close," said Nathan.

"No you weren't," said Will. "But I can't have you using up all of the napkins. Now paint it white and try again."

Nathan held up the bird and frowned.

"You don't have to paint the whole thing, just the tail where you blew the paint," said Will.

"I splattered all over the thing."

"Well, white it is."

"How long did it take you to get that right?" asked Nathan.

"A while," said Will. "I just use the electric gun now. It's up in that cabinet over there."

Will gestured to the cupboard above the sink.

Nathan's voice was somber, "Above the coffee pot?"

"To the right."

"You didn't tell me you had an electric airbrush."

"You didn't ask."

"I did," said Nathan.

"Oh. Well, you'll find it up there."

Nathan went over to the cabinet and opened the door.

Inside on the shelf next to the airbrush kit were bottles of wine, all unopened except one. Nathan had not seen Will with a Dixie cup in his hand since Abby had left. Nor had Nathan seen Will drink any brandy. What he had seen was Will working endlessly in the studio without reprieve, that is until he had finally taken that long sleep. Since then Will had been going nonstop.

Nathan took the airbrush kit down from the shelf and carried the case over to the table.

"You know how to set that up?" asked Will.

"Yea, my friend used to have one of these when I was in school," said Nathan. "We used to paint t-shirts."

"Good. Then you know how to clean it too."

Will stood up, walked over toward the window, and grabbed an extension cord. Will plugged the cord into the wall and brought the other end to Nathan, uncoiling the cord as he did. "Use this cord instead of the table socket, you won't have to have it right on top of you that way."

"Thanks," said Nathan then proceeded to set up the kit. Will walked back to the window and stretched his arms above his head, clasping his hands in the air.

"Storm's a comin'," said Will faintly.

"What's that Will?"

"Nothing, something I heard about the weather. I'll be back in a minute, I got to stretch my legs."

Will grabbed the jacket he kept by the door and stepped out into the light. The glare of the sun caught him off guard and he quickly brought his hand above his eyes to correct his vision. From where he stood the sun was shining through the willow and the branches played games with the light. He shifted his head. In the side yard he heard the loud knock of a woodpecker pounding into a tree and out on the lake the soft buzz of a chainsaw cutting into the ice. He walked the path to the willow and ducked beneath the canopy of branches to stand next to the trunk. Will placed his hand on the willow. He patted the tree twice to test the solidity and peered up at the cables that attached themselves to the tree from the house and the studio. He flattened his hand and gave the willow a solid forward push. The tree did not budge or make a sound within. The branches above did not waiver to surrender any ice or snow and looking back at the cables again, neither seemed anymore aware of him then before. He decided the tree was solid and patted the bark again, this time gently, biting his lower lip as he did.

The sky was crystal clear and the blue contrasted the snowy earth. Will took the few steps down toward the ice and turned toward the tree. There was no way he could easily see the foundation of the willow in the bank beneath the snow. Slowly he backed away to get the entire tree in scope. His boots crunched on the snow above the ice. He kept walking backwards until he could see the willow, house, and studio all in front of him. Surrounded by leafless trees the Bellen yard appeared tranquil. Will guessed the yard was. He tried to think if there were ever any truly bad times that came to this house and he could not. Even with the loss of family, through generations, the home had been peaceful. He inspected the dock pulled up by the shed, the deck covered with tarp, the wheels peeking out beneath. Will had not put the dock in the lake last year or the year before.

Will focused on the ground where the willow stood, his eyes gazing into the past. The willow now stood where he and Emily spent many nights on a blanket watching the stars in each others arms as the children slept inside. As a child he had learned to walk on that yard and so had Michael and Abby. There used to be a swing set in front of the studio he remembered now. And by the shed beneath the snow, was the remnant of a sandbox that he had played in as a child.

With a thousand drooping branches covered in ice and light snow, from where Will stood, the willow was a large crystalline gazebo on the lake edge. Periodically a glimmer appeared that danced back at the sun above. Will thought how Emily would have loved this grand tree in full lacy dress.

In the studio window Will could see Nathan watching him. Will raised his hand and gave a wave. Nathan waved back and disappeared into the shadows. Will put his hands in his front pockets and turned to the expanse of the lake. He squinted his cool blue eyes out toward the shanties and started to walk. Will did not remember the last time he went for a walk on the lake and decided that today was a good day for one.

* * * * *

CHAPTER 62

Late afternoon the sky turned overcast and dusk quickly followed. Already house lights began to sparkle through the tree line along the edges of the lake. Nathan had initially peered out the window periodically and then by late afternoon he sat fixated in the direction of the lake. He could barely see Will's silhouette against the bluing snow as he approached the property, stopping intermittently, then trudging forward again. When Nathan saw Will mount the bank to the yard he got up from the window and slipped his jacket on. He flipped the switch to the outside light and stepped outside the door of the studio as Will moved up the path from the willow. Nathan could see a pleasant look on Will's face.

"You warm enough?" asked Nathan.

"Yes," said Will stopping next to Nathan. His voice calm, relaxed, "It's not as cold as you would think out there if you keep moving around."

"You're probably starting to give yourself hypothermia," said Nathan. "Let's go into the house and I'll make dinner."

"Ok," said Will.

The two went into the house and per Will's request Nathan boiled some pasta. Will built a fire in the lake room and the two ate their dinners on TV trays while watching the television. The television was issuing warnings about the blizzard moving across the state. When the radar came on Nathan was surprised. The sky was overcast outside still very calm, no wind, no snow. The radar on the television showed half the screen blocked off by a huge dark patch representing the blizzard that was bearing down on Willow Lake.

"It's probably best you head home, before the weather sets in, unless of course you want to stay for the night," said Will.

"I think I'll take your advice then I'll see you in the morning," said Nathan. He quickly cleaned the kitchen and left for the evening.

Will had enough of the television and turned the box off. He did not need the weatherman to tell him there was a storm on the way. He felt the weather in his bones. He was ok with the weather.

Will went into the kitchen and opened the freezer. Abby had a sweet tooth and she certainly would have left some ice cream in there. Yes there was some vanilla. Will put some ice cream in a small bowl and placed the container back in the freezer and then went back into the lake room to eat his dessert.

Will sat on the arm of the sofa and looked out toward the lake. Because of the lamp by the window all he could see was his reflection staring back at him. He did not see a sixty-seven year old man with white hair eating vanilla ice cream. The reflection washed out the lines in his face so he appeared younger and the amber light of the room made his hair shadowed, almost brown. Will thought he looked satisfied and he liked that. Will straightened his back and peered deep into the glass. Yes, Will affirmed, satisfied.

Will finished his dessert and took the bowl to the kitchen. He stretched his arms over his head and yawned. He may have appeared youthful in the reflection of a window yet he was tired. Though still early Will decided to take an after dinner nap, after which he would go back out to the studio.

Will went into his room to rest on his bed, falling asleep in moments. He slept deeply and still, much longer than he had planned, late into the night.

As the storm moved in Will took no notice. As reported a blizzard of wind and ice bore upon the lake. Will sat up abruptly when something blew down by the shed making a loud crash. Once awake he heard the sounds of howling gales blowing against the house. The gales caused the house to creak when the wind was strongest.

Will got up from his bed and went to the lake room. The light was still on so he could not see out of the bay window. When he turned off the switch, the bay window illuminated with the outside events of the storm. Will could see the willow swaying in the wind, her large canopy of branches were a shifting dress of snow and ice. Will thought the tree might blow down. He put on his boots and his heavy jacket and opened the door. The wind caught and pulled the door from his fingers slamming the wood back into a snowdrift that was forming by the house. Will grabbed and pulled the door shut. Icy sleet cut into his fingers as he did. The wind was carrying icy rain and sleet, coating everything. Will threw the hood of the jacket up over his head to keep the ice off his ears and made his way toward the shed. The wind pushed against him and he almost fell over more than once in the deep snow that covered the way to the shed. When Will finally got to the shed he was able to pull the wooden door open enough for him to fit in. Once inside the world quieted, Will did not realize how loud the gale was until he was clear. He went to the corner of the shed to get the coil of thick nautical rope he had bought for the dock a few years back. He got a deal on the hundred-foot coil that now would be put to use. Will figured he could further anchor the tree to the house with the rope, at least through the storm.

Will reached down to pick up the heavy coil. With both

hands, he lifted the coil onto his shoulder and made his way back to the door. When Will slipped back out the door, the wind pushed against him, making the move forward that much harder. Still Will tromped through the snow where there was no path to get directly to the tree. He leaned into each step, sometimes landing on his knee.

When Will got to the willow an ice laden branch cut his check. The smaller branches were flailing like whips with each gust. Will kept his head low to get close to the trunk. The trunk moved elastically above the snow. Will's fear was for what was happening to the roots. He dropped the rope to the ground and wrapped one end around the tree several times before tying the rope off. The sleet beat upon him as he worked. When Will felt the rope was secured to the tree he tied the other end to himself. Then Will pulled the rope tight between himself and the tree so he could manage the slack as he moved closer to the house.

Will eased away from the tree. With each step Will pushed his feet hard into the snow and kept leaning back so the rope would stay taut. The tree swayed with the gales, pulling him forward with each gust. Slowly Will released the slack of the rope until there was not anymore. The house was only a few feet behind him yet could not be reached. He pulled on the rope as hard as he could to get farther back with no success. Will decided that if the house could not be the anchor then he would. He rolled his body into the rope, pulled his hood down over his face, and then slowly anchored himself down in the snow. Each time the trunk of the willow swayed toward him, he would claim the slack. Will believed that the rope around his waist would be enough to hold the willows girth through the last of the storm. Will had prevailed. Then off the lake came a gale so forceful that Will could see the snow push out from underneath. The snow spun with the gust and formed a cyclone. Howling toward him the large funnel pressed upon the shore. The cyclone enveloped the yard, Will was deafened, and all around him shook within the wind and the icy rain. Water came across his face too quickly to bead. His hands squeezed the rope and began to bleed pink with the icy rain. Through squinting eyes Will saw the large anchor cables fly over his head with broad curls and rolling curves. The steel slowly furled with the parts of the house and studio they were fastened to flailing to the end of them. The willow and Will remained yet the ground was no more. Time suspended and the world around Will moved slowly and gracefully. The air was thick with snow from the funnel and Will could only discern the cables and the willow. Large branches were to and fro though the willow for the most part floated intact in the stormy sky. The gale forced the cables out past the willow, taking with them all sound to be heard. Will saw one cable snap free of burden and oh so slowly extend from the snow-hazed darkness to where the sunrise was beginning to peek through a break in the storm. The sunrise had light hues of fuchsia and tangerine. The tension on the rope eased and the cable mesmerized him. Floating above Will's head the cable appeared to hover, then slowly fell back at him, directly to him, until all went black.

There was a depth, a sense of warmth.

* * * * *

CHAPTER 63

Abby lifted the lace curtain of her apartment window to find the red rental car Mitch was driving.

"I see you," Abby said into the cell phone. She could see the four door red sedan turning the corner onto her block. "I'm on my way out."

Abby hung up and placed the cell phone into her bag. She scanned the apartment then paused. A notion that she was forgetting something, that something was lost, passed over her. Abby went to the door, picked up her suitcase, and headed for the street.

Mitch was double parked outside of Abby's building when she came out. He stood next to the car and opened the back door as she approached so that she could deposit her suitcase quickly, which she did. Abby then turned to him and gave him a hug.

"You didn't have to do this," said Abby.

"It's the least I could do. I couldn't see you taking a train and Caroline and Brian have their hands full at the lake," said Mitch.

"Of course. That's still so sweet of you. You must have gotten up so early."

"Don't mention it," said Mitch. Abby walked around

the back of the car and got in. Mitch watched her then got into the car as well.

Mitch had gotten up early. Mitch rented the car from Fremont the night before and left for the city around five in the morning so that he could get in early enough to get Abby out before rush hour began. This was a good plan because the streets were empty as the two drove away from the building.

Mitch had a tea waiting in the car for which Abby was grateful. All Mitch had smelled all morning was his coffee, until Abby got into the car. Now the car had a sweet feminine smell of cosmetics and shampoo. Even in the midst of a grey morning, Abby appeared radiant. Expressionless, her eyes still sparkled and her cheeks still glowed. Mitch was pleased to see Abby yet he could see the shadow behind the veil.

There was little traffic as they left the avenues and entered the expressway. Neither said a word as the roadways got bigger and they progressed farther from the city center. Mitch stole glances at Abby and she just stared forward at the road, sometimes veering to the side to something in the distance: a billboard, a building, nothing. Sometimes her gaze just hung in the air. Mitch said nothing. They rode together in silence.

An hour outside the city Abby reached over, placed her hand on Mitch's shoulder, and squeezed. Her eyes pleaded for his and her mouth let free a melancholy smile. Mitch smiled back.

Morning traffic had picked up yet flowed evenly through this scenic stretch. The rest of the drive would be scenic, particularly if one were partial to snowy evergreens. Abby tuned the radio to a station playing classical music. The music went well with the trees passing by her window so she leaned back in her seat and watched as they fell by, one by one.

"Mitch," said Abby.

"Yes, Abby."

"Caroline said the house and studio were damaged."

"I had the boys patch them up so the weather can't get in."

"Oh... Thank you."

"It's alright," said Mitch.

When they got to Willow Lake, Abby started to become noticeably uncomfortable. There were things that needed to be done in Fremont yet that would wait until later. Mitch was taking Abby to her cousin Caroline's in Willow Lake first. Mitch understood Abby's uneasiness when he realized she was looking into the cemetery. He had driven past that cemetery countless times and the place meant nothing to him. Mitch realized that to Abby that cemetery had a great meaning, the place held her family, her mother, brother, and soon would hold her father. Mitch reached over and caressed the back of her neck. Abby leaned her head back in his hand and rested there.

As Mitch drove through the village Abby continued to gaze vacuously out the window with a somber expression. The Stone tavern was still dark at this time of day. People seemed to be walking slowly. The sky was overcast grey, gloomy. Abby did not shift her view over the lake. Her gaze did not fix on any one point or any one thing. At the edge of the village Mitch turned onto Willow Lake road. The next stop would be Caroline's house. Abby knew that she was getting close so she started to compose herself. She had already talked to Caroline on the phone a couple of times since the storm, since the accident. Caroline had told Abby what had happened after Nathan found Will. Caroline had begun the arrangements. Abby felt that she was being so unfair to her cousin due to Caroline's proximity.

When Mitch and Abby drove into the driveway they could see that all of the lights were on in the house. The atrium lit up amber against the cool colorless woods. Caroline came out of the door and onto the porch and ran down to her cousin. Abby opened the car door and went to her cousin's embrace. The two held each other tight.

"Are you alright?" asked Caroline.

"I don't know," said Abby. "How about you?"

Caroline responded by just shaking her head.

Neither Caroline nor Abby shed tears. The pain in their hearts poured through their eyes as they met.

Mitch eased out of the car. He was moved to see these two strong women surrender their emotions to each other. He walked over and put his arms around them, still holding each other tight, and led them back to the house.

* * * * *

CHAPTER 64

"Brian's not back yet," said Caroline as she brought Abby and Mitch into the kitchen. "He took the twins to a friends down the lake."

"Are they okay?" asked Abby.

"They're not really aware of what's going on. Hey, I know it's a little early for lunch but the two of you have been on the road, and we have plenty of food."

In disbelief Abby saw that every counter was covered with foil and plastic containers, "Where did all of this come from?"

"Most from my parents. Tom and Mary sent a delivery boy over from the IGA with enough salads, prepared meats, and cold cuts to insure no one would have to bother cooking."

"I'm sure that Tom and Mary won't be cooking either," said Abby. She thought about them missing Brian's birthday party because they were away in Florida. Abby would now be seeing them soon.

Caroline took three plates from the cabinet and set them down in front of the makeshift buffet. Abby started to take the covers off from the food.

"You two just have a seat," said Caroline.

On each plate Caroline put an assortment of the salads and meats. She placed the plates in front of Abby and Mitch and then took a seat across the island from them. Abby had not realized how hungry she was. Once she started eating, the food went down easily.

Caroline asked, "Have you eaten anything since we talked last night?"

"I'm not sure," said Abby. Everything was confusing for Abby right now.

Mitch went to the refrigerator, took out a pitcher of lemonade, and set the pitcher on the island. Caroline told him which cabinet to get three glasses from so that she could fill them. The more Abby ate the more color came to her face and the faster she ate as well.

"I guess eating was a pretty good idea," said Mitch.

"That's what you're supposed to do at times like this," said Caroline.

They ate silently and then Abby reached across the island and took Caroline's hand and smiled. Mitch was glad to see a smile on Abby's face. Mitch picked up his glass of lemonade and gestured a toast, "To Tom and Mary for this great food."

"Here, here," they toasted back.

"I almost forgot," said Caroline. She got up from the island, went over to the side counter, and lifted a towel from a tray. Below the towel was a plate of frosted sweet biscuits. Caroline picked up three from the top and covered the plate then brought them back, distributing one to each plate.

"I made these this morning. They're good," said Caroline.

Abby picked up and held the biscuit in front of her, "All of this food and you still baked these?"

"That's not all I baked," said Caroline, pointing to a sidebar lined with towel-covered trays. "I was baking all evening."

Mitch bit into his biscuit and with his mouthful he said, "Some things never change."

Abby asked, "You've seen her bake like this before?"

"Any time she get's stressed," said Mitch. "I remember back in college heading to Caroline's around midterms and finals for all of the cupcakes you could eat."

Caroline and Abby laughed.

"My dear Caroline was a chronic baker way before she went off to school," said Abby. "I remember when she was waiting for Bobby Collins to ask her to homecoming. She came to my house and we made every kind of fruit pie possible. Two of every kind."

All three laughed at this.

Caroline continued, "We kept sending Michael to the Orchard Hill farm stand to get more fruit and each time he would come back with something different."

Abby added, "We moved the pies out to picnic table to cool and when we went to check on them they were gone. So we go out to the studio and there was Will with a pie on the workbench and a fork in his hand and a bunch of empty pie tins in front of him. We asked him what he thought he was doing and he looked up and said," Caroline joined in unison, "Waiting for some ice cream."

The girls laughed again harder. Caroline held up her glass of lemonade again, "To Uncle Will."

"To Will," said Mitch raising his glass.

"To Will," said Abby.

Then they fell silent.

Mitch asked Caroline, "Did you bake any pie?"

"Just apple, that's all I had around," said Caroline.

"I love pie," said Mitch.

"Me too," said Abby.

"You know, I do too," said Caroline, and she brought the pie over.

Caroline took out three pie plates and then cut three pieces. She offered to heat the pie in the microwave and both declined. Caroline then offered ice cream to which all three laughed yet still declined. All were satisfied to eat the pie as is.

Mitch and Caroline could see a noticeable difference in Abby's strength and color. Food had been what she had needed, at least one of the things. Being with family was helping as well.

After lunch Mitch stood and took the car keys out of his pocket. " I need to take the car back and get my truck. I'll be available for anything you need once I pick it up."

"Where is your truck?" asked Caroline.

"The Fremont Airport."

"What's it doing out there?"

"The only rental car I could find last night was at the airport. Do you want to go into Fremont Abby?"

"No, I think I am going to stay with Caroline for now. I'll see you when you get back," said Abby.

"Ok then, let me get your bag out of the car. I'll be right back."

Mitch brought Abby's bag into the house and the girls met him at the door. Mitch gave each of the girls a tight hug then turned and went back out to the car. From inside the atrium Abby watched Mitch drive out of the yard. Her arms were crossed and her head tilted, she sighed lightly as he pulled away. He did not see her.

"You're like an old couple already," said Caroline as she stepped up next to her cousin and put her arm on her shoulder. The two let the sides of their heads rest together.

"I knew you two would be a match," said Caroline.

"He's a great guy. There's no doubt about that," said Abby.

"But what?"

"No buts. Just a lot to ask from him so quick."

"It was nice of him to drive in this morning and pick you up."

"He's a doll," said Abby.

"You look like you could use a nap. Why don't you lie down? Everything is set up for tonight. Will had it all together, surprising enough."

"You gotta give him that."

Abby turned and began walking the length of the room toward the lake. Without looking back at her, she asked Caroline, "Have you been over to the house?"

"Yea. Brian and Mitch took me over there. Mitch had the guys patch it up."

"Yea, he told me," said Abby. "How bad was it?"

"Architecturally? I don't know. Not bad I think. Honestly, I couldn't focus," said Caroline. "I had just been over to see him."

"Of course," said Abby. She had sauntered to the sliding glass doors overlooking the deck. "I'll have to ask Brian what it takes to fix it."

"The boys already have it worked out. I don't think it's that much. They just haven't discussed it with me," said Caroline. She too was now staring out onto the lake with Abby, each seeing nothing.

"Right," said Abby. "They're good guys."

"Yea, they are," said Caroline.

* * * * *

CHAPTER 65

Abby carefully applied the mascara that Caroline had shared with her. She had not worn hers in so long, the tube had dried out. How odd she felt to wear make up to a funeral viewing. Abby assessed herself in the mirror. The globe bulbs surrounding the glass cast off an amber light that she thought made her appear tan. "Tan in winter," she thought, "and in a cocktail dress." The black dress Abby wore was not a cocktail dress, though the dress was elegant, perhaps she felt too elegant. Abby thought she appeared as if she were going to a fancy party. She had even blown her hair out and she never blew her hair out. Abby turned to her right and Caroline was standing in the door. She was wearing a black dress and had blown her hair out as well. They smiled girlish smiles at each other.

"You look silly," said Abby.

"Not as silly as you look," said Caroline. Caroline stepped up next to Abby and peered intently into the mirror. With the end of her finger, she rubbed her eyebrows.

"You're beautiful," said Abby, admiring her cousin in the mirror. "I don't want to do this."

"Who would? Are you ready?" asked Caroline. "Brian has the car running."

"Yea, sure. As ready as I'll ever be."

The two hugged each other tightly again then went downstairs. Caroline produced two winter shawls for them to put on.

"The way we're dressed, we should be going to dinner," said Abby.

Caroline gave her another hug and the two went to the waiting car.

* * * * *

CHAPTER 66

The Bennington Funeral Home was a prominent funeral parlor in Fremont. The Bennington family had run the business for generations and the Bellens always used their services as a matter of tradition. The Funeral Home was a large Victorian House the size of a small mansion that sat on the corner of Second Avenue and River Street, Second Avenue being the grand estate avenue of Fremont. An ivy branched garden wall, naked in the cold, ran along River Street for almost the full block concealing a parking lot behind. There were several viewing rooms in the funeral home and at any time there could be two or three families mourning a loved one there. When Brian drove up to the home, both sides of the street were already lined with cars and the three could see people moving along the sidewalk and up the stairs into the building.

"The parking lot must already be full," said Caroline.

"It's alright. There's a deli parking lot two blocks up," said Brian as he trolled the car passed Bennington's.

"There must be a lot of viewings tonight," said Abby.

"I don't think so," said Caroline.

"They can't all be there for..." Abby drifted off. She kept her gaze in the direction of the funeral home, slowly turning her head back as the car drove forward.

"Sure," said Caroline.

Brian pulled the Subaru into the parking lot and parked below a large lit sign that had a picture of a tubby boy eating a long sandwich. Brian turned off the engine and he and Caroline stepped out of the car. Abby stayed inside. Over the top of the car Caroline arched her eyebrows high at Brian. Brian nodded his head and shut his door, then without a word walked around the car and opened Abby's door. Brian reached in and took Abby's hand to help her out of the car.

"Be careful on the ice hon," said Caroline.

Abby put her hand beneath Brian's arm and he walked her out of the lot and up the sidewalk. Caroline led the way a step ahead of them at an easy pace so that Abby would not get overwhelmed. When they got to the bottom of the wooden porch that wrapped around the front of the house Caroline stopped. Abby let go of Brian's arm and took Caroline's.

"Shall we," said Abby.

"Let me get the door," said Brian, and he side stepped around the two to make his way up the porch to get the door opened for them.

When the door opened the girls could feel the flood of heat and were washed in a sweet floral smell that permeated the funeral home. The interior of the foyer was classic Victorian in style with lush wallpaper in shades of peach and pink. Abby remembered the room all too well. Nothing had changed since her last visit. As they stepped in they could hear low talking in the sitting room to their right. By the sound of the chatter they could tell that a lot of people were in that room. Abby stopped Caroline at the edge of the French doors to the sitting room. She could see the back of a dark suit and knew that the next step would expose her to the visitors that had come to mourn and pay their respects. Once Abby was exposed a chain of events would be set off that would entail small talk and discussion and ultimately the journey to the adjoining parlor where Abby knew there would be a coffin, a coffin with yet another member of her family inside. Her chest tightened and her breath was short. Abby felt something brush her shoulder and was startled. Brian was removing her shawl. Abby turned her head to Brian then to Caroline and smiled. The distraction was appreciated. Abby took Caroline's hand and squeezed, then released and walked into the sitting room.

The large sitting room was full with people sitting on the sofas and chairs, and standing in every available space. All were talking amongst themselves, sipping coffee, and eating cookies from silver trays in the corners. The reception could have passed for a formal party with the attire and the décor except the theater was not what was in the next room.

The people, mostly of her father's age, took notice to Abby and Caroline's entrance. The chatter dropped off to a silence as all in the room looked in the direction of the black clad women at the door. Abby distinctly heard her name whispered in a tone of pity in the back of the room paired with the phrases, 'poor girl', 'so beautiful', and 'so sad'. The expressions on the faces of the group were saddened smiles. Abby looked across the room and brightly greeted everyone. "Hi everyone," said Abby, as exuberant as she could sound and still maintain an appropriate tone. Immediately the expressions of grief lessened and cheerfulness replaced them. Murmur picked up again as she was greeted by old friends of the family. Abby heard other phrases with her name that pleased her, like 'she is so much like Emily' and 'her parents would be so proud'. Men and women alike took their turn to pull her aside and offer condolences and anecdotes from times years passed.

Caroline tried to stay near Abby's side yet she herself was pulled away after stepping into the room. Caroline's mother and father would not be flying in until the morning, and in lieu of their presence she became their proxy.

Abby smiled at each and every mourner as they shared

with her their joy for her father. With each person the theme was common, celebration not sadness. So many funny stories, Abby soon realized that she had not stopped smiling since she entered the room, and people were still waiting their turn to speak with her. So many people, so many she did not recognize, and more were coming through the door. Abby could see that more people were floating in then out, she did not know how all of these people were fitting in the room. Caroline touched her shoulder and whispered in her ear, "You have to see this." Abby did not want to go. Caroline eased her over to the parlor doors. Abby took a breath and tightened her chest. If the funeral chamber were as she remembered, she expected to see with her father's coffin across the room to the right. Abby lifted her head and her eyes widened. Abby did not see a coffin before her. Rather, the partitions between three viewing rooms had been removed creating one large room. That large room was occupied with over a hundred people.

"Oh my," said Abby.

"Oh my, is right," said Caroline. "I think we better go say hello."

* * * * *

CHAPTER 67

Abby and Caroline stepped into the larger room and began the ritual again, condolences, stories, smiles, and adoring kisses upon the cheeks. Sometimes Abby would see Caroline and for a little while they would try to hold conversations together. Before too long they would be separated, having to wait for their opportunity to get back together again. Brian kept up a constant supply of coffee and did his best to seek out Caroline if she had drifted too far to get back by herself.

Abby and Caroline were in the adjoining rooms for quite some time before Abby saw the coffin in the far corner of the last room. What drew her attention were large wreaths filled with white mums bordering the long dark polished wooden box. Abby could see that the lid was up yet from the far side of the room could not see inside. People sauntered up to the side, singly and in couples, some crossing themselves, others holding vigil momentarily over the coffin. Occasionally someone would reach inside to touch Will's arm or hand or to place something next to him. Abby continued speaking to all that approached her, keeping one eye on the corner of the room. She stayed near the entrance of the room and made no attempt to cross.

Caroline joined Abby in thanking Mister and Missus Bauer for coming. As the older couple stepped away Abby whispered into Caroline's ear, "Take me to the bathroom." The bathrooms were downstairs by the main entrance. To get to them they had to retrace steps already covered, that wasn't so hard, and nobody new was entering now to stop them. Caroline squeezed Abby's forearm and led the way back to the entrance excusing the two as they made their way. When they were in the bathrooms Abby threw her arms around her cousin, "Thank you so much for being here."

"It's alright Abby. I'm always here for you," said Caroline.

Abby asked, "Have you seen Will yet?"

"I saw the coffin in the far corner but I haven't worked up the nerve to get close yet," said Caroline. "You'd know if I had though. There would be no way I'd still be this composed."

"Well it's inevitable," said Abby. "Can you go with me to see him?"

"Of course dear. Just give me a minute to freshen up."

Abby stepped out of the bathroom ahead of Caroline. She thought the wallpaper in the hall tawdry with the pink background and deep red velvet fleur-de-lis print. How old that paper must be she thought. Abby inspected the trim along the ceiling for faults of age, finding as she expected, yellowing and bubbles from the old glue in a corner above a framed picture of a bouquet in a vase. This paper had been here in her teen years Abby remembered.

Caroline opened the door of the bathroom and Abby turned toward the stairs. Caroline touched her shoulder and gestured toward the other end of the hall where a stairwell would lead them to the other side of the house, the side of the house that held the entrance to the viewing room where Will was in his coffin.

At the top of the stairs another sitting room held a group of people, some Caroline and Abby had spoken to prior.

Caroline and Abby were focused in the direction of Abby's father in the room beyond. This time no one directly approached, rather nods were shared with lightened brows of sympathy. As the two entered the room Caroline took the lead by holding her cousin's arm once more. This last section of adjoining rooms had folding chairs lined up in rows back to the door with an aisle between them for a direct path to the coffin. When those occupying the aisle saw Will's daughter enter the room they stepped into the rows clearing the aisle for her. Caroline and Abby found the action strange though knew better than to react inappropriately, besides, seeing the coffin at the end of the aisle caused the girls to relinquish any comedy they may have found in the situation. Abby's jaw clenched and she reached for Caroline's hand on her arm.

Abby could now see Will inside the coffin, next to him a photograph of an unsuspecting family twenty years passed, her father, mother, Michael, and her propped up in a black wooden frame. The room shrank as Abby glided to the side of her father.

"That's a nice suit," said Abby in a soft voice. She reached in and felt the lapel.

"Brian got it from the house. It was set aside per Will's instructions. Brian said he had a few of them, I was surprised."

Abby sighed, "He wore them when he was young, Mom and he used to go to the city."

"Oh, I never knew that," said Caroline.

"He looks good," said Abby.

"Yes, he does."

"He would hate that."

"What?"

"People always say things like that, 'He looked good'. Will would hate that I said that," said Abby.

"Well," Caroline paused, "Well, he does. Look at him. He looks great."

"He does, doesn't he," said Abby.

"Are you ok? Do you want a minute?"

"Yea, a minute."

"I'll be over hear hon," Caroline kissed Abby on the forehead and then squeezed her arm tight before walking to the row of chairs where Brian was waiting for her. Brian handed Caroline a packet of tissue wrapped in plastic. She quickly removed two tissues and dabbed her eyes.

Abby placed both hands along the smooth edge of the casket and looked long into the pillow. She had not seen Will's usually disheveled hair neatly combed or cut. Now he wore the style of a man she did not recognize. Not that Will could not pull off a look so debonair, even in the coffin he was a handsome man, still this was not his look. This was not her Will, the Will in the photograph with the perpetual boyish charm. Abby did see before her a peaceful Will and in that she took solace. That solace alone must have subdued her, for she could find no further feelings or thoughts at that moment. There was no misting of the eyes, no churning stomach, her jaw relaxed. Abby raised her hands lightly from the coffin and placed them back again. She would have more time to spend with Will at the funeral. The final goodbye to her father and the deliberation of what to do would not have to come right now.

Abby turned away from the coffin to face the room. Brian and Caroline stood and stepped forward to embrace her. Abby felt the familiar peculiarity of all the adjoining rooms silencing to a murmur again. Not about to be made the center of attention due to sympathy Abby wanted to quell any unneeded tension before the tension arose. An overt smile to Caroline and Brian and an open embrace relaxed the tension in the rooms before uneasiness could mount.

Over Caroline's shoulder Abby saw Nathan for the first time. He sat against the wall with his hair pulled back and head hung low. Abby excused herself and Caroline whispered, "He has been taking this hard, he found Will and all." Abby walked over to where Nathan sat and took the empty seat next to him. Nathan kept his head hung low not noticing that Abby had sat down. She placed her hand on his back and he slowly lifted his head. Nathan's glasses were misty and his face red, and his nose running. In his hands was some crumpled up tissue.

"Oh, Nathan. You poor dear," said Abby as she gestured back to Caroline to bring over more tissues.

Nathan sniffled and smiled, "I'm ok. How are you?"

"Best as can be expected," said Abby.

"I have been praying for you," said Nathan.

"I'm sure you have. You're so sweet."

Abby put her arm around Nathan and pulled his head on her shoulder, "It's alright. Don't cry. Will's in a better place." Abby could hear herself consoling Nathan with the same words she had heard all evening.

"Do you think so?" asked Nathan.

"Sure."

"Because I'm not so sure he was a believer. He liked to make fun on my account."

Abby thought about what Nathan said and responded, "Will liked to have fun. But he was a believer all right. I don't think I ever met anyone madder at God than him. He had to believe in him to be that mad."

"He was mad?"

"Not when you knew him, but when Mom was sick, and after she died. He finally made his peace."

"You think so?"

"I know so," said Abby, realizing that she and her father had shared something all along.

Nathan took tissues from the package that Caroline gave him and the girl's consoled him until his sobbing slowed. Abby stood and once again embraced her cousins and whispered into their ears, "His timing couldn't be better." Caroline and Brian turned to see Mitch at the parlor door shaking hands with Josh Colden from the lumberyard. Brian stepped to the side, keeping his arm around Caroline and she continued to keep her arm around Abby in turn.

Mitch matched eyes with Abby and the two shared a subtle smile. Mitch patted Josh on the arm and approached Abby. Mitch shook Brian's hand and kissed Caroline's cheek. Then Caroline handed Abby off to Mitch and the two embraced each other.

"How are you doing?" asked Mitch.

"I'm so glad you came. Now let's get out of here," said Abby.

"Sure thing," said Mitch.

* * * * *

CHAPTER 68

The lake appeared pristine. The overcast sky made the ice a subtle blue among the grey shadows of the small snowdrifts. Abby stood with her arms crossed, white wine in hand, gazing out through the glass doors of Caroline's kitchen. The kitchen buzzed with people moving about behind her. Though there had been a marathon of mingling, the lake took her attention when she passed by the doors. Abby had survived through the funeral service earlier in the day as a matter of course. The memorial service at Bennington had gone much the same as the viewing, with an even greater number of people, though Abby was not as surprised as before. Her vision of Will as obstinate and distant had overshadowed his pervasive charm that she knew now had such an affect on others. She did what she felt her duty, to greet everyone and share their celebration for her father's life. Now at a second reception at Caroline's, a smaller group of Willow Lake people gathered to pay their condolences. All of the greeting and congeniality had a toll that Abby started to feel.

As Abby peered out across the lake, she realized that she needed to see the house. In the few days that Abby had been back at the lake, she had not been to the house or the studio. There had been no obstruction to a visit. There simply had been no real reason for her to go. Everything Abby needed was at her cousin's house, the necessities of living, a room for herself, and family for support.

Abby sighed and slowly turned from the glass doors. She scanned the faces of everyone in the room and, with a smile, excused herself. She made her way to the outer room toward the stairs. As Abby took the first step of the staircase she saw Caroline talking to Emma Shaw. Caroline raised her brow in Abby's direction and Abby nodded back, and then went up the stairs to her room.

In her room Abby slipped out of her skirt and blouse and put on blue jeans and a sweater. Then she pulled her skates out of the travel bag, sat on the bed, and placed them next to her. She crossed her arms and leaned forward, slightly bowing her head. A light knock came at the door and Caroline entered, "Hey, I thought I better check to see if you were surviving the marathon."

Abby turned her head to the side, grinned softly, and then said, "It keeps going doesn't it?"

Caroline took a seat on the bed on the other side of the skates, and then picked them up and held them. "Thinking of going out on the ice?"

"Yea, I was. Do you think that's stupid?"

"You need some air. You should go for it. I'll hold down the fort. It's about to wrap up anyway."

"Thanks," said Abby. "You know I don't even know why I brought them. They were by the door when I left the city. I don't know what I was thinking."

"Well," Caroline held the skates out for Abby to take, "it's a good thing you did."

Abby chuckled and then said, "Caroline."

"Yea."

"Mitch went to the IGA with Brian. He'll be back soon."

"Don't worry about Mitch," said Caroline.

"Caroline."

"Yea."

"I don't suppose you have a jacket I can wear. I don't have a good one for the lake."

"Sure, let me get it for you."

The two went to the hall and Caroline took one of her jackets out of the closet as well as some gloves and a hat. "These will be better than whatever you have. Go out the front door so you don't have to explain yourself to anybody. You can take the side deck around and then down to the lake."

"Thanks again," said Abby, "for everything."

Abby did not bother to slip her sneakers on. She followed Caroline downstairs and per her cousin's advice slipped out the front door without making eye contact with anyone. The crisp air washed against her as the door closed behind. She felt liberated from the duties of ceremony that had burdened her over the last few days. Abby moved hurriedly with quick short steps around the corner to get out of view from the atrium before putting the jacket on, and then she scurried just as quickly down to the deck by the lake. Abby only then glanced up at the house with some notion that she may have been followed before resting to put her skates on.

For the first time since Abby had received the call about Will she felt light and rejuvenated. Abby laced her skates tight and put on her gloves and then eased onto the ice. With a few strides Abby launched herself out onto the surface of Willow Lake. At first she skated out toward the center of the lake. Her mind clear, only the sounds of each skate cutting into the frozen mirror below her and faintly off to her left, a quad runner pulling a skiff away from a shanty. From the distance the skiff was floating across the lake rather than being dragged on the ice. Abby picked up speed and let her legs go limber below her. On the edge of the lake the trees and houses were sleepy under the grey sky. The tree line pulled the grey from the sky, absorbing the dark though still early afternoon. Once out on the lake

Abby let herself turn in the direction of her family home. Abby's arms were by her side, she put her gloved hands into the wide pockets of the jacket, and she settled into a rhythmic motion, breathing slowly, moving effortlessly. She was honed on the direction that she had skated so many times before as a child.

It was not until Abby came to the outcropping of the point before Bellen cove that her heart began to race. Around the point would be the house and the studio, The Bellen studio. Abby's chest tightened and her mind raced with the name Bellen. Abby was now the only Bellen. Abby slowed then stopped. Abby wanted to be prepared for what she would see when she rounded the point. Pulling her hands from her pockets Abby shook her arms to loosen her body in an attempt to fight off the oncoming tension.

Abby skated on. Her heart beat harder and her stomach ached. As Abby cleared the tall pine on the point the first thing she could see was the willow. Abby's eyes widened and filled with tears. Abby skated forward stiffly. The willow spread shattered across the ice. A soft blanket of snow lightly covered the tree, broken midway in two, with branches scattered out into the cove. Held up like a large fan, the roots of the willow were pulled from the base of the shore.

Abby tried to determine what the blue painted object was alongside the length of the tree. Abby coasted to a stop. She realized the object was part of the eave of the studio roof. Then Abby shifted her eyes to the house and the studio behind the tree.

Abby dropped to her knees.

* * * * *

CHAPTER 69

Because they had been patched Abby had not initially noticed that the ends of the eaves were missing. The materials the workman used to cover the holes were the same color of the buildings and from a distance blended with the rest of the buildings. Now closer, Abby could see that the top corners of each building had been torn away.

Abby took a deep breath and tried to brush her tears away. The tears still came. She wept softly at first. Her breaths drew deeper and the weeping grew to a wail. Abby tried to rest on her feet behind her, and then slipped to the side so that she sat upon the cold lake. And there Abby sat on the ice reclaiming the grief that had bottled up inside her, the grief that she could not find or let loose at the funeral home. Abby leaned upon one hand and bawled out loudly, "We were just working things out!" and then after sobbing some more, "Damn you Dad!"

Abby hung her head and sobbed loudly, she had nothing more to yell at the empty yard and the fallen willow before her. Though she had lashed out she was not going to let herself be angry with Will, no more than any anger she had harbored for her brother or mother before. Abby knew that she and her father had made their peace. Abby had never doubted his love for her. She grieved for time that had been lost that she wanted back and now would never get. She grieved the finality of Will's absence. Abby grieved for the loss of her father.

Abby's nose was running and her cheeks were flush. She sat crumpled and sobbed heavily. Abby wrapped her free hand around her head and continued to break down. Minutes went by as Abby cleansed her heart of the agony that had bottled up. Abby sobbed until her sobs became cooing whimpers. Still Abby sat and wept. When she could sob no more she started to catch her breath and breathe deeply. Picking her head up Abby looked at the willow lying next to her. "Poor old girl," said Abby. She raised herself back to her knees. She began to wipe her face with her gloves. Strands of hair matted by her chin. She put her hand into her pocket and fished around and then pulled her hand out, took off the glove and reached in again. This time she produced some tissue to wipe her eyes. Abby took yet another deep breathe. She picked herself up from the ice and made her way to the shore.

Close to the base of the willow Abby could see the deep hole from where the roots had torn free. Carefully she pulled herself up on the bank, almost sliding back down for lack of footing for the skates. Once in the yard Abby examined the house, and the studio.

Leaning on the corner of the house with his arms crossed was Mitch, his right hand scratching his chin. "I just missed you. Caroline thought you would come straight over here. She knows you pretty well."

Abby sighed, sniffled, and wiped her eyes, "That she does."

"The damage isn't as bad as it looks. Just the ends of the eaves were torn free. I can have the boys fix it up in no time," said Mitch.

"Good. I want to move back in as soon as possible," said Abby.

Mitch stood up from the wall and took a few steps from

the house. He turned and gestured to the eave, "The patchwork is pretty much sealing the eaves. I'll check it out myself. But you could move back in now."

Abby motioned her head toward the studio, "What about that? It looks a bit worse."

"That's just the siding," said Mitch. "Easy enough to repair. I don't think there is any foundation damage but we'll do a full inspection."

"That would be great," said Abby. "I tried to talk to Will about it before. But now I know what I need to do."

"What's that?"

"This is my house now, my studio. I'm the last Bellen. I'm going to find a way to make it work."

"You really thought this through?"

"Not at all, but it just seems right. You know, Bellen pots from Bellen hands? I think I can make a life for myself here."

"Are you sure that's what you want to do?" asked Mitch.

"It's been a long time coming," said Abby.

Abby then turned back toward the willow. On the other side of the crater from where the roots had been torn, the split log bench still sat undisturbed.

"I could use a little help," said Abby. Abby held out her hand behind her. She waited for Mitch. Mitch took her hand firmly, leaned beside her, and kissed her cheek. Abby led him over to the bench and the two sat down facing the lake and the length of the willow shattered on the edge of the ice.

* * * * *

* * * * *

THE END

* * * * *

ABOUT THE AUTHOR

Daniel Arthur Smith is the internationally bestselling author of The Cathari Treasure. American born, Daniel has traveled to over 300 cities in 22 countries, residing in Los Angeles, Kalamazoo, Prague, Crete, and New York.

Daniel was born and raised in Michigan, graduating from Western Michigan University where he studied philosophy and comparative religion. He has been a teacher, bartender, barista, poetry house proprietor, technologist, and a Fortune 100 consultant across America and Europe. Daniel resides and writes in Manhattan with his wife and young sons.

* * * * *